WAGESOFSIN

The Protective DETECTIVE SERIES

D0916362

ALSO BY YOLONDA TONETTE SANDERS
In Times of Trouble

WAGES OF SIN

The Protective DETECTIVE SERIES

YOLONDA TONETTE
SANDERS

SBI

STREBOR BOOKS

NEW YORK LONDON TORONTO SYDNEY

SBl

Strebor Books
P.O. Box 6505
Largo, MD 20792
http://www.streborbooks.com

© 2014 by Yolonda Tonette Sanders

ISBN 978-1-59309-473-7
ISBN 978-1-4516-9564-9 (ebook)
LCCN 2013950689

First Strebor Books trade paperback edition April 2014

Cover design: www.mariondesigns.com
Cover photograph: © Keith Saunders/Marion Designs

10 9 8 7 6 5 4 3 2 1

Manufactured in the United States of America

For information regarding special discounts for bulk purchases, please contact Simon & Schuster Special Sales at 1-866-506-1949 or business@simonandschuster.com

The Simon & Schuster Speakers Bureau can bring authors to your live event. For more information or to book an event, contact the Simon & Schuster Speakers Bureau at 1-866-248-3049 or visit our website at www.simonspeakers.com.

*This book is dedicated to law enforcement officers
and all those who risk their lives to keep others safe.
Thank you for your sacrifice and service.*

ACKNOWLEDGMENTS

One of the challenges I have when writing acknowledgments is finding new ways to thank many of the same people. I am very grateful for my core group of wonderful loved ones who stand by me through thick and thin. I first thank God for blessing me with all of you. I also thank Him for the gift of writing and the opportunities He has provided that allow me to share my gift with others. Without Him, there would be no me or *Wages of Sin*.

To my husband, David, thank you for being my protector, confidant, and giving me the leeway to explore my many endeavors without hesitation. I love and appreciate you.

To my favorite son, Tre, and my favorite daughter, Tia, despite being nearly grown, y'all are still my babies. As growing teens, you will make mistakes, disappoint me from time-to-time, and downright tick me off, but know that you will never be able to escape my love. May you each grow up to be and do all that God has for you. I am very proud of you both!

To my mom, Wilene, you may not be technologically savvy in such a way that you can forward an email, tweet, or post information on Facebook, but you can work a telephone like none other, and I know you will call everyone from here to China, telling them about this book.

To my dad, Eddie, anyone who truly knows you knows that you

are likely to be playing golf or billiards on any given day. Though you may read books, you are not a novel reader. Yet, I know you are going to read this story immediately upon receipt because I am your daughter and you are very proud of my accomplishments. Not only will you read it, but you will promote it to no end.

To my mother-in-law and friend, Janice, if I could handpick any mother-in-law in the world, I would still pick you. You are a key member of my support group. You are a proofreader when I am developing stories or drafting emails; a mother when I need advice; and a friend when I need to vent. Thank you for the many roles you play in my life. Each one is appreciated and needed.

To Tiffany, you are my favorite sister-in-law ever! ☺

To Big David, my father-in-law, the best dressed chess player in Cincinnati.

To Teresa, you are not just my friend, you are my sister. Sometimes friendships vary in terms of closeness and strength from time-to-time, but our relationship has remained consistent from the very beginning. You are irreplaceable. Thank you for everything you have done to help with this story and with Yo Productions, in general. I love you, girl!

To Kesha, I miss our weekly Monday phone calls, which would start off with us talking about business and end with us mentioning everything under the sun. You know I love you, cousin. I am proud of you and I am always here for you.

To Tyree, thank you for being my sister, not only in Christ, but also in love. We have talked, cried, and prayed each other through many life trials during our many "therapy" sessions. Thank you for all the times you've lent me your ear.

To Jenn, you are loyal and such a sweetheart. I love and miss you. I also miss our sleepovers. One of these days, Tia and I will come hang out with you and Hannah. I look forward to getting to know her.

To Barb, thanks for never failing to look out for my family.

To Kim, thanks for always giving a helping hand whenever I call.

To Suzy and the entire Tobin clan, you all will forever be in my heart.

To Jeff, my trips to Kroger have not been the same since you've moved. LOL

To my sister-friend, Angie, thanks for constantly cheering me on and praying for me. I love you, girl. You know that I am here for you.

To my girls in Business by the Book and our leader, Nancy, I look forward to our time together. Through it all [we are] royally aware that Christ leads us boldly to success.

I want to give a special shout-out to everyone in my original hometown of Sandusky, Ohio. There are so many of you who continuously show me love and support. I am blessed to come from such a small community that's so mighty in love.

A very special thank-you goes to Pastor Clayton Howard of Ebenezer Baptist Church in Sandusky for always going the extra mile to support my endeavors. I thank everyone at Ebenezer for adopting me as one of your own. I did not grow up in that church and yet it feels like home.

To the members of churches that I have had the privilege of calling home, First Church, New Hope, and Providence (my second home as a child), thank you for all the love you show me as well.

To Anthony and Nicole Redic and all the members of Family Fellowship Church of Christ, thank you for being so loving and welcoming to my family.

To the residents of my current hometown of Columbus, Ohio, I hope I make you proud.

To the Columbus Police Department and Officer Betty Schwab, thank you for hosting the Citizen's Police Academy class. I tried to use the information I learned to help with this story. I hope I have adequately represented the department as I have a lot of respect for you all.

To my favorite member of the CPD, Regina Dudley, thank you for always being willing to help in any way possible.

To my aunts and uncles—Mildred, Pat, Nita, Phine, Big Irby, June, Fish, and Bud, I love you all dearly.

To my crazy and loving sister-cousin, Tonya, you keep me praying by always giving me something to pray about! Lol.

To my best kiddie friends and "adopted" niece and nephew, Dionna and Michael, y'all are so much fun to be around. You make it easier to cope with the fact that Tre and Tia are growing much faster than I had anticipated. Know that "Aunt Londi" loves you both a whole, whole bunch! Tifani and Derrick, thank you for trusting me with your children. It's an honor to be part of your village.

To Sara and Stephen, I don't know how you do the things you do, but I am very grateful to have both of you in my life.

To my entire Strebor family and everyone at Simon and Schuster, thank you for everything you do to make sure that the best possible product gets into the hands of readers. I know that there are many who serve behind the scenes whose names I do not know, but I appreciate all that you do.

To my many relatives, friends, associates, church family, book clubs, stores, Facebook fans, Twitter followers, students, and you (the reader), thank you for your continued support over the years.

To my author friends with whom I've had the privilege of sharing this journey, thank you. I don't have to explain anything to you because you already understand.

If I have forgotten anyone, it was not on purpose. Feel free to send me an email and fuss at me, but ultimately, I ask that you forgive me.

Much Love and Many Blessings,
Yolonda

Website and Social Media Info:
www.yoproductions.net
www.facebook.com/yoproductions
www.twitter.com/ytsanders

"The Columbus Police are asking for your help in their search for a missing woman. Thirty-four-year-old Lolita Gordon was last seen yesterday morning when she dropped her son off at school. Workers became concerned when Mrs. Gordon failed to pick him up at the end of the day and called her husband who contacted the police. Her car was later found abandoned on 315 North not far from the Henderson Road exit with two flat tires. Investigators say that the tires appear to have been tampered with and there is further information not yet released to the public, which leads them to suspect foul play. If you have any information about the whereabouts of Lolita Gordon, please call the Columbus Police at 614-555-TIPS. You may remain anonymous."

With an increasing heart rate from the day's excitement, the Avenger cast a look to the woman sitting across the room on the floor. "I have information that could help solve this case. Do you think I should call?"

Bound and gagged, Lolita cried. Her muffled pleas remained unpersuasive.

The Avenger smiled, approaching Lolita and gently pulling loose strands of dark hair from her face. "Calm down, dear. Your cheeks are so red you're starting to blend in with the furniture. I promise that they'll find you after I'm done."

Looking her directly in the eyes, the Avenger asked, "Do you know why I've chosen you, Lolita?"

She frantically shook her head no. Her eyes were sad and pitiful. What pretty eyes she had—a shade of emerald green that sparkled underneath the steady flow of tears. No wonder she was loved. Lolita's eyes were mesmerizing. Anyone could be captivated by her stare. The Avenger quickly looked away. This divine assignment had already been initiated. No backing out now. Holding up two photographs, the Avenger delighted in watching Lolita's expression turn from general fear to terror. Killing her was not only the righteous thing to do; it would also be fun.

CHAPTER 1: IMPECCABLE TIMING

"Yeah…" Detective Troy Evans wasted no time answering his cell.

"Can you get down to the station ASAP? There's a guy here who says that he has information about that missing lady and will only talk to the lead detective," said one of the night duty officers.

"I'm on my way." He tried getting out of bed without waking his wife, but she had heard the phone.

"What's going on?"

Moonlight illuminated the room, shining directly onto Natalie as she sat up, suddenly alert. The satin sheet she held over her chest covered everything but Troy's imagination. With memories of their last encounter only a few hours old, it took great restraint on his part to keep from sliding back into bed with her. "There's a possible lead in Lolita Gordon's case."

"Is that the woman who disappeared last week?"

"Yep."

"Bless her heart. I hope she's okay."

Troy wasn't optimistic. It had been exactly six days since the Gordon girl disappeared. "I appreciate you wanting to see me out, but you stay in bed," he said when Natalie began searching for her nightgown. "If I'm fortunate, maybe you'll still be here when I get back so we can work on baby number two."

Giving him a half-smile, she slipped on her gown, leaving the room and heading downstairs. To a casual observer, she would seem upset, but Troy understood her actions. She was praying, something she always did during these late-night runs. Having been on the force for over eighteen years, he'd spent most of his time working homicides except for a temporary assignment a couple years back in sex crimes. The units in which he worked had no bearing on the amount of time he committed to his cases or his compassion for the victims, dead or alive. Troy didn't have a set shift. He was there whenever duty called and it summoned him now. Though there was no proof that Lolita Gordon was actually dead, there was something unsettling found in her car indicating that her life was in danger and Troy had been given the case due to those suspicious circumstances.

Once dressed, Troy peeked in on his son. The toddler slept like a log, not flinching a bit when the bright light burned in his face. Pictures of Spider-Man hung on the walls. He was Nate's favorite action hero. "See you later, li'l man," he whispered before heading down the stairs. With impeccable timing, Natalie handed him his thermal coffee cup when he got to the kitchen.

The early May humidity was turned up high and Troy really didn't want the coffee, despite the pleasing hazelnut aroma. He'd rather get his pick-me-up via an energy drink, but since Natalie had thought enough of him to make it, he graciously took it without complaint. "Thanks, babe," he said, quickly kissing her goodbye.

"You're welcome."

Troy scanned her from head to toe one last time. The short satin gown clung to her tall, light-skinned, and very shapely frame. Once an aspiring model, she could be a little high maintenance at times. Though she came short of ever truly breaking into the industry, her measurements were superb, in his book, and well worth the attention he wanted to give them. "Hopefully, I'll see you soon." He gave her another quick peck before heading to the garage. "Don't forget to lock up!"

CHAPTER 2: PERSON OF INTEREST

roy had interviewed a lot of people over the years, but none as peculiar as Eric Freeman, who, at one o'clock in the morning, sat in the interrogation room, dressed in black pants with a long-sleeved white shirt and a red sweater vest that seemed at least a size too small. His hands were cupped under his chin. His eyes were closed and his lips were rapidly moving, but no sound came out—the first clue that this dude was extra special. "Eric Freeman, correct?"

"Pastor Eric Freeman."

"Alrighty then. I'm Troy Evans, the lead detective on this case. How are you?"

Freeman responded, "Blessed and highly favored. I was communing with the Father about the soul of the young lady that prompted me to come here. The Lord has brought to my attention something pertinent." That was clue number two.

*"O-*kay. Let's get right to it, Eric. What is it that you know?"

"Detective Evans, I am a man of the cloth and I ask that you respect my calling. I happen to be the Pastor of The Tabernacle of Jesus, a church in Sandusky, and it offends me that you have overlooked my unique anointing."

Clue three!

"I know for a fact that Mrs. Gordon is dead. You will find her body behind Saint Joseph Cathedral downtown."

Scribbling down notes, Troy asked, "And how do you know this? Are you responsible for her death?"

"Absolutely not! I would rather not say how I came across the information, but it is true. Check it out for yourself and if I can be of further assistance, please let me know."

Criminals always thought they were smarter than the cops. Freeman was arrogant to say the least, standing like Troy had taken up enough of his time. He was in no way as intimidating as he wanted to be—average height, average weight, and specks of gray that put him somewhere between Troy's age of forty-one and fifty. Troy returned the cold stare Freeman gave without budging from his seat. "Sit down."

Freeman folded his arms and then tapped his foot impatiently on the floor for several seconds before finally obeying. "Detective Evans, I have nothing else to add at this moment. I've told you everything that I know."

"You will need to hang tight until we check this place out."

"Am I a suspect?"

"If Mrs. Gordon's body is where you have said—"

"It is."

"Then you're definitely a person of interest."

"But, I didn't kill her."

"Then you'd better start writing a statement, detailing everything you know."

The ride to Saint Joseph brought mixed emotions as Troy rushed to confirm or deny Freeman's allegations. People made up stories to the police all the time. What would be Freeman's motive? *Attention?* The way he emphasized his title had to be a result of some deep-seated insecurity. *Pastor* Eric Freeman. Who cared? If this was some type of wild-goose chase, Eric would pay dearly.

Troy saw her as soon as he pulled into the lot. He cursed as he called in a 10-28, the homicide code for the CPD. Naked, Lolita's body had been positioned so that her legs were straight and her arms spread wide. Something had been placed on her chest. Troy kept his lights shining as he walked up to the body. It was a pocket-sized Bible splattered with blood. A single gunshot through her temple appeared to be the cause of death. Troy started taking pictures on his cell while waiting for the Crime Scene Investigation team to arrive.

Stretch marks testified to Lolita's claim to motherhood. A child was now left motherless, a husband now a widower. Troy couldn't help but think of how devastated he and Nate would be if something were to happen to Natalie. When CSI got there, he sent Natalie a text stating that he wouldn't be home any time soon, ending it with *"I luv u."* Several minutes passed with no reply. Maybe she'd gone back to sleep. Hopefully she remembered to lock up.

"We found some footprints," said Paula J. Kyser, the lead CSI agent. Even in above-eighty-degree weather, the entire crew was in their usual wardrobe, covered from head to toe. *"A safety precaution,"* he'd been told many years ago. A lot of the officers referred to Paula as "Plain Jane" for her lack of physical bells and whistles. With limp, short auburn hair, a flat chest, and an even flatter butt, few guys took a second look her way, but everyone knew she had an unparalleled commitment to her job. A young widow, her husband had been robbed and killed seven years ago. Sam's murderer had never been brought to justice and Troy felt that was part of the reason Paula worked as hard as she did to help catch others.

"Hopefully, these footprints will match up to the suspect."

"Time will tell."

Knowing the scene and Lolita Gordon were safe in the hands of the CSI crew and coroner tech, Troy headed back to the station.

"I was awakened about ten o'clock Wednesday night when my prayer partner called about a pressing matter. See, as a man of God, I believe it is important we have people in our lives on whom we can count. The Bible, Proverbs 27:17 to be precise, says that 'Iron sharpeneth iron; so a man sharpeneth the countenance of his friend.' Thus, my friend and I have become a source of iron for each other. After prayer was over, I was on my way into the kitchen to get a glass of water as I was a bit parched from being caught up in the Spirit and that's when I saw it. A message on my wall, written by the Hand of God, that read, 'My dearly beloved son, tell them that her body is at Saint Joseph Cathedral.'"

"This dude can't be for real," Troy said to Jonathon Knight, his friend and fellow detective, as he continued to read through Freeman's statement.

"I realize how absurd this sounds. I was skeptical at first, but no one had been in the house all day except the Lord and me. I started to drive to Saint Joseph before coming into the station, but I decided to step out on faith. You know the Bible tells us that faith is important in our everyday lives and because I wanted to demonstrate to the All Mighty that I trust Him, I came straight here to report all that the Lord told me. I, Pastor Eric Joshua Freeman of The Tabernacle of Jesus church in Sandusky, Ohio, declare that everything written herein is true.

In God I Trust, Pastor E. J. Freeman"

"This is the most outrageous story I have ever heard!"

"Let's put him on the box." Knight's voice had a rich, James Earl Jones sound. Some officers had nicknamed him "Danny DeVito" because of his height and round frame. Officers could be cruel! To his knowledge, besides being playfully called a "country bumpkin" because of his faint Southern accent, Troy had escaped unflattering nicknames. He was in excellent shape for his age and was what his wife described as "eye candy." Jon was noticeably taller than DeVito. To Troy, he looked more like the Caucasian, slightly slimmer version of CeeLo Green. "Once he fails, that'll give us an advantage."

"Cool. We need to check him for gun powder residue as well. You handle crazy man while I talk more with the husband."

In another room, Chad Gordon sat hunched over, bawling, not even bothering to lift his head when Troy entered. Troy waited a second. For a moment, Troy wished he'd traded places with Jon. It was hard enough to see a man cry, but seeing a thirty-four-year-old, six-three and two-hundred-something-pound man shamelessly wailing was an even bigger pill to swallow. His detective instinct said that Mr. Gordon was not involved, but Troy still had to ask him the tough questions. "Were you and your wife having marital problems? Can you think of any reason why someone would have wanted to kill her? What's your affiliation with Saint Joseph Cathedral?"

Chad Gordon tearfully answered every one of the questions and, once he finished, started asking some of his own. "What am I going to tell our son? How can I raise him without her? Will you please find out who did this?"

"You are free to go," Troy finally spoke up after a brief pause. No response from Chad, only more tears.

"I'm going to set my card on the table. Feel free to call me if you have any questions or think of anything else that can help us with your wife's case." Still nothing. "I'll leave the door unlocked so you can go out when you're ready. I'm sorry about your wife and please believe that we are working diligently on this case."

"Thank you." Chad lifted his head long enough to choke out those words. Troy backed out and let him be.

A week after the discovery of the Gordon girl's body, Troy had taken Natalie out to dinner and a movie for her thirty-seventh birthday. Their time together was interrupted when Troy was again called to the station to meet Eric who revealed where the body of a local college student, Myesha Turner, could be found. She'd been abducted several days earlier from her dorm room. A dorm with nearly a thousand students and no one saw a thing! They found the killer's same calling card in Myesha's room that was in Lolita's car, provoking a sickening feeling that a serial killer was on the loose.

The following weeks would replay like a bad nightmare with the disappearances of two other women on separate occasions. The third victim was a soccer mom, Amy Howard, who went missing one evening after she'd called 9-1-1 to report suspicions that someone was lurking outside her home. By the time officers got to the house to check things out, she was gone. The fourth was a physical therapy assistant, Michelle Rossi, who was in the middle of a patient visit when she went out to her car to get supplies and never returned.

Sadly, within six weeks of Lolita's murder, late-night calls had become the norm as Myesha, Amy, and Michelle all met with Lolita's same fate. Troy feared that an additional discovery would come soon since another woman, Sarah Matthews, was missing. The killer had managed to escape detection all this time. Though Eric Freeman remained at the top of Troy's list of possible suspects, there was nothing concrete to tie him to any of the murders. He passed a lie detector test, had alibis during the times of the disappearances, tested negative for gun powder residue, and voluntarily allowed police to search his home which yielded no results, leaving

Troy puzzled and frustrated. After the second victim was found, Troy knew that this case would take over his life if the killer wasn't brought to justice soon. Now, in mid-June, four, perhaps five, victims later, every move he made revolved around this case, making it very difficult for him to balance work and family.

The department had held several press conferences within the past month to provide some answers to a demanding public that was on full alert. News reporters covered some aspect of the murders daily. The most perplexing thing for Troy was the fact that none of the victims had anything in common—different races, different ages, and different stages of life. The killer had been their only connection. They had all been kept alive between three and seven days; all had been stripped naked, but with no evidence of sexual assault; all had been found with a single gunshot wound in the head; and all discoveries were "revealed" supernaturally by God to one Eric Freeman within forty-eight hours of their deaths.

CHAPTER 3: HIGH MAINTENANCE

"It's been five days since the disappearance of Sarah Matthews and police are no closer to finding her than they are to catching the 'Bible Butcher' who, so far, has abducted and killed four women. It was early last month when we first broke the story of Lolita Gordon, who disappeared after dropping her son off at school. Her body was found nearly a week later behind the church where she'd been a member for several years. In the following weeks, the bodies of Myesha Turner, Amy Howard, and Michelle Rossi were also discovered at various locations and now family and friends of Sarah Matthews fear that she may face the same fate. Police are not saying how they are finding the bodies of these women, but sources say that information is coming from an unidentified third party whom investigators are not releasing much information about at this time. The family of Sarah Matthews has issued a twenty thousand dollar reward for anyone who can offer details leading to her safe return. Stay tuned for the latest news and information as we will provide any updates we have about The Bible Butcher the moment they come in. Next up, your weather forecast for the weekend."

"I don't like that name," Natalie said as they sat in bed late Friday night. The killer had been dubbed "The Bible Butcher" after the media learned of the Bibles found on each woman's chest. "It's stupid. It makes it sound like he's cutting up the Bible. They should call him the 'Mysterious Murderer' since y'all don't know who he is yet."

"You do realize you just poured salt in my wounds, don't you? I'm trying, babe." He held up the notes he'd been going through like it was evidence in a trial. Chad Gordon called him on a weekly basis, asking if there had been any breakthroughs.

"I know, honey. I didn't mean to imply anything. I just think the media goes too far sometimes."

He wasn't in the mood for this conversation. She'd get on a roll and not stop. "What time is Corrine bringing Nate home?" Their son was spending the night with his big sister, something that occurred at least once a month. Tonight was technically supposed to be their date night, but neither seemed up to going out. Natalie had gotten a few movies from Redbox® and ordered pizza, but she'd dozed off before the first movie even got started, waking up about forty minutes ago to fuss at him about working when he was supposed to be spending time with her.

"Sometime early tomorrow afternoon. She's leaving Sunday for a business trip to Chicago, so I'm sure packing will be an all-day adventure. You know how Corrine is."

"If she's anything like her mama, then yes, I do know how she is." Natalie playfully smacked his arm as he was writing a note to himself. His hand streaked across the paper and he ended up poking himself in the left arm. "Ouch. I should arrest you for assault."

She kissed him softly on the cheek before whispering in his ear, "If you put your work away, I won't mind being detained. Matter of fact, why don't you go ahead and read me my rights."

Troy smiled. He was more than happy to oblige her request.

"We found her." It was after two the next morning when Jon called. Troy sighed. *Sarah*... "Same M.O.?"

"Exactly the same. From the looks of things, rigor mortis has completely set in so she's been dead at least twelve hours, but we'll know for sure after the autopsy."

Troy swore loudly enough that Natalie stirred. She hated when he cursed, but right now he didn't care.

"Did the whack job report this one, too?"

"Yep. Claims he received another message from God. He volunteered to wait at the station. You'd better get here quick if you want to survey the entire scene. The techs are moving fast. It won't be long before they take the body."

Troy got the location from Jon and wasted no time getting out of bed.

"Another body?" Natalie asked.

"Yep." He didn't want to let on how much this case was getting to him. "You know the routine." They'd been married nearly four years, but Troy knew that Natalie didn't like nor had she gotten used to his job. He enjoyed what he did, for the most part. He'd sworn to protect the citizens and catch those who violated the law. But, he was having a hard time catching the killer or proving that Freeman was guilty. Be it Freeman or someone else, this maniac had killed five women in a little over a month. Time was of the essence.

As Troy dressed, Natalie did her usual routine—she silently prayed while getting up and heading downstairs. "I don't want any coffee!" he yelled after her. No response. Had she heard him?

Man, he loved that woman! Marrying her was the best decision he'd ever made and he never wanted to take her for granted. He remembered all too well how he almost foolishly lost her when they were dating. But now he thanked God, not only for her, but for their soon-to-be three year-old son. The two of them brought much needed joy into his life. He hoped they'd fill at least one of the two empty rooms with another little one in the near future.

Nowadays, his wife and son were the only reasons he ever really took the time to thank God. That's not to say that he didn't believe in Him. Troy's faith had been strong at one point, especially when a buddy of his got killed during a routine traffic stop several years back. It was definitely strong when he and Natalie initially married. It went downhill the last few years as all the crap he'd witnessed on his job began to get under his skin. Sometimes he wondered how true it was that God never slept nor slumbered. Where was He when the father shot and killed his two young sons because he didn't want the mom to get custody? Where was He when the Hampton girl's murder was being plotted? Where was He during this last month or so when some sick scum bag blew out the brains of defenseless women? He could only imagine what Chad and the other victims' families were experiencing. So much tragedy in life seemed to happen under the watchful eye of The Almighty that Troy wasn't sure what to believe anymore.

Troy started to peek into little man's room before remembering he wasn't there. Downstairs, Natalie was in the kitchen at the island reading her Bible. *Seriously?* It was too early in the morning for that. At least there was no coffee thermal waiting for him.

They said their usual good-byes and shared a quick kiss and then he said, "Make sure you lock up and turn on the alarm."

"Bye, Troy." She nudged him out the door, rolling her eyes. She hated his "dumb" instructions as she called them. Yes, Troy *knew* that Natalie would lock the door and turn on the alarm, but with an apparent serial killer on the loose, he needed to say it. If not for her sake, then for himself.

He hopped into his Navigator, cranked up the AC and backed out of the garage, not daring to leave until the door had come down securely. He then peeled out and headed to where Sarah Matthews, aka victim number five, was waiting.

CHAPTER 4: THE MOST HIGH

"Evans! What's up, man? How's that pretty-looking wife and son of yours doing?" one of the investigators asked.

Ignoring the question, Troy slipped on shoe covers and coldly brushed his way past everyone to find Jon Knight. He was not one to engage in small talk at moments like this. Everyone should know that by now!

Sarah had been found in an abandoned warehouse on Columbus's west side. The strong stench of her body was apparent way before Troy reached her. Knight was speaking with Paula when he arrived. "You got any information for me?" he asked while taking pics of her on his cell phone in case it took longer than he wanted to get the official ones.

"Not a single thing," Knight replied. Troy was actually speaking to Paula, but he really didn't care who answered him, he was hoping for some new discovery. "As you see," Knight continued, "her legs have been straightened and her arms spread in cross-like fashion, just like the others."

Troy nodded. That was the first thing he'd noticed along with the Bible that lay across her chest.

"There's something interesting about this victim," Paula chimed in, kneeling next to her body. She pulled loose strands of her blonde hair to the side and took a picture. "She has a bruise on the side of her face."

"From what?" Troy moved closer to get a better look.

"We'll have to get her to the lab and let the M.E. analyze it for sure, but it looks like some type of blunt force trauma…maybe from a gun?"

"Anything else?"

"Footprints," Jon answered. "But you know the deal with that."

Various sizes had been found at the other scenes, none matching each other or Eric. "Unless we find a print that has Eric Freeman engraved on the sole, we might as well have nothing."

Hours later, Troy was at the station ready to interrogate Freeman once again. He was determined to catch this jerk and when he was that motivated to wrap up a case, it was hard for him to delegate questioning to someone else.

Eric Freeman sat in the interrogation room, dressed in an outfit eerily similar to the one he wore when Troy first interviewed him. It was probably ten degrees hotter this night than it was six weeks ago—way too hot for a sweater vest.

"Detective Evans, what a shock to see you." Freeman's sarcasm did not go unnoticed.

"I'm surprised you're not communing with the Father tonight. He must not have any additional dead bodies to secretly reveal to you."

"I am not a killer."

"I see someone's feeling self-conscious."

"I'm as tired of this as you are. I've continuously prayed that you are able to find the person who is hurting these women. I've prayed for all their souls, even the lady who was found tonight."

"Her name was Sarah." He threw down pictures of her body that he'd printed from his phone. "Eric, why did you do this to her?"

Troy watched as Freeman's face tensed. A reaction he'd expected. "How many times must I tell you, it's *Pastor* Freeman." Though Troy found humor in the great offense Freeman took whenever anyone called him by his first name, comedy wasn't what he was after. He wanted to unnerve Eric, get him on edge and hopefully talking. "You really need to learn to respect the Lord's anointed. I did not do this." He closed the folder with the pictures and slid them back to Troy's side of the table.

"How did you know where her body would be?"

"Like I have told you on several occasions about the others, God specifically told me where to find her."

"You know what, Eric?" Troy's voice was stern. "I'm not buying this vision crap. You are like any of the other coo-coo birds who come in claiming to be psychic—"

"I am *not* a psychic!" The table shook when he pounded his fist. "I am a prophet of the Most High, not some devilish psychic. It is my Heavenly Father who makes it possible for me to do what I do."

This was the first time that Troy had gotten this far under Freeman's skin. The first time he'd witnessed such aggressiveness that was indicative of his ability to kill. "Is that why you hit Sarah Matthews? Did she call you a psychic instead of a prophet as you claim to be?"

Clenched jaws and short quick breaths, Freeman seethed with anger. "Detective Evans, you are antagonizing me. I'm done talking to you. Since I'm not under arrest, I assume I'm free to leave. If not, I'd like to call my attorney."

The man had never before asked for an attorney. By law, Troy had to oblige. Against his own desire, he softened his tone and played into Freeman's ego. "Pastor Freeman, you are free to leave or call an attorney so we can continue questioning. It's up to you. I want this to be over before anyone else gets hurt. If you know more about these murders than what you've let on, now is the time to talk—after you call your attorney, of course."

"What more do you want from me? I've been subjected to all kinds of invasive procedures. You've searched my home, my car, and I spend hours here each time one of these women goes from life on to eternity. I have told you everything I know. I can only reveal to you what is made known to me by my Father at the time of His choosing."

"Danggit, Eric! I'm tired of playing this game with you. Five women have been murdered and you have been connected to all of them! Quit screwing around and tell me what you know!" Troy leaped across the table, grabbing Eric by his collar. Within seconds, Jon and another officer burst in the room and pulled him away.

"Evans, chill!" Knight ordered. "You went too far this time."

Moments later, as Eric was escorted out of the interrogation room, he and Troy glared at each other. *Just wait, you fake prophet punk. I will get you!* Troy only hoped that no one else had to die before he had the evidence to put Freeman away for good.

CHAPTER 5: PRICELESS

I t was around two on Saturday afternoon when Troy finally made it home. He saw his stepdaughter's silver Eclipse out front and walked into his home to find Natalie and Corrine sitting at the kitchen table playing a game of Leap Frog with Nate.

The "Hey, babe," from Natalie and the "What's up, Troy?" from Corrine was followed by the thrilled cry of *"Daa-dee!"* from Nate who immediately ran and jumped into his arms, causing Troy to nearly drop the case file he had on all the murders. It felt good to have his li'l man in his arms—especially after spending the night questioning and interviewing Freeman and other witnesses. Worst of all, he'd spoken with Sarah Matthews' grieving parents. Though he'd been trained to deliver news without getting emotionally involved, his heart still went out to the families of the victims.

In the past, Troy had always been able to do his job without being consciously aware at how the pain of others tugged at his own heart. Not that he was callous. He definitely cared, but he was able to handle the emotional aspects of his job by doing one of his three favorite activities: basketball, playing Xbox, or exercising. Since meeting and falling in love with Natalie, he had really gone soft. And after the birth of his son, he'd gotten even softer. When he looked into the eyes of Sarah Matthews' parents and saw the depth of their pain, he was more determined than ever to stop

Freeman or whomever from hurting anyone else in Columbus. What if it had been *his* only child? What if it had been Nate?

Troy gave Nate a harder than normal squeeze as Natalie kissed Troy on the cheek while grabbing the files from his hands and laying them on the island. Nate immediately threw up his fists. "Let's fight," he said as he started playfully punching Troy, saying "boom" with every thrust that successfully landed. Troy, who had been dead tired, suddenly found the energy to participate in this activity.

"Ouch!" Troy pretended to shriek while Nate laughed. Troy sat him down and the two of them playfully went at it. Troy had to get on his knees to even the playing field so Nate could feel like he got a good hit in. When Nate delivered the final blow, Troy toppled over on the granite floor in defeat. "Okay, you won, son. Daddy is no match for Nate the Great."

"Yay!" Nate threw up his arms in victory and ran around Troy shouting, "I float like a butt-fly and sting like a bee."

Natalie, Corrine, and Troy all laughed. Nate was a precocious child. A few days shy of his third birthday, he spoke well compared to other small children his age, but whenever he tried to say Muhammad Ali's signature line faster than his lips moved, it always came out as "butt-fly" instead of "butterfly." Part of Troy thought his son did it on purpose to get the laughs. He sometimes showed off a little "all eyes on me" mentality like his mama.

"Nate, why don't you show Daddy what Sissy bought you?" Natalie suggested.

"'Kay. Be right back." He strutted away proudly as if he really had won an actual fight.

Troy got off the floor and joined Corrine at the table just as Natalie brought him a cup of orange juice.

"Rough night?" she asked.

"Very." Though it wasn't unusual for Troy to talk about his work with his wife, he was careful not to share too many details to not jeopardize any of his cases, and he definitely didn't talk in front of anyone else. "What did you and Nate do last night?"

"Nothing much, I took him to Chuck E. Cheese's and then we went back to my place and watched movies. I was dozing off because he wore me out."

Troy chuckled. "I bet. That boy has a lot of energy."

"You think?" Dressed in a plain white T-shirt, blue-jean shorts and flip-flops, Corrine's hair was pulled back into a very simple ponytail. No makeup or jewelry, except the locket she always wore with Nate's newborn picture. Yawning at least three times since Troy had been home, she looked like she could use a nap.

"Look, Daddy!" Nate ran back in with a model airplane, making noises and swerving it in the air.

"Wow. That's nice, li'l man."

"Sissy go bye-bye tomorrow and her said I can't fly in 'da big plane wif her, but I can fly 'dis one."

"That was nice of Sissy, wasn't it?"

"Yep! Her always nice to me," Nate said smugly, continuing to occupy himself with his plane. He flew it all around the kitchen before buzzing back into the living room.

"Um, Corrine, you do realize his birthday isn't until Wednesday and he's not having his party until *next* weekend, right?"

"And your point would be?" Her words sounded sarcastic, but her expression was soft.

Natalie amusingly shook her head. "She spoils that boy to no end."

Corrine stuck out her tongue. "Chill, Natalie. That's what big sisters are for."

Moments like this were priceless to Troy. He saw the pure joy in Natalie's face whenever she and her daughter were together. He saw it in both of them. They had an atypical mother-daughter relationship. In fact, they were more like sisters, being only thirteen years apart. And though the two had only met when Corrine was eighteen, if Troy didn't know their story, he would swear they'd known each other all their lives. He truly admired his wife for all she'd been through and her ability to overcome. She was beautiful, both inside and out. Natalie was tall with dark, long, silky hair and a honey-brown complexion. Corrine was a younger, lighter-skinned version of her mother. Their mutual love for one another was also evident.

"Sissy, come 'ere!" Nate called from the living room. Corrine wasted no time going to see about him. When he said jump, she did—a habit that would sometimes get Nate in trouble with his parents when he tried to be demanding with them as well.

"You look like crap," Natalie blurted.

"I feel like it. I doubt I'll feel any better until we can catch this creep. Each time it gets harder to notify the families. Mrs. Matthews cried so hard that she had to be rushed to the hospital. Her husband said she has a bad heart and I don't mean to be pessimistic, but this might do her in. It's incredibly frustrating to have so many victims and not a single lead."

Natalie gently cupped his hands with hers. Her skin was so soft. Troy relaxed a bit. "You will get him, babe. I'm sure of it. I hope you plan to get some rest before going through those files you have over there." She nodded toward the island.

"If I don't, will I be punished later?" He pulled her from the chair over to him. She straddled his lap, wrapping her arms around his neck. Her long dark hair fell into his face, her lips inches away from his.

"If you do, it will only guarantee you'll have enough energy later to handle me because I intend to be a very bad girl." Instead of going for his lips, Natalie leaned to the side and kissed his neck. Troy had begun to imagine helping her out of her V-neck, short-sleeved shirt, and capris. One of the things he'd feared before they married was that she'd let herself go—part of the horror stories he'd heard from other husbands about how their wives took increasingly less care in their appearance as the years went by. Thinking back, Troy should have known that Natalie was too vain for that. You can take the girl out of the modeling world, but you can't take the model out of the girl. True to her style, she had on high-heeled, open-toe sandals that attractively displayed her red painted toenails. He found the sparkling ring on her middle toe very sexy. He would have her leave all of that on while everything else came off. Troy's body began to react to his daydream. He grunted passionately as she made her way from his neck to his ear and finally to his lips. Wide-eyed, they kissed as his hands tightened around her body and hers around his neck. He saw the desire for him in her eyes. They'd managed to communicate without saying a single word. Suddenly, her look changed from passion to...*embarrassment?*

"*Yuck!*"

Troy turned around and saw his son run out of the kitchen back into the living room. He'd seen them kiss before. This was for sure another one of his theatrics.

Corrine looked like she wanted to gag. "For real? Y'all are getting all freaky when Nate and I were in the next room? Um, ever thought about going to *your* room?"

"Yeah, I thought about it," Troy said aloud. Corrine rolled her eyes and followed Nate. Troy grinned slyly at his wife. "Want to go upstairs for a while and work on our baby project?"

Her body stiffened. She was obviously getting as impatient with the process as he was. "Naw. I'm sure Corrine is ready to get going. We'll finish this another time." She got up, taking his hand and headed toward the living room.

He stopped her for a second, kissed her lightly. "I love you." There was a time when he feared saying that at all and now he wondered if he said it too much.

If he did, Natalie didn't seem to mind. She smiled. "I love you, too, babe." And they headed to the living room, dropping hands before entering.

CHAPTER 6: NOTHING TO ADD

Natalie sat in Aneetra's living room flipping through a magazine while waiting for her friend to get ready. She liked Aneetra's house. Sitting smack dab in the middle of a cul-de-sac, with three bedrooms, a living room, kitchen, two bathrooms, and a basement, it seemed a perfect fit for Aneetra, her husband, and their two girls. The living room had such a warm and inviting feel. Natalie would have added a third contrasting color to the navy blue and tan scheme, but it worked and was a true match to Aneetra's simplistic style.

Sometimes Natalie wondered if she and Troy had made a wise decision by building a large four-bedroom home. It was starting to feel overly spacious, especially now that Troy was pushing for another child. They'd built it with the intentions of having at least two children, but seeing how much time and energy Nate took up, Natalie was having second thoughts and she didn't know how to tell Troy that she hadn't stopped taking birth control.

"Are we taking Cu-tee or my car?" Aneetra yelled out to Natalie from her bedroom.

The license plate on Natalie's car read "QT PIE," but instead of simply saying "your car," Aneetra always referred to it as "Cu-tee." Natalie had had that plate ever since she got her first car. At the time, it went well with her model-like mentality. Now, in her late thirties with a stable career as a financial analyst and a mother, wife, and devout Christian, she didn't really think the license plate fit so well. "Cu-tee" was no longer a spotless little sports sedan as was her custom before Nate. Over the years, the plate had transferred from car to car and now sat comfortably on what she called her "tweener" because it was a cross between a sedan and SUV. It was also filled with Nate's toys and crumbs of whatever he ate while riding in the backseat. "Let's take mine since Nate's car seat is already in there." She hoped the backseat wasn't *too* bad. She'd meant to sweep it out.

"Cool," Aneetra said, coming around the corner putting her earrings on. The two of them met about six years ago when Natalie first started at Dennison Financial Solutions. Aneetra befriended her immediately, but it took some time for Natalie to warm up to her. Now they were "besties" no doubt. It didn't matter that they worked together all week; hanging out today came as naturally as anything else.

Natalie loved Aneetra. She'd been a true friend to her even during those early days of their friendship when Natalie thought she was annoying. She hadn't wanted, needed, or embraced Aneetra's friendship at first. Thank God Aneetra never gave up on her. She was the type of person whom Natalie could share anything with and not feel like she would be looked down upon. Aneetra didn't know *all* her business, but Natalie had spilled enough about her not-so-perfect past that if Aneetra was the type to hold her mistakes against her, she could have done so without hesitating. "Girl, we have to do something about your hair!" Natalie eyed her friend cautiously. "I may have gotten out of modeling, but not fashion. How are you going to have on a fly sundress and then rock a big bun?"

Tall like Natalie, Aneetra was heavier in the hips with a slight mommy belly she opted to cover up rather than work to get rid of. Aneetra wasn't drop-dead gorgeous by society's standards, but to Natalie, she was absolutely beautiful. Aneetra was only thirty-nine, but sometimes she dressed like she was a decade or so older. The olive green sundress was one of her more tasteful styles and complemented her dark brown skin. Whereas Natalie would have worn heels, Aneetra opted for decorated flats. They were cute, though. Aneetra looked great from the forehead down. That bun added several years to her appearance.

"Girl, it's too hot out for me to wear my hair down. I don't see how you're doing it."

"You know I'll pull my hair back in a ponytail in a minute. You don't have to wear it down; just not in a bun. Or at least wear bangs because that's not cute."

Aneetra chuckled, rolling her eyes. "Why do I need to be concerned with being cute? My man won't be back in town until late tonight. I trust that after being gone for a month, my bun will be the last thing he's thinking about."

"*Please* don't let that brotha come home to that hairstyle. You know military men like to fantasize about what their wives will be wearing when they get back. I'm sure the picture he has of you doesn't include you looking like you borrowed a hairstyle from someone named Mamie."

"Ha! Be quiet. I'll fix it up special for him tonight, but I am not worried about looking cute right now so you, miss diva, will be left with an image of me and my bun." Aneetra stuck out her tongue before calling for her girls and Nate to come from the play room so they could go.

"Aunt Nee Nee, Lauren hit me," Nate quickly complained.

"No, I did not!" objected twelve-year-old Lauren. Her chubby cheeks flared with anger.

"Yes, you did!" said eight-year-old Ashley, whose physique was completely opposite of her older sister's. Little miniature versions of Aneetra, both girls had their hair platted in corn rows. Thankfully Aneetra had enough sense not to give them buns!

"I know Lauren better not have put her hands on anyone or else she's going to find herself in big trouble."

"He hit me first," Lauren argued, storming past her mom and out the front door, but not before calling both Nate and Ashley "crybabies."

"You better adjust your attitude before I do it for you!" Aneetra shook her head in disbelief. "That girl is getting a mouth on her. It's something about the sixth grade. Kids go in innocent and come out crazy."

"Come here, Nate." Natalie doubted his complete innocence. He trudged over, looking like a puppy that had peed on brand new carpet. "Why'd you hit Lauren?"

"Her hit me, too."

"*Why* did you hit her?"

"Her not share her candy wif me," he explained as though it was a reasonable justification.

"Lauren, if you have candy, give this baby some right this second!" Aneetra yelled.

"No," Natalie objected. "He's not going to hit people to get what he wants."

"But she shouldn't be eating it in front of him. She knows better."

"And so does he."

"Don't be too hard on that baby. Lauren is much older than him. She should've set a better example." Aneetra brushed loose strains of Ashley's hair back in place.

As Nate's godmother, Aneetra was no better at babying him

than Corrine. Natalie gave him the *look* and made him sit down next to her. "Mommy, I sorry."

"Aww…Aunt Nee Nee is going to buy her baby some candy when we go out."

"Me, too, Mommy?"

"Of course, sweetheart," she said to Ashley.

Natalie was unmoved. She was used to Nate's run-of-the-mill apologies. "You need to go out there and apologize to Lauren."

"Okay. You come wif me." He hopped off the couch and grabbed Ashley's arm.

As they walked by Aneetra, she reached out to Nate. "Can Aunt Nee Nee have a hug and kiss?" He nodded yes. She picked him up. "I love you."

"I love you, too, but I not like your hair!"

Natalie fell out laughing and Aneetra couldn't stop from doing so herself. She put Nate down and stared amusingly at Natalie. "I guess I *should* rethink this do, huh?"

Several hours and a few hundred dollars later, Natalie and company were seated in the food court at Polaris—the largest indoor shopping mall in Ohio. Aneetra was reading a magazine, while Lauren sighed every so often to indicate her boredom—she was still grumpy from being yelled at earlier—Ashley and Nate were in their own world playing a game on Natalie's iPad. Natalie flipped through her iPhone, looking at show times. It was difficult finding something to suit all the kids, especially with the age difference between Nate and Lauren. Nate had asked to see the new *Spider-Man* movie, but she was glad it wouldn't be in theaters until next month. Hopefully, Troy could stop working long enough to take

Nate to see it because Natalie wasn't very interested in the newest version that did not have Tobey Maguire as lead.

"Every day doctors are finding a new link to cancer. It's no wonder with all the chemicals they put in food nowadays."

Ever since her mother died, Natalie had been very active during Breast Cancer Awareness month. She liked participating in various fundraising walks whenever possible. Though it had been over six years since her mom's passing, Natalie still missed her greatly. It hurt to know that Nate would never know her. "I think it's over for the movies unless you want to split up."

"It doesn't matter to me. It's not like—"

"Aneetra!" Both she and Natalie looked up to see Lynn walking toward them.

"Auntie Lynn!" exclaimed Lauren, running up to hug her mother's friend, followed by Ashley. Nate simply stared at the unfamiliar woman.

"Hey, girl, what's going on?" said Aneetra.

"Nothing. I came out here to look for stuff for our cruise next month. I can't wait until we get our girl time together. I started to call and ask if you wanted to meet me, but I had to show a house earlier and didn't know how long it would take. Oh, hey, Natalie." Lynn spoke as if she noticed for the first time Natalie was there.

Natalie's greeting was also dry. She wasn't sure why they didn't exactly gel. Lynn had actually helped Natalie sell her mom's house after she'd died. She'd been real cool then, but the more they'd been around each other, the less they clicked. She was fair-skinned with coarse reddish-brown hair and freckles—a feature that few African Americans have—but she was very pretty. She seemed to know it though. Maybe that's what Natalie didn't like—that Lynn reminded her of how she used to carry herself.

Natalie continued flipping through her phone. It was more of a ploy to appear occupied rather than sit looking stupid with nothing to add to the cruise conversation between Lynn and Aneetra.

"Has Marcus come home?" Lynn inquired.

"Not yet. He's supposed to be back late tonight."

"Oh, well, tell him I said hi. He's been gone for quite a while."

"I know, girl, I miss him."

"I bet. You girls having fun?"

Ashley yes; Lauren no. Aneetra rolled her eyes. "With that attitude she may not live to go on the cruise next month. She's been working my nerves."

"I'm sure it goes both ways." Lynn winked at Lauren who smiled; both pretending not to see Aneetra's curt look. "Lauren, you want to come with me?"

She looked at her mom. "Can I?"

"I don't care as long as you bring her home before it gets too late."

"*Yes!*" Lauren transformed into a totally different child. "Did you drive your blue car or the red one?"

"Blue." She smiled as Lauren's face lit up. She liked riding in Lynn's convertible. "You want to come, Ash?"

"No, thank you."

"Brent has a blue car, too," Nate chimed in.

Who's Brent? Natalie thought, but didn't speak up. Lynn and Lauren left soon after, making the movie selection a lot easier.

CHAPTER 7: BLAST FROM THE PAST

Troy was physically exhausted, but his mind could not rest. Though he tried, he couldn't fall asleep. Images of all the victims' bodies and expressions of heartbroken family members stirred in his head. He called Knight. "Hey, Jon, you asleep?"

"Naw, man. I was sitting here going through this case."

"Same here. You want to come over and go at it together?"

"Are you sure? We were at it all last night. The coroner won't be in 'til Monday so I'm not sure what else we can do. You go ahead and spend time with your family, I'm cool. I'll give you a call if I find something."

Troy appreciated how Knight tried to look out for his marriage. A recent divorcee, Knight now lived with his elderly mother in a small two-bedroom home. He'd been divorced for less than a year and his ex-wife had already remarried and moved their teenage son to Michigan with her new husband. Knight didn't really talk much about his feelings, but Troy knew he had a hard time coping with the sudden change. Knight admitted that he believed his job played a part in the demise of his marriage. Long hours, heavy caseloads, and emotional withdrawal were some of the things that Knight cited for sending his wife into the arms of her current spouse. "Do not repeat my mistakes," he often told Troy when he felt Troy might be focusing too much on a case. The two had been friends and partners for many years, except for the time when Troy was temporarily reassigned.

"Don't worry, man, I'm not neglecting anyone around here. Natalie's gone. She took Nate with her over her best friend's house so it's just me for the next few hours. I can't sleep because this case is nagging me."

"Alright, let me get my stuff together. I'll be a minute because I need to pick up a prescription for Mom. Give me about an hour."

Troy got out of bed and slipped on a plain white T-shirt and a pair of sweats over his boxers before going downstairs to put a pot of coffee on. No energy drinks around, he needed the caffeine. The case files still lay on the island where Natalie left them. While the coffee brewed, he flipped through pictures of the victims and the crime scenes.

Most serial killers had a common type of victim, but these ladies were so different from each other:

Victim #1—Lolita Gordon—a thirty-four-year-old Hispanic wife and mother; Victim #2—Myesha Turner—an African-American local college student from Oklahoma; Victim # 3—Amy Howard—a redhead divorced soccer mom; Victim # 4—Michelle Rossi—an Italian physical therapy assistant; Victim #5—Sarah Matthews—a young, blonde Caucasian female in law school. Each report had the same note: *Victim was lying on her back with arms spread out wide. Body did not appear to have been disturbed before CSI arrived.*

Death became their common denominator. All had been shot in the head with a .38-caliber handgun, all their bodies spread out in the form of a cross, all had a copy of the Bible placed on their chests, and all their locations were revealed by a "message" Eric Freeman claimed to have gotten from God. Troy got his coffee and case files and went downstairs.

Though this was not a federal case, the CPD had called in the

FBI Behavioral Analysis Unit to put together a profile right after the third victim was killed. Troy had not worked so closely with the FBI before so the only thing he knew was what he'd seen on television about how the local PD and Bureau bumped heads because of territorial issues. His experience wasn't anything like that. He'd expected to see an older white guy dressed in a black suit and dark sunglasses, but got the surprise of his life when a blast from the past, Agent Cheryl Hunter, walked in.

The two had dated for about a year when they were in their early twenties. He'd known her as Cheryl Bivens back then. Standing barely above five-three, she was still very attractive decades later although her hair was now cut boyishly short. Dressed casually in jeans and a fancy T-shirt, she had the cutest dimple in the middle of her chin. If Troy had wanted to take a trip down memory lane, which he didn't, Miss Lady made sure he would go alone. She pretended not to know him and got right down to business.

"There are several major types of killers," Cheryl said. "A visionary killer is the type who claims to hear voices. They're usually psychotic. The lust killer is driven by sexual motivation, but since none of the victims were sexually assaulted, I would rule that out. The thrill killer simply enjoys the experience, and the power seeker gets a kick about having total control over the victims. Based on the evidence, I think the guy you're looking for is what we call a missionary killer."

"Why wouldn't he be a visionary one?" Troy asked. If Eric claimed to get written messages from God, hearing voices wasn't too far off.

"I get the sense that this individual feels like he is doing something for the good of society—*hence* the name, missionary killer."

That felt personal.

"Considering the note left behind, it's clear that these individuals are being punished for something, be it a real crime or a perceived one in the mind of the killer. Since none of the victims have criminal records, I'd say it's something more personal. Also, the lack of true evidence left behind suggests this killer is extremely organized. You are only finding what he wants you to discover. I bet he'd watched these women for months, maybe even years, before abducting them. Like I said, visionary killers are often psychotic. These categories are not exclusive, so it is possible that the perp is a combination of both, but I would expect more disorganization if he were strictly psychotic." Cheryl sounded very matter-of-fact, but Troy picked up on the underlying offense in her tone. Or was he being paranoid? They didn't have what would be considered an amicable split. "I would put your perpetrator as a Caucasian male anywhere between thirty and forty years old. Chances are, he had a troubled childhood or a traumatic event later in life. Either way, something has triggered this string of killings."

"But these women don't have anything in common?"

"To the killer they do."

Cheryl had given him her contact information and said to call anytime if she could be of any further assistance. Since then, they'd spoken briefly several times as she'd called or texted to inquire about how the case was going. In the meantime, two more women had been killed and Troy was as clueless now as he'd been then. The only one who had any answers at all had been Freeman and *if* the profile was correct, he'd be eliminated because of his race. Could Freeman be *the* guy? Maybe he had an accomplice or maybe Troy was simply barking up the wrong tree. The whole supernatural thing was too far-fetched. He had to have some kind of connection. Troy continued searching though the files, looking for clues, *anything* that could shed light on this case. He hadn't realized how much time had passed until he looked at the clock. He'd called Jon nearly two hours ago. What was taking him so long?

CHAPTER 8: THE SIGNATURE HOOK

The Avenger sat on the park bench and watched as Mindy Lee walked by with her dog. "Good evening."

"Hello, how are you?" Mindy politely replied right before her greyhound jumped into the Avenger's lap. "Sparkie, get down!" She pulled her long, dark hair to the side and knelt down to scold him. "Bad! I'm so sorry about that. I hope he didn't get any dirt on you."

"Oh, I'm fine. He must've smelled these treats in my pocket. Do you mind if I give him one?"

"He doesn't deserve it."

"Even dogs deserve a little mercy from time-to-time, don't they?"

She laughed. "I guess you're right."

The Avenger pulled out a treat.

"Where's your dog?"

"Me? I don't have one."

"So…why do you have dog treats in your pocket at a dog park?" Mindy slowly began to back away, suspiciously. She glanced nervously to see if anyone else was around. There were several passersby. She looked a little more at ease.

"Some idiot hit my dog and then ran off." That was a lie. "These treats were still at the house. I didn't want to throw them away and since she and I used to walk this same trail, I started coming here and giving them to other dogs. I know it sounds crazy, but for me, it's sort of like therapy. I had Lula for seven years. I didn't think I would mourn the loss of an animal like this, but I miss her. She was all I had left after my spouse died from cancer. Somehow she'd gotten out the back gate and when I came home, she was lying dead in the middle of the street! If the person had half the heart and called it in, they tell me that Lo—um, Lula would have still been alive."

Mindy's countenance relaxed and she moved closer to the Avenger. Her mutt jumped up again, but she quickly yanked him away. "I'm sorry to hear about your dog. I know I'd be upset if something happened to Sparkie."

The Avenger pulled out more treats. "Here, why don't you take the rest of these?"

"Wow! Thank you." Sparkie started going crazy. "I better move on. Thanks again! I pray you heal soon."

The Avenger fought hard to keep from laughing when she used the word pray. Mindy Lee was a hypocrite and soon, she'd be forced to pray that God have mercy on her soul. Having those treats tonight was no accident. The Avenger had watched Mindy for quite some time and knew this was a park she frequented. She'd appeared to be a good person, but the Avenger knew better. Mindy Lee would pay for her sins.

Knight finally arrived about seven without any explanation. He and Troy had gone over the case files until both of them had bloodshot eyes. "I don't get it, Jon, what are we missing?"

"I don't know. We need to go back and interview the families. There has to be a commonality somewhere."

"You think doing another search of Freeman's home will help?"

"I doubt it. The shell casings are useless without a gun to match it to and he doesn't have one registered. It would be a waste of time unless you're dying for him to show you where God revealed the message again."

"Oh yeah, looking at a blank wall did us a lot of good. I can't believe that nut job passed a polygraph."

"He's convinced himself that he's telling the truth. Under those circumstances any psycho would pass."

"There's something we're overlooking with him. He spends a lot time between here and Sandusky. Maybe our clues are up there. He said he has a church there, but I did some digging and turns out the only two members are him and his mama."

"Well, Jesus does say '...[W]here two or three are gathered together in my name, there am I in the midst of them,' so technically he could be telling the truth."

"Nice try, Jon, but he's still a few eggs short of a dozen."

Knight laughed. "I know, man. He's definitely an interesting character. Do you know anything about Abundant in Christ church? It says here that he was a member there before starting his own church."

Troy's veins tensed. He was very familiar with the shady dealings of that church. "Are you sure?"

"It's right here in his case file."

"Let me see that." Knight handed him the paper. Sure enough, there was a later statement in which Freeman had mentioned his former affiliation with Abundant in Christ. "Man, how'd I miss that?"

"You're working too hard. Maybe you need to take a day or two off."

"I'm cool. Besides, I'll be off all next weekend for Nate's party. I know we have to be careful about interviewing associates of Freeman's since he's only a person of interest, but I know someone who used to belong to this church. I'm thinking I can do an unofficial interview that will hopefully help us eliminate or confirm his guilt."

"Great! Go for it, brotha. The sooner we have answers about this cat, the better."

If Troy didn't know any better, he'd swear Jon was as black as him. The guy used words like "cat" and "brotha" on a regular basis, claiming his "urbanization" came from growing up in an area called Seven Hills in Cincinnati. Jon also made no secret about his love for sistahs. Not only was his ex-wife black, but he flirted with almost anyone with an Ebony hue.

Troy watched Jon's face light up when Natalie yelled, "Hey, babe, I'm home," and came down the stairs. It seemed like all the guys in the department thought his wife was "hot," but Jon was the only one bold enough to make his crush on her public. Troy wasn't the least bit concerned. Since his divorce, Jon was flirtatious with a lot of women—a coping mechanism, perhaps—because when he was married, it was clear that Jon only had eyes for his wife. Jon could flirt with Natalie all he wanted; Natalie wasn't into short or fat guys.

"Hey, Jon." She smiled when she saw him and he stood up to give her a hug. "I didn't know you were here. I didn't see your truck outside."

"I parked across the street. Good to see you. When you gon' drop that zero and get with this hero."

"Man, that line is about as old as them Hammer pants you're wearing." Troy cut in as Natalie laughed, coming over to give him a hug and quick kiss.

"I'm sorry, Jon, but Troy will forever have my heart even after 'death do us part.'"

Not even close to being a singer, Knight belted, "And I-i-ee-I will always love you," the hook from Dolly Parton's song that was once remade by the now late Whitney Houston for the *Bodyguard* soundtrack.

"*Wowwww!* You left me speechless with that one."

"A brotha knows how to take a woman's breath away," Jon said to her.

"Um, Jon, you're not a brotha, dude."

"Man, I need to get a new partner because you always messing up my game with the race card."

"You couldn't leave me if you wanted to. You know they say once you go black, you never go back."

Jon laughed. "Yeah, well, going white makes ev'ry thang all right!"

"Y'all are just too much for me," said Natalie. "I'm going back upstairs; I just came to say hi."

"Where's Nate?" Jon asked.

"Knocked out. Aneetra and I took the kids to Polaris, the movies, *and* to the park."

"If nothing else wore him out, I'm sure the mall did since his mama is one step away from being a shopaholic. Did you break the bank?" asked Troy.

"Whatever and no, I didn't go crazy. I bought a few things we needed for the house and some other stuff that I'll show you later."

Troy and Natalie had different ideas when it came to what their home "needed." "I'll try not to be too long because I know you wanted to, um, talk to me about something. Remember the conversation we started earlier in the kitchen when Corrine was here?"

She giggled. "Sure thing; I'll be waiting. Good to see you, Jon. Tell your mom I said hi."

"Will do. Good to see you, too, lovely lady."

When Natalie shut the door, Jon turned to Troy. "I guess you're ready to call it a night."

"Yeah. I wish we would've closed this case tonight, but that's too much like right. I'm going to follow up on the lead about his former church affiliation. Right now, I need to get some rest though. I haven't been asleep all day."

"All right." He gathered the stuff he'd brought over and the two of them talked for about fifteen more minutes before they walked upstairs.

"Let's touch base tomorrow."

"Okay. I hope you and the missus have a nice *talk*." As much as Troy tried to be discreet, he should have known that Jon had been around them long enough to pick up on their sexual innuendos.

"Get out!" Troy gently nudged him as Jon laughed all the way to his truck. Troy shook his head and made sure to lock the door before turning on the alarm. Jon Knight was a character, but he was also one of the most dedicated, caring, and genuine detectives that Troy knew. What Troy did appreciate was how he looked out for his marriage, despite all the jokes.

Before going into his bedroom, Troy peeked in on Nate. His little guy was snoring away. Troy couldn't believe how much he enjoyed fatherhood. He'd once been uncertain about whether or not he would be a good father because he didn't have a good role model. Though he still had his insecurities, Troy knew he was giving Nate his absolute best. His son didn't deserve to grow up in a world where serial killers prowled the earth. "I'm going to catch you, jerk!" He pledged aloud as though the killer could actually hear him.

Eager to get to his wife, Troy gave Nate one last glance before leaving. Tired couldn't even adequately sum up how Troy was feeling, but he would conjure up enough energy for Natalie. He walked into his bedroom, hoping to find his wife in her birthday suit or with a sexy outfit on, but instead she was still fully dressed and sprawled out on top of their satin comforter. She'd fallen asleep with her iPhone in hand. The bags of "necessities" she'd gotten lay untouched on their ottoman. He shook her lightly. "Hey, babe, do you want to change out of your clothes?"

"Huh?" She groaned. It was no use. When Natalie was tired she slept like a log. Any other time, he may have been more persistent in attempting to wake her so they could have their recreation time, but he, too, was beat. Instead, Troy gently, but forcefully got his zombie-like wife out of her clothes and into a nightgown. He kissed her lightly before sliding into bed next to her and drifting off.

CHAPTER 9: BAKED TO PERFECTION

orrine was up and packed early Sunday morning. Two pieces of luggage stood by the front door of her small two-bedroom apartment. The second room was supposed to be her office, but over time it turned into a room for Nate. Her desk now sat in the corner of her already crowded living/dining room.

With plenty of time to kill, she lay on her sofa, scrolling through the TV guide and making sure the DVR was set to record her shows while she was away, but not before updating her Facebook status to *Chi town, baby!*

A month shy of turning twenty-four, Corrine was doing well for herself. A marketing analyst for Victoria's Secret, she was required to make business trips on occasion. Already this year she'd been to Indianapolis three times and Philadelphia twice. She was more excited about this current trip because it was an opportunity to truly mix business with pleasure.

"Hey, Mama," she answered her cell phone when her adoptive mother rang.

"You on your way to the airport?"

"Not yet. My flight doesn't leave until eleven. As long as I'm there by nine-thirty, I'll be straight."

"Is Natalie taking you?"

"No. A friend is."

"You be safe, honey. I know you have a lot going on with your job, but I hope you can find some time to come visit this summer. I miss you, Corri, and so does everyone else. You moved to Ohio and it's like you forgot all about us."

Three summers ago, Corrine left her home in Jackson, Mississippi after graduating college and came here with the intentions of staying a short while to help Natalie after Nate was born. She interviewed for the heck of it and ended up getting the job. "Mama, you know that's not true. I was home for Christmas—even stayed an extra week in Jackson after New Year's so I could hang out with you guys."

"That was nearly six months ago. I haven't seen you since."

"I'm sorry. Things have been busy. I'll try and get there this summer. You do know that the airlines run both ways. You could always come visit me."

"No offense, but when I see you, I want to be with *you*, not you *and* Natalie."

Corrine knew this was a dead-end discussion. Her mother would likely always have a jealous streak about her relationship with Natalie. Corrine used to try and defend her reasons for moving to Ohio, saying that she wanted to get to know her little brother and be in his life only to have her mother not-so-kindly remind her that she had siblings in Jackson, too, and their lives were as important as Nate's. Corrine didn't know how to tell her mom that Natalie could never replace her. She loved them equally and yet differently. She would forever be grateful for the sacrifices her mom made to adopt her and she loved her father and siblings more than words could explain. When Natalie came into her life, it was like finding a missing piece of herself. She had no desire to meet her biological father. Natalie was the one who mattered.

They'd lost eighteen years together and these last several years of being around each other and bonding was not something that Corrine was willing to forgo. How could she make her mom understand that her heart was big enough for both her and Natalie to share? "Mama, I love you. If you do decide to come up, I will make sure that it will be Corrine and Toni time. No one else will be invited."

"Girl, you dun lost your natural born mind if you think we're about to be on a first name basis. I'm not into this new age parenting. Your sister came home from school one day tryin' that mess and was put in place real quick. That girl is so different than the rest of y'all. She's going to be the one to make me go completely gray."

Corrine laughed. She could only imagine. Dorrinda was the only other girl besides Corrine out of the five, and she was also the youngest. Spoiled rotten to the bone, she would be starting her freshman year of high school this fall. Growing up, Corrine had felt like maybe their mother treated Dorrinda a little more special because she was her actual daughter. Looking back, she now understood that those feelings were birthed from her own insecurities about feeling out of place in the Shepherd household. Corrine had always known she was adopted, but she didn't know anything about her biological parents growing up. With Natalie being half-black, half-white and her father fully white, that made her only 25% black, but she could technically pass for "light-skinned." Being the only fair one in a home full of dark-skinned people was a constant reminder that she didn't fit in. There was nothing that her mother or father did to isolate her. In fact, they probably overly compensated for her and consequently that's likely why they felt so hurt when she moved to be with Natalie, who happened to be beeping in at the moment. Corrine didn't dare mention this out loud. Instead she said, "Mama, I'm going to get off the phone because my ride will be here soon. I'll call you when I get to Chicago, okay? Tell everyone I said hi."

"Okay, baby, you be safe. I love you."

"Love you, too." She clicked over in time to catch Natalie's call. "Hey…"

"You all set?"

"Yep, I'm waiting for my friend."

"The name of your friend wouldn't happen to be Brent would it?"

The question caught her off guard. She'd planned to tell Natalie everything about him later this week. She wanted to introduce them at Nate's party next Saturday. "Uh, yeah. Why?"

"Nate mentioned his name several times yesterday and when I asked who it was he said 'Sissy's friend.' You know I don't let anyone around my child. What in the world was Nate doing in his car? Did you let him take Nate somewhere alone?"

"No! You should know I wouldn't do that. Brent took us to Chuck E. Cheese's."

"How long have the two of you been dating?"

"I didn't say we were."

"Cut the crap, Corrine. No man is going to take you and a child to Chuck E. Cheese's unless something's going on. So, how long has it been?"

"Four months."

"*Four months!* I thought we were better than that. Why haven't you said anything about him?"

"Sawree! I didn't know I was supposed to tell you all my business."

"You do if it's someone you plan to have around my son. You've kept him secret for a reason, so what's wrong with him?"

Danggit, Nate! She'd forgotten how much little kids talked! "You probably won't believe me, but I did plan to tell you about him this week." Corrine looked up to see Brent coming in the door. Her adrenaline, already racing, was kicked up a notch. She put her finger over her mouth to make sure he stayed quiet. He looked confused. "My mom," she mouthed.

"Which one?" He mimicked back, displaying an endearing smile. She loved the way his dusty blonde hair slicked to the side. It made him look younger. She noticed that he'd been tanning recently. He was baked to perfection with a golden bronze glow that shined. He leaned in for a quick kiss and Corrine longed for more, but Natalie's yelling in her ear killed the moment.

"Are you listening to me? I deserve to know about this stranger you had around my son!"

Corrine felt like she was overreacting, but given all that Natalie had endured in life, she understood. "Sorry, Nat, I got distracted. You're right." She motioned to Brent that she'd be back and headed down the hall to her bedroom where she prepared to give Natalie a full exposé.

CHAPTER 10: GIRL GONE STUPID

"*P*ut that airplane down and get over here so I can put on your clothes or I'm going to take it and you won't see it ever again!*" The shrilling sound of Natalie's voice woke Troy.

He'd gotten good at ignoring morning mayhem when he desired to sleep in, but it was time for an intervention before more drama ensued. "You want me to get Nate dressed for church?"

Looking both relieved and yet still irritated, she nodded and threw his pants onto the bed, turning around to do her hair. Dressed in a towel robe that Troy wouldn't mind undoing the Velcro to, Natalie had already showered.

"Come here, buddy." He patted the bed. "Do you have to take Corrine to the airport?"

"Nope. She's riding with a *friend*. That girl has lost her ever-loving mind! I wish I could beat some sense into her."

"What's wrong?"

Natalie exhaled. "I don't even feel like talking about it right now. I'll tell you later."

"All right." Part of Troy was relieved as he didn't feel like playing counselor at that moment. Normally, she and Corrine got along fine, but when they did bump heads, Natalie got overly emotional and insecure about her parenting skills. "Later" would give the two of them time to patch things up and hopefully eliminate his role as emotional therapist.

Knowing Natalie liked to leave the house by ten-thirty, Troy had about twenty minutes to get Nate together. While Troy was zipping his pants, Nate, with the airplane still in hand, started "zooming" and bouncing up and down on the bed.

"Nathaniel Troy Evans, quit jumping on my bed right this minute!" Natalie glared through the mirror.

Nate jumped up in the air one last time, landing on his bottom.

"Baby, he can stay here with me."

"I take it that means you have no intention of coming."

It was a rhetorical question. He knew she would like him to go with them and most times he did even though he wasn't convinced that church attendance and having a relationship with Jesus were one in the same, but he went anyhow because that's what "good Christians" did. Today, he simply didn't feel like it and even though Natalie didn't say anything, he read the disappointment on her face. "I was planning to go over the case again, but you look like you need some alone time. I'll hang out with Nate and we'll stay here and pray for you to come back with a better attitude."

She tried to hide it, but he saw her crack a smile.

"C'mon, Nate, let's pray. Say dear Jesus…"

"Dear Jesus…"

"Please give me a new mommy."

"I not want a new mommy."

"Boy, you're messing things up. She'll look the same, only a lot nicer. She won't be a snapping turtle."

"Ha! You silly, Daddy. Her not a turtle; her my mommy."

"Oh, son, you have a lot to learn about women."

"Ain't that the truth!" Natalie finished pinning her hair and came over to the bed. "I'm sorry, babe. I didn't mean to snap at you." She bent down and gave Troy a quick kiss on the lips. Doing so allowed him to get a very clear look at her cleavage in that robe. If Nate weren't in the room and she wasn't trying to leave, he would have grabbed her and played out the scenario that should have happened last night.

"*Yuck!*" Nate covered his eyes and his airplane tumbled to the carpet.

Natalie grabbed his hands and started tickling him, "What are you yucking about?" Troy took in the moment. Natalie was a phenomenal mother. He couldn't wait until they brought home a new addition to their family. They hadn't even really tried with Nate and it happened, but making this second baby proved much more difficult. After several months of regular activity, there was still no bun in the oven. "Relax, honey, these things take time," Natalie had said when he shared fears of perhaps being unable to produce. He hoped it didn't take too much longer. He was already past forty and wanted to attend his next child's graduation before he was eligible to collect social security.

Troy jumped in on the horseplay between Natalie and Nate and the three of them tumbled and tickled each other ferociously. Natalie wasn't even upset that her hair had gotten messed up. *Thank You, Lord, for my wife and son!* He'd spent so much time during his younger years avoiding any type of long-term commitments that he never wanted to take his family for granted. Though he didn't understand why God allowed such craziness in the world, the one thing Troy knew for sure is that he was truly blessed. That was something not even the worst day on his job could make him deny. Troy may have a few issues with God, but he didn't doubt His existence or goodness in his own life. Troy's two greatest earthly blessings were right before his eyes.

Troy took a quick shower before Natalie left. Once she was gone, the two Evans boys ate nachos and cheese dip—a breakfast Lady Evans would despise—and went down into the basement where they played several video games. Despite his age, Troy had not given up his Xbox 360 and he would have preferred to play one of his sports or war-like strategic games, but Nate wasn't ready for all of that. Instead, they played a more age-appropriate game on the Wii. Troy's only enjoyment of "Jamario Brothers" as Nate called it, was the interaction with his son.

As if two gaming systems weren't enough, soon a Kinect hook-up would be added because Natalie *insisted* they get one for Nate's birthday. Troy wasn't convinced that it was so much for Nate as it was for his mother—especially after looking through her bag last night and seeing a Zumba exercise game she'd bought during yesterday's shopping spree. *A real necessity, huh?*

By the time he heard Natalie come in from church, Nate was asleep on the futon and a phone call from Chad Gordon had prompted Troy to work on the case. He also had an email from Agent Hunter asking how things were going. He wished he had more to tell them both. Unfortunately, answers continued to elude him.

Troy waited a few minutes, expecting Natalie to come down, but she never did. Her footsteps could be heard pacing back and forth upstairs.

"Corrine, think about what you are doing! I've been down that road and I know what I am talking about!" Troy heard her speaking as he ascended the stairs. "No, I am not overacting. I don't want to see you make the same mistakes that I did. You're playing with fire. Keep striking matches and one of them will catch flame."

A writer at heart, Natalie often had crafty ways of tying her words together. Prior to Nate, she had been very active in a poetry group.

Her involvement had greatly declined over the years. "Your head is as thick as a brick! I don't know why I'm wasting my breath. You're going to do what you want anyhow." Natalie finally noticed Troy standing there. She gave him a weak smile, rolling her eyes. "Okay, I'm done talking about this. Call me if you need me to pick you up from the airport Thursday. I love you."

"It looks like my prayer was in vain and that Pastor Giles' sermon didn't do anything to put you in better spirits."

"Oh, hush, I'm fine." When Troy put his arms around her he felt her tenseness, despite the warm kiss she gave him.

"What's going on between you and Corrine?" He was still hesitant to get involved, but this thing wasn't working itself out fast enough.

Natalie blew out a deep sigh. "My daughter is dating a married man."

"Whoa…" The news was shocking enough to break Troy's hold on her waist. Corrine did not seem like that type. "Are you sure?"

"Yes, I'm sure." Natalie gently pushed him away and leaned on the counter. "Yesterday, Nate mentioned the name Brent several times and when I finally asked him who that was he said it was 'Sissy's friend.' So, I called this morning and demanded she tell me who it was since she had him around our son. She claims she was going to tell me about him although they've been together for four, five months—something like that. She wants to bring him to Nate's party next week and had the *nerve* to tell me not to trip about him being married. She said it all nonchalantly, like it's something I should overlook. " Natalie smacked her hand against the island. "Oh and it gets better from there. Not only is the guy married, but he also has three kids."

"Wow. How old are they?"

"I don't know. Does that even matter?"

"You're right, honey, it doesn't. I'm sorry. You know we detectives close cases with details."

"Well, this is the case of a girl gone stupid! I've been down that road before and I'm trying to tell her that it only leads to destruction. I don't want her making my same mistakes." When Natalie started crying, Troy gently pressed her head on his shoulder. Her tough shell always crumbled when it came to the kids or others she cared for deeply. "I don't want her to be like me...like I used to be!"

"Babe, calm down. Corrine is an adult and she will have to make her own mistakes, like we all do. You're doing your part by steering her in the right direction."

"I told her that I wasn't comfortable with her bringing him, considering the circumstances, but I don't want her to be mad at me and not come herself. It will break Nate's heart."

"You know she wouldn't do that to him."

"I hope not. I wish she would listen to me. I feel so powerless to help her. Man, I suck at motherhood!"

Troy gently grabbed Natalie's chin and lifted her head to him. The thirteen year age difference between Natalie and Corrine came with benefits and disadvantages. Since Natalie was close enough to Corrine in age, she was able to relate to her in a way that sometimes got lost when there's a large generation gap between parent and child. But times like this, Natalie felt like a failure. The situation with Corrine was more serious than he'd thought and he felt bad for downplaying things earlier. "Don't you even go there! You know that's not true. You are a wonderful mother. I'm sure Nate agrees and so will our next little one."

She swatted his hand away from her belly. "I'm not pregnant."

"Give me about thirty minutes and you can be."

She huffed, showing her irritation. "I am *so* not in the mood."

He figured as much, but a guy couldn't be blamed for trying. "Babe, relax. You've built a wonderful relationship with Corrine. She trusted you enough to tell you about him. I seriously doubt she told Toni."

"Oh, Toni would flip."

"Exactly! I think Corrine wanted your voice of reason even if she doesn't seem to be responding to it. She knows where you stand on things. She's listening, baby. Give it time to sink in and even if it doesn't, it's not your fault. Don't get all dramatic about being a bad mother. You're not. You're awesome. Corrine and Nate are proof of that."

Natalie remained silent as her tears continued to fall. Troy stared deep into her eyes and saw the mixture of confidence and insecurity as they wrestled inside of her. On the surface, Natalie often seemed overly confident. From the assurance of her footsteps to the assertiveness of her speech, Natalie never went unnoticed. But somewhere underneath, Troy knew there was still a layer of uncertainty. Perhaps it was residual pieces of her brokenness— the time in her life before they met, before they married, before she placed her trust in God. Natalie was not the type to allow people to easily get close to her. She had other associates, but Aneetra was her only true friend besides another lady in Mississippi whom Natalie knew as a child and reconnected with several years ago. Neither Troy's sister nor his best friend's wife had been able to really crack beneath her surface. Though he did think Natalie was overdramatizing a bit right now, he realized each time she'd let down her guard in front of him, she was exposing her vulnerability and he was not willing to risk crushing her any further. He looked deep into her narrow, copper-brown eyes.

"The mistake Corrine is making is no reflection of you. She'd be lucky to turn out half as good as you are."

"But—"

"There are not buts. If you ask me, Corrine and Nate have the best mother on the planet."

She smiled faintly. "I don't think your mother would appreciate you saying that?"

"She'll be all right." He kissed her forehead before slowly making his way to her lips. "I love you, Natalie Renée Evans."

"I love you, too," she whispered between sniffles.

CHAPTER 11: IN THE MIDST OF IT ALL

On Monday morning Troy stopped at Hope Ministries Rehabilitation Center, a drug and alcohol facility for recovering addicts owned and operated by Hope Ministries Church—a small, but well-respected organization in Columbus. Troy hadn't been here since the time he worked a high-profile case, but he was certain that the man he needed to speak with would still be around. Leaning across the desk, he flashed his badge. "Hi, I'm Detective Troy Evans with the Columbus Police Department. Is Robert available?"

"Um…just a sec." The receptionist quickly dialed him on the phone. Seconds later, Robert appeared.

"Detective Evans, it's been a while. Nice to see you." The two men shook hands like they were old friends. Roughly the same age, both men had built physiques. The first time that Natalie had met Robert and his wife, she later told Troy that she'd thought Robert was "cute" and that his wife was "pretty." Troy appreciated how he and Natalie could openly compliment others without stirring up feelings of jealousy. While he would agree that Robert's wife was indeed attractive, Troy's masculinity would not allow him to even fathom describing Robert as "cute." Robert was a dark-skinned guy of average height who happened to keep himself in shape—something that another guy *would* notice. If that's what Natalie considered cute, then *whatever*. "What brings you by?"

"Does the name Eric Freeman ring a bell?"

"*Wow.* It rings many bells. C'mon, let's go to my office." He turned to the receptionist. "Debbie, please hold all my calls unless it's Pastor B or my wife."

Robert's office hadn't changed much since the last time Troy had been there, if at all. A newspaper clipping of Robert wearing boxers and being escorted by the police in handcuffs still hung on the wall. Someone had written a scripture underneath it. Troy had always wondered about that picture and why in the world Robert had it hanging up like it was something to be proud of. He didn't know much about Robert's past, but he did know about the troubles his family had endured the last few years. Yet the guy was so full of life, always wearing a smile.

"You want to know about Eric Freeman, huh? You mind me asking why?"

"I'm investigating several cases."

"C'mon, you have to give me a little more than that. My mind is wondering."

"Eric is a person of interest in a case I'm working. I'm fishing for as much information about him that I can gather. Anything I say to you must not be repeated."

"Not to worry, you have my word."

Troy believed Robert. Troy's life experiences and eighteen years of on-the-job training had made him an expert in character judgment. Through his limited, professional interaction with Robert, Troy could tell he was a cool, trustworthy person and perhaps that's why Troy felt comfortable enough to come to him. A man doesn't go from being in handcuffs to the director of a drug and rehabilitation center without proving his integrity somewhere down the line. "Is Eric a friend of yours?"

"Hardly…I don't know him well at all. I've only had a few inter-actions with him, but that was enough for me."

"You and your wife used to attend Abundant in Christ, correct?"

"I *never* went to that church," he said adamantly. "Lisa did. They all went there."

Troy didn't need clarification of who *they* were. He knew exactly where Robert's mind had drifted. "I'm sorry, man. I don't mean to dredge up any bad memories. I'm just—"

"You're cool. I take things one day at a time. Some days are easier than others, but that's life. Anyhow, Eric and Lisa were, um, *friends* at one point. Like I said, I was around him only on a few occasions, but that was enough for me to figure out that the man is not playing with a full deck."

"Please elaborate."

"I think he suffers from some type of god-like complex. Of course it would take a psychiatrist to diagnosis him for sure, but I think he's a Christian narcissist, if there is such a disorder."

A narcissist? That certainly would fit the profile of someone who could commit these murders. Cheryl had said the killer was on some kind of a mission. Perhaps Eric wanted to show these women that they weren't as knowledgeable about Christ as him. "Have you ever witnessed him show any signs of aggression?"

"Yep! Say something about the Bible that he doesn't agree with and you're in for the fight of your life. I know you're trying to be discreet, but can you tell me what he may have *allegedly* done? The worst thing I can imagine him doing is going off on some-one for misquoting scriptures."

"No, I'm afraid it may be much more serious than that."

"How serious?"

"I'm investigating several murder cases." The room went jarringly silent. "You okay?" Troy finally spoke up several minutes later.

He nodded slowly and smiled. "I'm good. Anyhow, regarding Eric, he is a lot of things, but the last thing he strikes me as is a murderer. Then again, who am I to say that he doesn't have a dark side?"

"Do you think Lisa would be willing to answer a few questions about Eric if need be?"

"She definitely knows him much better than I do, but I'm sure she'd tell you the same thing. As anal as Eric is about the Word, I can't fathom him taking anyone's life, but I've learned the hard way that you never really know what people are capable of until they actually do it. If your case against him becomes official then, by all means, contact her. But, I don't want her involved if this is only a fishing expedition. She's been through so much these last few years. We are finally getting used to our new sense of normal. I don't want anything to upset her."

Detective to citizen, Troy felt that Robert's lack of willingness to involve Lisa was impeding his investigation. Sure, Eric was officially classified as a "person of interest," but that was all jargon. They needed to gather as much information about him so he could be cleared or charged. How many women would have to die before this case came to a close? But, man to man, husband to husband, Troy understood exactly where Robert was coming from. He'd do anything to protect Natalie. She'd had a troubled childhood and if he thought for a moment that something or someone could cause her to regress, he'd put a stop to it immediately.

"It's not that she can't handle it," Robert continued, "She's probably way stronger than I'm giving her credit for. But I don't want her to have to deal with it unless absolutely necessary."

"I gotcha. For now, I'll let her be. But, if this case does advance against Eric, I won't be able to avoid talking with her."

"Understood."

"Well, I have taken up enough of your time. Thanks for meeting with me."

"Not a problem. You've done so much for my family, it's the least I could do."

"I only did my job."

"No, it was more than that. I'm from Baltimore, man, and I know the difference between a cop only doing his job and you. You're good people, Detective Evans. Believe that."

"Please, call me Troy." He snickered to himself, recalling how bent out of shape Eric gets about being addressed by his first name.

"Okay, Troy. Is there anything else I can help you with?"

"No, not at this time. I'll be in touch should there be any new developments."

"So, you're not going to ask me?"

"Ask you what?"

"I saw you eyeing that clipping on the wall. You want to know what happened, don't you?"

"Guess I'm not the only detective in the room."

"You'd be surprised about the things I pick up on from time to time."

"I admit I'm curious. What's your story?"

For the next twenty minutes or so, Troy listened intently as Robert shared with him the events of his past and how it was that night of getting arrested by the Baltimore PD that changed his life and propelled him into his purpose. Robert even admitted his infidelity, which shocked Troy to the core. He didn't seem like the type. Troy's expression must have revealed his thoughts because Robert said,

"My actions were a shock to everyone, including myself. The thought of cheating on my wife was detestable to me. Something I'd never imagined doing. You wouldn't believe how jacked up the chic was that I cheated with. It made no sense at all. Man, I wasn't even attracted to her, but it goes to show how people get tangled up when they stray from the Word of God. I was going though all the motions, but my heart was rebellious against Him."

"Do you ever get angry with God for the way things ultimately turned out? I know you and Lisa are back together, but it came at a hefty price."

"Not at all. I've learned not to praise God when things are good, but even when they are not. My divorce, remarriage and even…" he took a deep breath. Remnants of sadness were felt during the pause. "Well, you know the rest. The point is that God is good and nothing that happens in my life will make me doubt that."

Troy had been a Christian for about five years, but unfortunately his faith had weakened quite a bit over the last few. He couldn't exactly pinpoint one thing in his own life that caused his spirit to diminish. As a matter of fact, Troy had to admit to himself that his life was pretty good. There was no room for complaints. Both he and Natalie had good-paying, steady jobs, despite the economy. Besides the mortgage on their four-bedroom, two-and-a-half-bathroom home, and the payment on Natalie's car, the Evans' didn't owe anyone for anything. They had a joyous young son with no medical conditions, the entire family had full coverage health insurance, and they were planning on expanding their family. Essentially, all of his family's needs were met and there were many wonderful aspects about Troy's life. It was his job and the devastation he saw happen in the lives of others that started to get to him. Robert was one of those individuals and yet, his faith hadn't been shaken at all. What was Troy not getting?

"These last few years have not been easy, but no one can ever convince me that Jesus is not real. There's no way my wife or I would have survived all we've been through had the Lord not been with us. I may never understand why things turned out the way they did, but I know *Who* has been the key to my having peace in the midst of it all."

"Wow, man, that's deep. Are you sure you're not a preacher because I could swear that was a sermon you just gave."

Robert laughed. "Ministry isn't only about being in the pulpit. I am where I am supposed to be. What about you? Where does your relationship with God stand?"

Troy hadn't expected Robert to be so direct. Being so spiritually grounded, Robert reminded him of his best friend, Elvin, who had been very instrumental in leading him to Christ. Elvin and his family lived in Chicago and though the two spoke on a regular basis, it was usually about catching up with the happenings in each of their lives. When biblical things did come up, Troy was able to talk a good game to make it seem like his faith was still strong, but he'd never shared with Elvin the doubts that arose the last couple of years. Elvin never called him out the way Robert had done, though Troy was certain he wouldn't hesitate to do so if given the chance. "I believe in God."

"Man, even the devil believes in God. I asked you about your relationship with Him. Belief in and fellowship with aren't exactly the same thing. "

Troy respected a man who didn't beat around the bush, but Robert was getting way too personal now and Troy wished he'd kept his mouth shut. "I—um, well—" As Troy struggled to string together a sentence, his cell phone rang. A welcomed interruption! "Excuse me for a moment. Evans here..." It was the voice of one of his colleagues informing him of some disturbing news. "All right,

I'm on my way." Troy turned to Robert. "Good talking to you, man, but I have to run. Sorry to end things so abruptly."

"No problem. We'll finish this conversation another time." Robert smiled, but this time it wasn't only a smile. There was much more behind it—like Troy had become a spiritual charity case or something. It felt eerie and Troy didn't know quite how to respond. "I wish I could have been more help to you."

"You were very helpful. Thanks again." Troy extended his hand as Robert got up and opened the door. "I can see myself out. You take care."

It looked like Robert was going to say something else, but Troy made his exit before giving him the chance.

CHAPTER 12: A REASONABLE EXPLANATION

Natalie noticed Aneetra's downcast spirit all morning, but it wasn't until later in the day that she was able to get her alone. The two hadn't spoken since their outing on Saturday. Normally, they would see each other at church, but Aneetra wasn't there yesterday and Natalie didn't blame her. If Troy had been gone for weeks before returning home, she wouldn't have been at church either, or work for that matter. She would still be "ministering" to her hubby at this very moment. Unfortunately, she and Troy didn't get any recreational time in over the weekend. Not for lack of trying, but rather opportunity, convenience, and the fact that he kept ruining her mood with that crazy baby talk. "Our lunch was just delivered. See you in our spot in five." Natalie walked by her friend's cubicle, carrying the Chinese she'd called in.

"What makes you think I don't already have lunch plans?"

"I know you don't. Wrap up and meet me there," she gently ordered and kept moving. Their spot was the conference room on the second floor where they worked. Every blue moon the ladies would eat in the cafeteria with their co-workers, but neither enjoyed the nonstop hour of office gossip or the let's-talk-about-the one-who's-not-here-today routine that often took place. Thus, if they didn't go out to lunch, normally they would eat at one of their desks or in the conference room, which was usually free during that time.

The room was huge. The sky-blue walls created a peaceful atmosphere and the ceiling-to-floor back wall-to-wall window overlooked the I-270 overpass. Plaques lined the walls, revealing tidbits about the company's history. Aneetra walked in as Natalie finished unpacking the food.

"You're awfully bossy today." She was only half joking.

Natalie smiled. "I love you, too."

"Yeah, yeah, whatever. This smells good. What did you get?"

"Orange chicken and fried rice. Here…" She handed Aneetra a paper plate. "You first, or rather crab lady before boss lady."

"Whatever. I'm not crabby."

"Something's going on with you, but go ahead and eat. You can tell me what's on your mind after your belly is full."

"There goes that bossy thing again. Girl, you better be glad I like you *and* that I'm hungry, because nobody can tell me what to do around here except Alex and she's out today."

"You didn't get the memo? I'm second in command, boo. Now eat." Aneetra laughed and they ate their lunch in unusual silence while Natalie thought about her own dilemma.

Nearly four years into their marriage, Natalie was still very much attracted to her husband and his ever-so-slight, but very sexy Southern accent. Her entire body tingled when she first saw his six-foot-one, smooth, dark chocolate, sculpted frame. Marriage, children and having a relationship with God were nowhere on her agenda. He was to be her booty-buddy. Somehow he'd penetrated her heart and that was scary because both of them had so many issues at the time. Despite everything, she'd felt God had been merciful. He'd blessed them tremendously, although their beginning was not-so-biblical and rocky. Troy was a wonderful husband and father. She knew how much he wanted another child and at first, she was cool with it, but now she continued to have second thoughts.

Besides the fact that he worked like crazy, she was also concerned about his increasing withdrawal from God. She'd tried to speak with him about his spiritual struggles before, but that didn't go too well. Instead, she prayed for him often and tried to be a godly wife to him. Natalie believed wholeheartedly in the Bible and she knew 1 Peter 3:1 which talked about wives being able to win over their husbands to the Word by their behavior. Troy knew almost everything there was to know about her past life. She surely hoped that the woman he saw on a daily basis served as a testament to him that God was most definitely real. She longed for him to be the spiritual head of their household, but until he was ready to take his rightful place, it was her responsibility to make sure Nate was raised in the "nurture and admonition of the Lord" as commanded in Ephesians 6:4. Spiritual leadership and being the primary caregiver for one child was enough. Natalie didn't think she could handle another one.

"Are things all set for Nate's party?"

"Pretty much. He should have a Spidey good time."

"That boy is Spider-Man crazy for sure. I need to get his present sometime this week. I should have picked something up while we were out, but I didn't want him to see. I don't know what to get him between y'all buying him a motorized car and Corrine getting him a swimming pool. Short of getting Spider-Man to make a real-life appearance, what's left?"

"Whatever you do, *please* don't buy him any video games. Troy got that covered. I guess I should be happy that at least he did add something educational to the mix." Natalie rolled her eyes. "The thought of my son playing video games for hours on end in his forties like his father makes me cringe. Don't get me wrong, I like Wii Fit and I'm eager to try the Zumba on the Kinect, but at least the games I play are beneficial because I'm exercising. Troy sits and wastes time."

"I think you're being too harsh. It's not like he spends hours every day playing and neglecting you and Nate. He works hard and deserves to relax however he sees fit. Give him a break."

"Since when did you become Troy's defense attorney?"

"I haven't, but I'm trying to get you to realize that there are worse things he could be doing. Be glad that he enjoys relaxing in the comfort of his own home even if he is playing a game. At least you don't have to worry about him running the streets."

"True."

"I wish I could say the same."

"What happened? Were Marcus' orders delayed?"

"No, he came home late Saturday night as planned, but then he got up early Sunday morning. He said he had to take care of some things, but he was gone for hours. Nat, I think he's having an affair."

Aneetra's normally bubbly personality had been deflated and Natalie saw strength wrestling with devastation in her friend's eyes. "Are you *sure?*"

"I don't have any concrete proof, but something is not right with him. You would think that after being gone for so long, he would have been ready to seriously jump me when he got back. It was close to midnight, the girls were asleep, and I was up waiting for him in the living room in a sexy nightie."

"Girl, did you put that bun back in your head?"

Aneetra chuckled. "I love how you can make me smile, even when I'm down. For the record, I was not sporting the bun. Nate talked me out of that one, remember?" Her demeanor turned solemn once again. "He came in, gave me a kiss—not the kind of welcome home kiss I was expecting—but a mere peck as if he'd returned home from the gym or something. Although I practically threw myself at him, he said that he was tired. He took a shower and went straight to bed. He got up at five o'clock yesterday morning to supposedly run errands. What kind of errands can a man have that early on a Sunday morning? As of this morning when I left, he *still* has not made love to me. We've been married for sixteen years and I have felt for a while that something wasn't right. But, now I'm certain. Oh, and he changed the code on his cell phone. Before you give me a lecture, I was *not* snooping. I was actually trying to get a number when I realized there was a new code. I don't even know how long it's been like that because I don't make a habit of going through his phone, but I've always been able to unlock it if I needed to. I asked him about it and he made up some excuse about having to reset it and that he couldn't remember the code off hand, but he'd get the number for me. By the time I went to the bathroom and came out he'd written it down."

"Maybe he changed it for security reasons."

"Yeah, right, that's weak. Marcus has always been so careless with his cell phone, but these last several months it's been glued to his hip. I didn't think anything of it until yesterday."

"Have you spoken with him about how you're feeling?"

"Not yet. But, I will. I'm asking God to give me the right words to say because I truly don't know how to approach this. If I give in to how I feel, Marcus would have a good old-fashioned beat down coming like my sister did her husband when she found out he was cheating. She literally cracked his skull with a baseball bat. They didn't talk until he was out the hospital and she was out of jail."

"You have got to be kidding."

"Nope. They were divorced shortly after. As crazy as her actions were, I can see how she snapped. They'd been together since high school and had four children over the course of twenty-something years. Marcus better thank God that I didn't give into my feelings because he'd have a lump on his head, too. But, I'm not trying to go that route. We've never been violent with one another."

Natalie wasn't sure what to say, certain that she'd be an emotional wreck if she even *thought* Troy was cheating on her. "His behavior does seem suspicious, but don't be so quick to think the worst. There may be a reasonable explanation for this." Natalie wasn't sure she even believed those words. It seemed like the right response.

"I hear you, Nat, but I have a bad feeling about all of this. I've been through enough to know that if it looks and quacks like a duck, then that's what it is."

"Well, I still hope it's not." She saw the pain that the mere suspicion of adultery lent in her friend's eyes. Pain that she was sure she'd contributed to wives in her past and that Corrine was helping another husband bring on his wife.

CHAPTER 13: AIN'T THAT SOMETHIN'

The rest of the afternoon Natalie did her work to the best of her ability, but she couldn't stop thinking about Aneetra, who'd left work shortly after lunch, stating that there was too much on her mind for her to be effective, so she took personal leave and went home. "Girl, pray for me," she'd said to Natalie. "I don't know what lies ahead, but I know I have to believe that God is with me."

"You know I got you covered. Holla if you need me."

That was several hours ago and Natalie hadn't stopped thinking about Aneetra since. As she drove from work to the preschool to pick up Nate, she hoped Aneetra would call this evening. Natalie didn't want to contact her because she knew Aneetra needed her space. If nothing else, she needed to spend time alone with God. Was Marcus cheating? He and Aneetra seemed like the perfect couple. Sure, no marriage was ever perfect, but they seemed close. Natalie looked at them as role models. Marcus appeared to be the example of godly leadership for his family that Natalie wished Troy was for theirs. If Aneetra and Marcus were having issues, was there any hope for her and Troy?

Seeing firsthand how adultery—or suspicion thereof—devastated the spouse, Natalie felt bad about the times she'd been the other woman. It was a gut-wrenching feeling to know that she'd caused the same type of pain she saw on Aneetra's face on someone else and apparently Corrine wanted to play "like-mother, like-daughter." She was going to have a good, long talk with that girl. And if that didn't work, she wasn't sure what to do. She was so grateful to have a relationship with her daughter and she didn't want to jeopardize what they'd built over the years. Corrine's moving here had been a source of contention between her and Toni. Perhaps if they'd had a better relationship with each other, Natalie would call so the both of them could tag-team and get Corrine to see that she was making a foolish decision. But, Natalie was as certain as Troy that Corrine had not uttered a single word of this to Toni, who was not good at handling her emotions where Corrine was concerned. And if Natalie were to mention it, somehow Toni would blame her. *If only Big Mama were alive…*Natalie missed her grandmother so much. Big Mama would know exactly how to handle this.

"Hi, Mommy," Nate waved to her when she walked into his classroom and then turned back to play with his friends. Part of her wished that he'd run into her arms immediately upon seeing her, but the fact that he wasn't clawing to get out of the building gave her peace knowing that her son liked his caregivers and peers. She'd feel even worse if he cried when she dropped him off and was still crying when she picked him up like a few other kids did. She had no qualms about leaving Nate and that was worth more than her desire for his immediate attention. She called for him to come while she spoke briefly with his teacher.

By the time she'd gathered his belongings, Nate hadn't budged. "Come on, Nate. Tell your friends goodbye and let's go." She walked toward the doorway and waited, but he still hadn't moved. *"Nathaniel Troy Evans,"* she began to say, but didn't have to finish. Nate knew his grace had expired.

Hand-in-hand they walked to the car while Natalie listened to Nate recap his day. With the exception of her former friend's baby girl years ago, Natalie had never spent much time around young kids before meeting Aneetra. Nate's intelligence amazed her. Only two days shy of his third birthday, he seemed ahead of his time. He spoke very well compared to the other kids in his class and he also understood things better than Natalie gave him credit for. She could actually have a conversation with him and it amused her to no end.

"And Ms. Frank made Jerry share 'da ball but him was cryin' 'cuz him not want to share," Nate was explaining to her when the cell phone rang.

"INCOMING CALL FROM DIANE," announced the Bluetooth surround speaker system in her car. "SAY 'HELLO' TO ANSWER OR 'IGNORE' TO SEND THE CALLER TO VOICEMAIL."

"*HELLOOOOOO*," yelled Nate at top of his lungs.

"Natalie?"

"Hey, Diane."

"Did I catch you at a bad time?"

"No. I just picked Nate up from pre-school and we're on our way home."

"*HI GIGI!*"

"You don't have to scream, Nate. She can hear you."

"Hi, Pumpkin, how's my boy doin'?"

"Fine. I got a star at school 'cuz I say all my ABCs like 'dis 'abcdefg...'" He continued all the way to z.

"That's good, sweetheart," said Diane.

"I count in Spanish, too, like 'dis 'uno, dos, tres, quantro, cinco—'"

"Very good, honey. Let Mommy talk to Gigi for a moment, okay?"

"'Kay."

"Di, you still there?"

"Yep. Girl, that boy just about know more than me. I can barely speak English good and he's talkin' in Spanish. Ain't that somethin'? I need to learn Spanish with all these darn immigrants we got down here." She chuckled. "Anyhow, what's up with that son of mine?" She went on to use expletives of how she called his black behind earlier that morning and he hadn't called her back.

"Aw, Gigi said black a—"

"Hush, Nate. That's not a nice word. Di, I need you to watch your mouth. Nate can hear everything you say." Her mother-in-law was sweet, but sometimes she cursed like a sailor. Natalie hated that her behavior seemed to have rubbed off on Troy who occasionally slipped when he was angry—even in front of Nate— and that irritated Natalie because she didn't want her son to be raised in that type of environment. At least in Diane's defense, she didn't profess to be a Christian. Troy didn't have an excuse.

"Girl, I'm sorry. I forgot I was on speaker that quick."

Natalie rolled her eyes. She'd told her mother-in-law on many occasions that she could count on being on speaker whenever she called and Natalie was driving. "Yeah, well to answer your question, Troy probably hasn't called you back because he's busy working on a big case. I talked to him through text messages today, but that's all."

"Oh, okay. Well, I wanted y'all to know that I that I mailed a g-i-f-t for someone today and it should be there by the time of the p-a-r-t-y."

"P-a-r-t-y," Nate repeated and then started laughing as though he really knew what she was spelling.

"It ain't much, but it was all I had. I told Tracy that she needed to send somethin' and she said she was going to, but then spent her money bailing that no good bas—um, husband of hers out of jail this mornin'."

Diane had no room to talk about her daughter's husband; Natalie's father-in-law wasn't exactly in the running for any awards. Troy may have gotten cursing from his mom, but Natalie thanked God that he didn't have any of his father's philandering ways. "That's okay. Thank you for sending your gift. I'm sure he will appreciate whatever it is."

"When y'all comin' down here? I ain't seen my grandbaby since Christmas."

"I don't know. I'll have to talk to Troy and we'll let you know. But, I'll be sure to send you some pictures of the party."

"Oh, yes, please do that. Well, I won't hold you any longer. Tell my son I said hi. If the package doesn't come, let me know."

"Will do. Thanks, again."

"Bye, Nate. You be a good boy. Gigi loves you."

"Kay. I luh you, too."

"YOUR CALL HAS ENDED."

Natalie wouldn't mind taking a trip to Houston sometime in the near future. Despite Diane's use of foul language from time to time, she was Nate's only grandmother and Natalie wished they saw each other more. Her mother died before he was born and he was too young to remember her paternal grandmother whom she'd affectionately called Big Mama. Natalie had no idea if her maternal grandparents were still alive. If so, she wondered if they were still in Jackson. All she'd known about them was that they'd disowned her mom after she'd gotten involved with Natalie's father, a black man. Not surprising, given racial tensions in the south, especially back in the day. Biologically, Diane was all Nate had because Troy's father couldn't be counted on.

Natalie was thankful for her mom's best friend, Sylvia, and her husband, Richard, who did try and fill in as local grandparents for Nate. They were cool, but it was still sort of weird since Richard and Natalie's mother were involved for many years before she died. She wouldn't have been able to break ties with either of them even if she wanted to because of Troy's professional relationship with Richard, who was a prosecuting attorney and worked closely with the CPD. In all honesty, Richard was the closest thing to a father figure that Natalie had, but he would never be able to replace her own father, who died when she was young. She still had faint memories of him held close to her heart. She could be crazy, but she swore Nate had his smile.

It was about a quarter to five when Natalie turned down her street. She glanced in her rearview mirror at Nate, who amused himself by continuously spelling his new word for the day, party. As expected, Troy's SUV wasn't in the garage when she pulled in. She didn't know what time he would get home. There was very little consistency in his schedule due to the nature of his job.

"Yay! We home," Nate shouted and smiled, trying to undo the seat belt of his car seat.

Extremely appreciative of her husband and son, knowing that based on her past, Natalie's marriage should be the one going through what Aneetra's was, she said aloud, "Thank You, Jesus!"

"Why you say 'dat, Mommy?"

"Because He has been so good to us, baby." While getting Nate and their stuff into the house, she silently prayed. *Lord, please be with Aneetra. I hope Marcus isn't cheating on her, but if he is, please fix this. Marriage is something You created and I believe it's Your will for it to survive and thrive. Please open Corrine's eyes to the destructive nature of her actions. Protect her from her foolishness. And God, thank You for just being You...no matter what.*

CHAPTER 14: MARRIED WITH CHILDREN

After leaving Robert, Troy's day was filled with more interviews and unanswered questions. The phone call he got was regarding a young lady, Mindy Lee, who hadn't been seen since Saturday night and also failed to report to work this morning. Not surprisingly, witness reports were inconsistent. Some recalled seeing a tall, dark-skinned man lurking around Mindy's house early Sunday morning while others said they saw a thin Caucasian male late on Saturday. No one thought to get the license plate of the F-150 or the suspicious sedan that some reported seeing on several occasions, including Sunday. Normally, the police would wait a full forty-eight hours before declaring an adult as a missing person, but there was a strange familiarity about Mindy's disappearance that was similar to how the other five cases began. Sure enough, when they stepped into her home, all officers observed the sign indicating that Mindy Lee was in the hands of a killer. At the most, she had a week to live.

Someone had been watching Freeman's every move since Saturday. There was no way he could have taken Mindy. Troy still believed he had some connection with the perp. Maybe he was an accomplice, but he was definitely not the main culprit. With few leads to go on, unfortunately, the only thing they could do was to wait for Eric to receive another "revelation" or for Mindy Lee to escape from her captor.

Troy had sent Natalie a text earlier saying that he'd be home late, but he'd actually got there about 7:30. He walked in through the garage door, slightly perturbed that the exterior alarm wasn't on, but the smell of lasagna on the stove and the sound of Natalie and Nate singing and dancing along with a *Blues Clues* video placated him.

"Here's the mail, it never fails, it makes me want to wag my tail and when it comes I want to yell, maaaaiiil!" Troy watched the sheer joy on Natalie's face as she and Nate screeched the last part together. She was an eleven out of ten in the looks department, but when it came to singing, she sounded as pleasant as a bull frog. Troy never had the pleasure of meeting Natalie's mother, but from the stories he'd heard from Natalie and others, her mom couldn't hold a note in a Ziploc bag and Natalie was even worse. Even Nate sang better than his mom.

"'Dat was fun, Mommy!"

"That was horrible," Troy teased, coming from around the corner.

"Hi, Daddy!" Nate ran to hug him, followed by Natalie who'd ordered him to "hush," but with such a bright smile that Troy knew she was happy to see him.

"You're home early." She planted a kiss firmly on his lips. Not too intense, considering the child was present, but deep enough that Troy recognized her foreplay and Nate ran and jumped head first on the couch screaming, "Eeeewwe."

"If that's how I'll be greeted from now on, I'm going to do my best to make it home early every day."

"Are you hungry? I'll make your plate."

"Yes, I am. Thank you, babe." Natalie went into the kitchen while Troy went over to the couch to play with Nate and ask about his day.

"I talk to Gigi and her said you have a black a—"

"Naaaaate! You say that word and I'm going to spank your bottom real good and I mean it! I told you earlier that wasn't a nice word."

"You know better, man," added Troy. Nate looked down and poked out his lips. "Stop that. You're not going to turn three if you act like that."

"*Nooa!* I wanna be t'ree."

"Then act like a big boy."

"'Kay. I sorry."

"So, you spoke with Gigi today?'

"Uh-huh. Her said p-a-r-t-y." He laughed.

"Do you know what that is?"

"I have my birday and Mommy said sissy come back from her airplane for my p-a-r-t-y."

Nate was tickled to death at himself. The boy often displayed one of two signs of sleepiness—extreme whining or excessive silliness—and it was clear he was ready to pass out at any moment. When Natalie announced that Troy's plate was ready, Nate laughed. When Troy finished eating and put his utensils in the dishwasher, Nate laughed. When Troy stated he was going to jump in the shower, he laughed. He kept laughing about the tiniest little things and there was only so much of it that Troy and Natalie could take before they put him to bed.

"And God bless my mommy, my daddy, my sissy and my birday party, amen." Nate was the last of the Evans clan to pray as he and his parents held hands in Nate's room. Troy gave his li'l man a high-five and left for the master bedroom while Natalie stayed behind to kiss and tuck him in.

"So my mama is mad at me, huh?" he asked when she came into the room. He was double-checking the lock on his gun safe to make sure it was secured. A cop can never be too careful about these things, especially with children in the house.

"Not really. She wanted to know why you didn't call her back."

"She left a message that she mailed Nate a present. She said to call when it arrived. I didn't think I needed to call and tell her that

I got the message." Troy was sitting on the edge of the bed when Natalie came and hugged him from behind, nearly knocking him over. "Are you okay?"

"Yes. I am so thankful for you."

He turned to face her. "I'm thankful for you as well." They kissed. This time it was a kiss that would surely lead them to "wrestling" as they'd told Nate they were doing one night when he walked in on them. He was planning to get on her for leaving the house unsecured, but the moment was seized by his hormones. Troy laid Natalie on the bed and they wasted no time getting straight to the point. Normally, they waited to make sure Nate was fully asleep, but neither took such precaution tonight as both seemed eager to please the other.

When their sweet encounter was over, Natalie lay on his bare chest while he held her tight. Initially he thought the wetness he felt from her cheek was sweat until she reached up to wipe her face. She was crying. "Baby, what's wrong? You and Corrine have another argument?"

She looked up at him, fear lingering in her eyes. "Would you ever cheat on me?"

"No! Where did that come from?"

"The Bible says that we reap what we sow and I've done my share of dirt. I don't want to be married for sixteen years only to discover that you're cheating on me. That would hurt too much."

"I am not nor do I ever intend to do so. I love you and I don't ever want to hurt you."

"Who plans adultery? I'm sure most people mean their vows when they say them, but then life takes over and stuff happens."

Her words reminded him of something Robert had said. *"The thought of cheating on my wife was detestable to me. Something I'd never imagined doing."*

"I know I've done wrong in my life. What if it comes back to me?"

"Babe, you are really trippin'. Don't fret on what could happen in our future. Let's enjoy each moment for what it is. I don't know what life holds and neither do you, but remember that God is merciful." *Maybe not so much in the lives of the recent murder victims.* How could mercy allow that to happen? "Isn't salvation supposed to wipe the slate clean?"

"Yeah, but—"

"Then why are you worried that I'm going to cheat on you because of sins you committed before you knew me or God?" Troy was amazed at how wise he sounded. He did believe what he was saying, but he was also still very conflicted about how to reconcile his beliefs about with his anger toward God.

"Can I see your cell phone?"

"For what?"

"I want to see it. Why won't you give it to me?"

Troy was starting to get irritated, but he remained patient and reached over to the night stand and got the phone for her. "Here, look through it all you wish, but you won't find anything. What have I done to make you question my loyalty?"

"Nothing." She laid the phone aside without investigating. "I'm so sorry. I'm thinking about Aneetra. She suspects that Marcus is cheating on her." Natalie filled him in on the conversation she'd had with Aneetra earlier that day. He agreed that Marcus' behavior was strange to disappear so early on a Sunday morning without explanation. *Sunday morning?* Marcus was tall and dark-skinned and drove a maroon F-150, same description neighbors gave of a mysterious man around Mindy Lee's place. Was it coincidence or could Marcus somehow be connected to her disappearance and the other cases? It wouldn't be the first time that a serial killer was married with children. Troy shook his head, dismissing the thought.

The description was so vague that half the men in Columbus could be suspects. Even Jon drove a black Ford truck, though he didn't quite meet the tall and dark-skinned criteria. Feeling bad for allowing his thoughts to drift while his wife was clearly in some kind of emotional distress—i.e. trippin'—he was sure to interject an "um hmm" or something similar from time to time so he at least appeared to be attentive.

"I haven't heard from her since she left work. I want to call, but I'm afraid that I will catch her at a bad time and I don't want to interrupt, especially if she's having any type of deep conversation with him."

"For real?"

"Troy?" Natalie sat up further.

"Hmm."

"Are you even listening to me?"

"Of course, I am."

"No, you're not." She grunted, smacking his bare chest.

"I'm sorry, honey. I may have zoned out for a second, but I promise that I heard *most* of what you said."

"What were you thinking about?"

"How bad my performance must have been if you're lying in bed with me thinking about another couple."

She laughed and leaned forward seductively. He was glad to see her smiling. "Trust me when I say that there is absolutely nothing wrong with your performance. As a matter of fact, if you're up to it, I'd like to see the second act."

Her words alone were enough to make his temperature rise and when she leaned down to kiss his chest that was icing on the cake.

CHAPTER 15: INSIDE SCOOP

The Avenger watched Mindy from the corner of the room, gun pointed in her direction. Today was only her third day and already she was working the Avenger's last nerve. She wasn't the least bit remorseful about her actions like the others had been. When confronted, she challenged every point rather than take the opportunity she was being given to repent. She was by far, the worst. The Avenger was losing patience with this one. Mindy hadn't even touched the Bible laid before her. The others seemed to go back to their roots, but this one had completely ignored the Word.

Mindy Lee was volatile. The scratches she'd placed on the Avenger's arms still burned. Mindy needed to seize the moment to repent and be changed. Maybe God had turned her over to a reprobate mind as Paul spoke about in Romans 1. No matter how much the Avenger tried to convince her of the error of her ways, she refused to listen. No use keeping her alive any longer. Though it hadn't been a full seventy-two hours yet, Mindy had to die. It would be better to wait until this evening, but the sooner Mindy was gone the better and the Avenger had found the perfect spot for her remains. Called to be the "angel of death," the Avenger carried out the mission, but where each victim spent eternity was up to them. Mindy was a lost cause.

"Go ahead and undress. It's time." The Avenger handcuffed, gagged, and stuffed her in the trunk of the car before making the ninety-minute-or-so drive southeast to a small Ohio city in Hocking County, and venturing deep into the woods. This was where the final showdown was to take place, but with the eyes on Eric now, there was no way to get a message to him, so Mindy's body would have to remain here until the whole thing was over. The Avenger hated breaking protocol. Things had been so meticulously planned out, but it was all good. God knew the Avenger's heart was ultimately to please Him. These women deserved to die.

Certain that no witnesses were around, Mindy was released from the trunk and led to her pending execution. The Avenger had found the perfect spot and made her kneel before the cuffs and the gag were removed. The Bible, opened to the appropriate scripture, was given to her. "This is your last chance. If you don't repent, you will die and go to hell. On behalf of God, I am extending His mercy to you one last time. Read it!" The ringing cell phone momentarily broke the Avenger's concentration. It was a split-second decision that gave Mindy the opportunity to knock the gun away and run. More annoyed than panicked, the Avenger ran after her, firing away. Mindy went down from a gunshot wound in the leg. "Stupid girl. Because of your rebellion, you've lost your chance for salvation." Several more bullets were blasted and Mindy Lee was dead.

The sound of a twig snapping caught the Avenger's attention. Someone had been watching.

Troy tried calling Jon several times all day but continued to get his voicemail. As the afternoon wore on, he'd decided to proceed without him, leaving one final message. "Hey, man. I'm headed over to Lang's. If you get this message, meet me over there. What's up with you? Call me a-sap. I think I may be on to something."

Troy spent the morning and early afternoon going over every shred of evidence and interview they had on record for each of the victims. He didn't find a direct connection between any of the victims, but he found a small detail that served as a common thread with some of them. It was a long shot, but right now anything to go on was better than nothing.

Jon finally called back. "Sorry, man. It's been a crazy day. You at Lang's yet?"

"Just pulled up."

"Give me about five minutes and I'll be there. What did you want to tell me?"

Troy worked with Jon long enough to know that his five minutes was more like ten or fifteen. For a white man, he sure knew how to operate on what was known in the black community as "Colored People Time." "We know they were all Christian women, so what if the killer targeted them because of some revealed struggle with sin? We know for a fact that Michelle Rossi and Amy Howard were no strangers to adultery. Interviews with Sarah Matthews' cousin also revealed suspicions of being involved with a married man she met online."

"We found nothing to validate that. To our knowledge, Myesha and Mindy were single and, from everything we've heard, Lolita and her husband had a good marriage."

"It doesn't mean that Turner and Lee didn't participate in the destruction of anyone else's marriage. Plus, Lolita and Chad's son is six, but they've only been married for five years. Maybe her sin was premarital sex," Troy reasoned.

"A killer targeting her for having a baby out of wedlock and then marrying the baby's father? I'm not buying it. Besides, how would the killer know anything about these women? We can't find anything that connects them."

"You're right. There's a piece of the puzzle missing somewhere. Whatever the case, I'm starting to think that Freeman's too convenient. Somehow he's getting the inside scoop about these murders, though. When we figure out his connection, we'll have our killer." Troy looked in his rear view mirror and saw Jon pulling up behind him. He hung up and got out of his Navigator to meet him. "So five minutes really did mean five minutes this time?"

"What? You thought I was rolling on CPT today?" His smile was bright, despite the apparent battle wounds on his face and arms. "You know a brotha won't let you down when it really matters."

Troy shook his head. "You're obviously going through an identity crisis. Why are you all scratched up?"

"I got into a fight with my cat and she won."

"When did you get a cat?"

"Oh, uh…a few days ago."

Strange, Troy thought as the two of them crossed the street to the tiny green house. He'd never known Jon to like cats.

CHAPTER 16: A ROCK AND A HARD PLACE

When Aneetra wasn't at work Tuesday morning, Natalie knew something was wrong, but she waited until lunch before finally calling.

"He cheated on me," Aneetra cried.

Natalie's heart sank. "Oh, honey, I'm so sorry. I don't know what to say."

"This isn't fair, Natalie! I have never been unfaithful to him. I thought he loved me. Why didn't God protect my marriage??? Why did He let my husband have sex with another woman???"

Tears ran down Natalie's cheeks. The pain she felt for her friend was like she was experiencing it as well. "Where is he now?"

"I don't know. We got into it again and he took off. He's probably over her house."

"You know who she is?"

"No. It's somebody he met online. Stupid jerk! He had the nerve to get upset with me because I was asking a lot of questions."

Natalie could think of a lot of things she wanted to call Marcus, but the Lord helped her to hold her peace. "I understand your desire to want to know details, but keep in mind that the more you know the more you have to forgive."

"Whatever. It's not like I was asking him what position he did her in. I wanted to know how long they'd been messing around and where they did it at. I'm his wife. I think I have a right to know if he was screwing this woman in our bed. *He broke our vows! Not me! He should tell me any and everything I want to know!*"

"You're right. I'm sorry. Where are the girls?"

"They're with Lynn. I called her last night and asked if she could pick them up."

Lynn was like a thorn in Natalie's side. She and Aneetra had known each other for a very long time. It seemed like Lynn took pleasure in bringing up back-in-the-day stories or other events that Natalie wasn't a part of. Natalie was sure she did it for the sole purpose of making her feel excluded, like last Saturday how she kept going on about the cruise they were taking. Natalie had never spoken her feelings about Lynn out loud, not even to Troy, for fear of being viewed as childish, but she didn't trust or care for the chic. She did value her relationship with Aneetra though and, for that reason, she dismissed the schoolgirl envious question of *"Why did Aneetra call Lynn and not me?"* She concentrated on how she could support her friend who shamelessly wailed over the phone. "I'm coming over."

"You don't have to do that," she said between sniffles. "I'm okay. Don't use up your vacation time for me."

"Nonsense, I'll use whatever I have for you. I need to wrap up a few things, let Alex know I'm leaving, and I'll be there soon."

"Ma'am, what can you tell us about Mindy's personal life?" Troy asked her friend.

The lady, a short dark-haired Asian woman whose first name was unpronounceable so she publicly went by Sophie, was understandably concerned about Mindy's well-being. "I don't know what you want me to say. Mindy was, *is*, a good person. The longer it takes to find her, the more likely it is that she won't be found alive. I've seen the news. Whoever is doing this doesn't wait long before killing these women."

"Even good people have some issues." Troy was having a hard time getting comfortable on her narrow sofa. He'd never seen anything like it before in his life. Was it even a couch? It looked more like a bleacher bench with a back. If that wasn't weird enough, the entire living room was the same color as the outside of the house. Natalie would certainly have had a fit about that. Thanks to Ms. Lang, green had now become his least favorite color. "Is there anything in Mindy's personal life that didn't quite line up with her faith?"

"What are you implying?"

"Nothing. It's that we would like to find her and any information about her that you can tell us will be beneficial."

"There was some things going on with her, but I-I'm not sure I should say. I don't think it has anything to do with her disappearance."

"You should let us be the judge of that."

"Look, lady, we are working our butts off to locate her before she ends up like the other victims. We can't do it without your help," Jon said bluntly. His intolerance was uncharacteristic. Troy was usually the impatient one while Jon remained the "good" guy.

"What my partner is saying," Troy remained calm, nodding to Knight that he would take over from here, "is that from everything we can find out about Mindy, she appears to be a fine, upstanding Christian citizen. Are there any indiscretions you can tell us? As her best friend, you would likely know information about her that we couldn't uncover by speaking with anyone else. If there is something, you need to tell us. It would help tremendously."

"Well…she is going to kill me if she finds out that I told you this."

"And she might get killed if you don't," huffed Jon.

"Mindy recently found out she is pregnant."

A pregnant single woman certainly fit into Troy's theory about why the women were being targeted. Could it go even deeper? "Was she planning to have an abortion?"

"Absolutely not! She would never consider such a thing. It violated her beliefs. I know it seems like an oxymoron—a Sunday school teacher getting pregnant out of wedlock—but I believe Mindy really did love God. She had a deep need to be loved and lost all wisdom when it came to men. She kept meeting these jerks online. In two years, she'd gotten involved with two married men. One stood her up when they were supposed to meet and the other got her pregnant."

Troy knew he was on to something now for sure. Even Jon was starting to give credence to his theory. The two looked at each other, sharing an *ah hah* moment.

"In her defense, she did think he was single. He didn't tell her about his wife and kids until after she told him she was pregnant. Mindy was devastated. She'd thought he was the one. I know she wasn't necessarily living right, but Mindy is a good woman. If she wasn't so insecure about being single, I don't think she would have ever been so vulnerable to these jerks she kept meeting."

"Do you know the name of her child's father?"

"Yes, I do. Excuse me for a moment." Sophie Lang went around the corner, probably to another green-painted room, and came back moments later with a Post-It note. "I don't know where he lives, but this is his name and cell phone number. Mindy called me from his phone one day when her battery died. I never told her I kept the number. I don't even know why I did. I guess part of me always knew something would eventually go wrong with their relationship because of the circumstances. I've spoken with him since Mindy disappeared, but I wasn't going to say anything about him because I honestly don't think he had anything to do with it."

"Let us determine that." When Troy looked at the name and number on that piece of paper, he knew that he'd stepped in between a rock and a hard place.

CHAPTER 17: A STICKY SITUATION

Natalie made it to Aneetra's house within forty minutes of their phone conversation. The front door was unlocked so she walked in, calling out her name.

"I'm in here," Aneetra yelled from her bedroom.

Natalie found her sitting at the edge of her canopy bed, sheets crumpled, surrounded by soaked tissue. Her reddened eyes and swollen cheeks bore witness to her troubles. "Oh honey!" Natalie hugged her tight. The drawn shades added an extra measure of gloom.

Aneetra relaxed in her arms, trembling as she cried. "I don't understand why God allowed this to happen. It's so unfair."

"I know, honey." Natalie's heart ached with a level of sympathy she'd never felt for anyone else before.

"I tried so hard to be a good wife. Why wasn't my best good enough? He has a wife and children and has to have a tramp, too? What kind of woman goes after a married man???"

Ouch! She knew Aneetra wasn't intentionally taking a shot at her character, but it still hurt. Natalie had done some low down stuff in her past. *If any man be in Christ, he is a new creature: old things are passed away; behold, all things have become new.* Natalie silently repeated 2 Corinthians 5:17, one of the scriptures she'd memorized after she got saved, which she'd used to encourage herself during times of insecurity. Though she had no doubt that she'd been forgiven of her sins, at times feelings of unworthiness and inadequacy would still pop up.

Upon learning that Aneetra hadn't eaten since their lunch in the conference room yesterday, Natalie tried to get her out of the house. "I don't have the energy to go anywhere."

Natalie was able to convince her to at least eat something. She scavenged through Aneetra's kitchen, finally settling on a frozen dinner that Aneetra ultimately let go to waste. Natalie had planned to stay with her friend for as long as she was needed, but she would have to leave to get Nate by six o'clock or the preschool would slap her with a three-dollar-per-minute late fee. She had texted Troy to see if he would get off in time to pick up Nate, but so far she'd gotten no response. *And he wants another baby!* Times like this are when Corrine's presence was missed greatly. She'd often picked up the slack. Natalie was about to ask Aneetra if she would mind her bringing back Nate when the front door slammed.

Marcus slowly walked into the bedroom. Beads of sweat rested on his bald head. His countenance was of a man who'd been given the death penalty. "I'll be out of y'alls way in a minute." His deep voice was painful and soft.

Natalie almost felt sorry for him. One glance at Aneetra reminded her of the real victim in this scenario. Aneetra stared at him, Natalie stared at Aneetra, and Marcus refused to look their way. He walked into their closet, grabbed a T-shirt and as he made his way out the room, Aneetra spoke. "Get lipstick on your clothes?"

Marcus turned to face her, pointing to a darkened stain on his shirt. "It's not lipstick; it's ketchup. I would like to change my shirt without any drama."

"There wouldn't be any drama if you weren't out there screwing around."

"Yes, I messed up, Aneetra, but life happens. I'm sorry I hurt you.

I'm hurting, too. Quit thinking that you're the only one suffering here!"

Aneetra got in his face. "Yeah, I'm sure it really broke your heart getting some from both your wife and mistress. I hope whatever she gave you was good because you've destroyed our entire marriage because of it!"

"You think the affair ruined our marriage? We've been messed up for a long time, but you've been too busy with your head up in the clouds to see that!"

"Oh, so this is *my* fault!"

Unsure of what to do, but no doubt feeling like a third wheel, Natalie crept out the room. Her standing there seemed so invasive though she could still hear everything they were saying to each other from the living room. She hated to leave Aneetra in the event that Marcus stormed out on her again, but she really had to go get Nate and there was no way she could bring him back here now. If this was how things were last night, no wonder Aneetra had had Lynn pick up her girls.

"It's freakin' ketchup for goodness' sake!"

"For all I know it could be anything! You've proven to be a liar!"

Natalie sent Aneetra a quick text apologizing for leaving and saying that she'd check on her later. The sound of the doorbell hadn't been enough to interrupt the couple's shouts. Natalie tried to lay low for a second, hoping whoever it was would go away, but the person was persistent. She would have to get rid of them however she could because she needed to go get her son. *"Troy!* What are you doing here?"

"Working. And you?"

"I came over because Aneetra was upset and I didn't want her to be by herself."

"You're a cheating idiot!"

"And you're too demanding!"

"Doesn't sound like she's alone now. You don't need to hang around here while they are arguing like that. You're putting yourself in harm's way."

Annoyed, Natalie frowned at him. "She just found out he was cheating on her. Do you seriously expect her not to be upset?" She noticed a figure across the street sitting in a truck. "What is Jon doing here? Better yet, you never explained why *you* are here."

"Natalie, we have ourselves a real sticky situation here. I suggest you go get Nate and call and check on Aneetra later. Right now, I need to speak with Marcus."

"About what?" She stopped Troy as he began to push his way into the door.

"Official police business. Go home! I'll talk to you later."

"Troy—"

"Leave, Natalie. *Now!*"

Natalie wanted to challenge him. Tell him that he better not ever speak to her like that again—that he could have responded to her text message—that simply because he was a detective, he didn't have the right to boss her around like some ordinary citizen; she was his wife and, police work or not, he'd better remember that. There was a whole bunch that she could say to him and that she probably would say to him at a later time. Right now, she knew better. As upset as she was with Troy, she knew how dedicated he was to his job and she saw his determination to enter the Bennett home. If she continued to protest, she could see her husband slapping handcuffs on her wrists to get her out the way. She saw it in his eyes. It was like the look she gave Nate when he had gotten on her nerves one too many times. Natalie pushed past him without saying another word. She hopped in her tweener and headed to the preschool, already late, hoping the light rain didn't slow down traffic too much.

CHAPTER 18: CONFLICT OF INTEREST

By the time Natalie got to the center, she had racked up a hundred and twenty dollars in late fees, which had to be paid before Nate would be allowed back at school. They didn't take checks so Natalie would have to leave a little early tomorrow in order to have time to stop at the ATM before work. The staff members, who were generally very pleasant to her, were visibly irritated. Nate was the last child left. His bag was already packed and sitting on the table beside him where he had fallen asleep.

Natalie almost regretted waking him because he did nothing but whine all the way home. The pit stop at Wendy's to pick up dinner didn't change his temperament. He cried as he ate. His nuggets were too hot, they weren't hot enough, a French fry fell on the floor, yadda, yadda, yadda. Natalie exhibited as much patience with him as she could, considering her own emotional state wasn't that great. She quickly gave Nate a bath and got him into bed. She tried to say prayers with him, but he cried all the way through and she gave up. Her mind was so jumbled she didn't have clarity with saying her own prayers. She lay on the bed, deep in thought.

8:37 p.m. Troy still wasn't home and no word from Aneetra. *Maybe Troy wanted to talk to Marcus man-to-man about marriage.* Nice thought, but far-fetched. Troy and Marcus didn't spend time together unless Aneetra and Natalie dragged them to a couple's outing. They got along well enough, but they never seemed to really click. They seemed to simply tolerate each other for the sake of their wives.

Troy wouldn't take the liberty to talk to Marcus about something so personal. Besides, in his own words, he was "working."

Troy's biggest case was the murdered women. How was Marcus connected? Maybe he was questioning Marcus about another case. No, all of his other cases had been delegated so he could focus solely on this one. The fact that he was questioning Marcus at all was unsettling. Anxiety overwhelmed her so much that she found herself calling both Troy and Aneetra, but neither answered.

To have so many questions and no answers was nerve-wracking. It would have been nice if, when her phone rang, it was either Troy or Aneetra calling her back, but from the caller-specific ring tones she'd programmed, she knew it was Corrine. "What's up?"

"Hey, Nat. Is Nate still up?"

"Nope. He's knocked out. He was really whiny tonight."

"Aww. I'm going to call him tomorrow and wish him a happy birthday. I miss my little bud. I can't wait until his party."

"I hope you're not still planning to ask your lover to come with you," she did not try to mask her sarcasm.

"Yes, I am. And please don't refer to him as my lover. He's my boyfriend."

"He's someone's *husband.*"

Her daughter sighed. "It's unfair for you to judge him without even knowing anything about him."

"I don't want to meet him. I'm sort of offended that you are so lax with bringing a married man around me. Would you be taking him to Toni's house?"

"No. What's your point?"

"That you are not respecting me. I may not be that much older than you, but I still deserve your respect."

"I wouldn't take him to my mom's house because I know how

she'd be. She never gives people a chance because she's too busy judging them from jump. I told you because we've always been able to keep it real with each other. I'm not trying to disrespect you, but I don't want to keep secrets from you, either. I know you're my birth mom, but for real, Nat, you're also my best friend and big sister all in one. I don't need you to approve of me dating him. I love him and he loves me and we're going to be together no matter what you or anyone else thinks about our relationship. You act all righteous, but you've dated married men before."

"And it didn't work out."

"Okay. That was your situation. Let me make my own mistakes, *if* this is a mistake. My point is that you are fine. You're happily married to Troy and you got there because you had something to compare your experience with him to."

"I don't want to see you get hurt. I also don't want you participating in the destruction of anyone's marriage."

"He's not happy."

"If his marriage is falling apart, let it happen without your participation. This is wrong, Corrine, on so many levels."

"I feel what you're saying, but—"

"Hold on a sec. Troy is beeping in." Natalie clicked over. "Hey, where are you?"

"Sorry I missed your call. I saw where you had texted me earlier about getting Nate. Anyhow, don't wait up for me. I got called to a murder scene."

"Hang on, let me get Corrine off the other line." Natalie promised to call Corrine back after she finished speaking with Troy, but Corrine didn't seem interested in continuing the conversation. She said she'd call Nate tomorrow. "Okay, I'm back."

"You could have stayed on the phone."

"No, that's okay. We were bumping heads about this married dude she's dating anyhow. Why did you need to talk to Marcus?"

"Babe, I can't get into that. I only wanted to check in and tell you what's going on tonight."

"Why is it you can tell me other things, but when I start asking questions, all of a sudden everything is off-limits?"

"There's clearly a conflict of interest here. I'm not going to tell you anything that could possibly jeopardize my case. I also don't want you going back over there until things calm down."

"You can't tell me what to do. If Aneetra needs me, I'll be there for her."

"You can be there for her without being at her house. Jon and I literally had to break up a fight between them."

"Did you arrest Marcus for domestic violence?"

"Marcus wasn't the one doing the hitting."

"You arrested Aneetra?!?!"

"*No.* We didn't arrest anyone. All I'm saying is that emotions are very high around there and you need to stay away from the house—not Aneetra—until further notice. I don't want you caught in the crossfire."

"Point noted, but not necessarily taken to heart."

"All right, Natalie, I don't have time to do this with you right now. I have to go. I don't know what time I'll be home, but I'll be there as soon as I can. Please make sure the alarm is on. Last night when I came in all the exterior points of entry were left unsecured."

"O-kaayy." Sometimes she hated his overprotectiveness, but it did creep her out a little being in a big silent house alone while her husband was out looking for a serial killer. The exterior alarm was on, but she got out of bed and turned on the motion sensor downstairs as well. *Better safe than sorry.*

CHAPTER 19: ALL AN ACT

orrine hung up feeling stressed. She hated the friction between her and Natalie. It hurt knowing that Natalie was disappointed in her, but she hoped she'd eventually come around. Sure, technically, she and Brent had no business crossing the line, but it wasn't as if they'd planned this. Working so closely together, they'd started out as friends and it evolved from there.

She stared out the window of the downtown Sheraton on East North Water Street where she would be staying for the duration of her business trip. Her room faced Navy Pier and overlooked Lake Michigan. Butterflies tickled her stomach as she recalled being at the top of the Ferris wheel earlier that afternoon.

"You okay?" Brent walked in, carrying hors d'oeuvres he'd gotten from the hotel club lounge.

"Yeah." She decided not to tell him about her conversation with Natalie.

"You have to taste this. It's really good."

He handed her a toothpick with lettuce, meat, and melted cheese. It looked like chicken salad on a stick, but it tasted so much better. "This *is* good."

"I should've asked the lady what it's called so I can have Hannah look it up and make it."

The mention of his wife's name caused her second bite to get stuck in the middle of her throat. "Do you think she would? I mean, with her being so distant toward you and all?'

"Oh, yeah, you're right. Then maybe you can make it for me." He scooped her up and led her to the bed where they fell on top of the comforter. "Something's wrong. I can tell. Spill it," he said while nibbling her neck.

"Natalie says that I'm contributing to the destruction of your marriage."

"Well, that goes to show that she doesn't know everything because Hannah and I are married by name only. I've told you plenty of times before that it's over between us. It was over long before I met you."

"When are you filing for divorce?"

He sighed, heavily, lying back on the pillow. "How many times must I tell you that I can't file for divorce until our youngest starts kindergarten? Hannah is not working and if I divorce her now, it will screw my son up. She's been his primary caretaker the only two years of his life."

"Why can't he attend pre-school like other kids? My little brother does and he's fine."

"Because he can't, okay? I know three years seems like a long time to wait, but it will happen."

"What if you decide you want to be with her again during this time?"

"I *won't.* We haven't made love since she got pregnant with our youngest son. Hannah is a good mother, but she's a lazy, fat cow. She's home all day and doesn't cook, clean, or do anything except watch soap operas and play Angry Birds. Oh, and I think she might have a drinking problem, too."

"But when she came to the company picnic last month, you guys looked so happy. She seemed very nice."

"That was all an act on both of our parts. We knowingly hate each other, but I am always very polite and cordial to her because I'm afraid that if I get her angry, she might take it out on our children in order to get back at me. Corrine, if I hadn't met you, I don't know what I'd do. Look at how much time we spend together. If I really wanted her, I'd be at home right now instead of enjoying this beautiful city with you. I'm with the one I love."

They did spend a lot of time together. Surely, everything he said about his wife was true and the way he said he loved her was so sincere. Three years would go by faster than she thought. Corrine could force herself to be patient if it meant Brent would ultimately belong solely to her. "I really want you to come with me on Saturday, but I don't think Natalie will be too friendly. I don't want you to feel uncomfortable."

"I don't know why you were pressing the issue so much. I honestly didn't want to go. I don't know all of her friends and it would be a disaster if I ran into someone I knew there. How would I explain that to Hannah?"

"You said she knows you're dating someone."

"Yeah, but she doesn't know who. Our friends and family don't know what's going on in our relationship. I took a big risk going to Chuck E. Cheese's with you and Nate. I don't want to do that again. Now that Natalie knows about me…I don't know. I'm only trying to protect you. I don't know what Hannah would do if she saw how beautiful you are. This is the first time I've ever stepped outside of my marriage. She'd be jealous for sure and might try to hurt you or even worse, the kids. She's vindictive like that."

Corrine felt sorry for him. His eyes were solemn. He really was in a bad situation. "I'm sorry I said anything."

"It's okay." He kissed her passionately and Corrine tried to erase the uneasiness she felt as Brent's hand slid up her shirt. It was a constant battle between her mind and body whenever they made love. She was slightly relieved when his phone buzzed, thinking that it might be about their business meeting tomorrow. As soon as she saw his face, she knew who had interrupted them.

"I'm sorry, I have to take this or she'll just keep calling." He hurried out of the room. As the door closed behind him, Corrine heard him say, "Hey, honey…"

It was all an act, she told herself.

CHAPTER 20: SWEET AND NAIVE

When Troy got the call that officers in Hocking County had found a body in the woods that fit Mindy Lee's description, he made it there a few minutes before Jon, but both had record times. Her body was found about a half mile from a murdered teenage boy. The police department had agreed to turn all evidence for Lee over to Columbus detectives, but they would oversee the case of the boy and share whatever they found. Apparently the boy had witnessed Mindy's execution and was trying to call 9-1-1 when he was shot.

Officers worked frantically to shield the bodies from the steady rain. Authorization had been given to get Columbus CSI out there to assist the smaller department. Troy wished they'd hurry. He had more confidence in his guys than strangers.

"Evans, chill. You know CSI will take care of this," Knight said when Troy started taking pictures.

"I know, but you know how I am." He looked toward the waning sunlight and shook his head in frustration. It would be fully dark soon and their crew was still about thirty minutes away. They'd gather what they could tonight and come back tomorrow for more, but Troy wanted as much of a head start as he could possibly get. Mindy's case was so different than the others. The Bible wasn't lying open on her chest. It was on the ground between the two victims and she had multiple gunshot wounds, unlike the others. The killer had been forced to break his pattern. That was crucial.

Troy took a few more shots with his smart phone before his people arrived, dressed in their usual head-to-toe garb. He and Knight moved out of their way, even the local crew yielded to them. "I never took you for a feline person, so when did you get a cat?" Jon's explanation about his scratches had nagged him all day. He had to know that Troy would inquire further. This wasn't exactly the most appropriate time, but Troy wasn't doing anything except staying out the CSI's way and Jon was eyeing the ground.

"Uh, a few days ago."

"What kind is it?"

"Um, a small orange and black one. She looks all cute and cuddly, but she's a mean li'l thing. She scratched the mess out of me earlier. Reminds me of my ex-wife. I hope you don't get scratched up when you finally make it home. Natalie looked really ticked when she left Bennett's place."

Troy knew he was lying, but why? And what was up with him trying to deflect the conversation? "I can handle Natalie. You need to worry about how you're going to handle your cat." He saw a new text from Agent Cheryl Hunter. *Heard abt hocking co...call if u need me.*

"Do you think she'll be all right?"

"Uh , yeah. She, um, she's understandably emotional right now. The two women closest to her are being affected by adultery."

"I know about Aneetra, but who's the other?"

"Corrine. She's dating a married man."

"Dude, for real? She doesn't seem like that type. She's so sweet and naïve."

"Yeah, well, apparently my stepdaughter is not as innocent as we thought." As lead detective, there was a level of austerity Troy liked to maintain when on the job. He'd realized that he'd opened the door to personal talk by inquiring about the cat and was glad to see Paula walking by. "You think we'll finally have some hard evidence?" He asked as she was headed from Mindy's body to the young boy's. Knight excused himself.

"Besides the shell casings? Hard for me to say. We're finding a lot of crap that we can't conclusively relate to the murders. But, don't worry, we'll go through these woods with a fine tooth comb and get everything to the lab so they can sort it out. Maybe you lucked out this time."

"Let's hope so. Why don't you focus on the girl and make sure everyone knows all evidence comes with us."

"Okay, but I want you to relax, Evans. I know these woods very well. My family owned property around here. I won't let anyone leave until I'm satisfied that the ground has been searched thoroughly."

Her saddened eyes revealed what she wouldn't speak out loud and what Troy already knew. This was the same area where her husband had been robbed and murdered—a case that had never been solved. He felt her pain and unwavering commitment to do all she could now. Her involvement brought relief. She was the most dedicated CSI tech he'd ever known. If the killer left anything behind, Paula and the rest of the gang would find it.

CHAPTER 21: ARMED AND DANGEROUS

I t was well after three o'clock in the morning when Troy got home. He poked his head into Nate's room to get a glimpse of him. Days like this were hard not seeing his son all day. There was no telling what Wednesday's work day would entail and though he wanted nothing more than to sleep through the morning uninterrupted, he planned to get up and see his wife and son off. If nothing else, he wanted to wish his boy a happy birthday.

Natalie and Nate were out the door by 6:45 a.m. It was around 6:30 p.m. when they would wake him up via their loudness for one reason or another. He was tempted to skip his shower after work, but washing was symbolic to him. It helped him purge, to take his mind from work back to home where peace and happiness reigned.

Natalie's Bible lay open on the sink, next to the toilet. She'd read that thing anywhere. Troy couldn't remember the last time he'd read his. *Where was it?* He remembered having it the last time he'd been to church. It was Mother's Day and he took Natalie out to eat after service. It had fallen out and he'd put it underneath the passenger's seat. *Wow.* It had been even longer than that since he'd read it.

It was clear that Natalie had put hers to good use, though. There were writings and highlight markings all over the place. Troy saw where she'd written today's date next to Philippians 4:7. *"And the*

*peace of God, which passeth all understanding shall keep your hearts
and minds through Christ Jesus.*" Next to that, she'd written Aneetra's
name.

Troy marveled at his wife's faith. Yeah, she had her moments of
trippin', but nothing seemed to calm her as much as the Word.
He got up and jumped in the shower. The warm water felt good
as it kneaded his muscles. There was so much on his mind. If he
wasn't so exhausted, he would have fired up the Xbox to help him
relax. As much as Troy tried to separate work and home, in this
case, it was impossible. If Natalie didn't already know why he and
Jon had gone to speak with Marcus, she would know soon. He
was concerned that this latest news would really unearth her. *And
the peace of God which, passeth all understanding...* This case was
siphoning any sense of peace Troy had left to hold on to.

Could Marcus be a killer? The thought seemed so outrageous.
But, he supposedly went on his last assignment around the time
the murders began and he was having an affair with the latest victim. Mindy had been murdered earlier in the day. Until his alibi
could be confirmed, he couldn't be ruled out.

If it weren't so late, he would call Cheryl to discuss the discrepancies between Mindy and the others. At this point, she seemed
like Troy's best ally because of trust issues he was developing with
Jon. Why was Knight lying to him? His behavior had been suspect—missing in action, scratches, lying—could he be harboring
some deep, dark secret that Troy should be aware of? Jon wasn't
really the type to share things about his personal life. Troy didn't
know that he and his wife were divorcing until the day before it was
finalized and that was only because he'd overheard Jon on the
phone with his attorney. The man didn't have to share all of his
business, but what was going on in his life that he felt the need to
lie to his partner?

After the shower, Troy slipped on his boxers and got in bed. Natalie was sleeping on her side. He wrapped his arm around her waist, taking in the pleasant scent of her freshly washed hair. She stirred without waking. "I love you," he whispered before drifting off to sleep.

Troy woke up in a daze. What day was it? Tuesday? He quickly retraced the week's happenings. No, it was Wednesday. It's Nate's birthday! He listened for sounds of his wife and son, but silence stood all around him. Was something wrong? No, it was a little after seven. They were gone. He immediately grabbed his cell phone to call her.

"Hey," she said dryly.

"I wish you would have wakened me. I wanted to see you guys before you left."

"Sorry. You were sleeping like a log when I got up. I didn't want to disturb you. Plus we left a little early because I needed to get money to pay the late fee from yesterday."

"Have you dropped Nate off yet?"

"Yep. I'm pulling into the parking lot at work now. I don't see Aneetra's car yet, but of course, you can't tell me what happened yesterday that could possibly prevent her from coming."

"Babe, don't let what's happening between Aneetra and Marcus affect us. I'm sorry that I was evasive with you. Anything I tell you at this point could mess up my whole case and my job means too much for me to intentionally do that."

"I know, honey. I'm sorry. Whatever is going on, I can't turn my back on Aneetra. She means too much to me."

"I don't expect you to. All I ask is that you not go by there—at least not until this blows over. I see crimes of passion all the time.

Not saying that Marcus or Aneetra would hurt one another, but I want you to be careful. They are both on edge right now and I don't want you caught in the middle. I probably would be a little more relaxed if you would carry your weapon, but—"

"You know that's not happening. I only went through the CCW training to please you. I hate guns."

"I know, baby. If I could be with you twenty-four-seven I would. I'd give my life to keep you safe."

"I really don't think I'm in danger, but you're obviously in your protective detective mode so I'll agree not to go over Aneetra's if that will make you feel better."

"It does."

"*But*, if Aneetra doesn't show up to work, I'm going to call her, okay?"

"Cool. I'm sure she needs you. Actually, I know she does."

"All right. Let me go ahead and get into work. Oh, for the record, I didn't appreciate the way you spoke to me yesterday."

"I'm sorry. I probably should have patted you down to see if you were armed and dangerous." Her flirtatious laugh combined with thoughts of "wrestling" put him at full alert. "I so wish you were lying next to me right now."

"Hold that thought. Hopefully I will get to see you tonight."

"I'm going to do my best to get home at a decent hour. I hate that I didn't get to wish Nate a happy birthday this morning."

"Oh my gosh, that boy was so hyper. He started crying because he thought it was Saturday and he was going to miss out on his birthday party."

"It may have been better if we didn't tell him it's his birthday today."

"That wouldn't have worked. Corrine called on my way to drop him off. She kept him occupied during the ride."

"Are things straightened out between the two of you?"

"We didn't really talk this morning. She said she'd call me when she got back."

"Hopefully she'll come home with some sense."

"That would be great, but I doubt it. I need to go inside now for real. I'll see you later." They exchanged "I love yous" and Natalie hung up.

He loved her so much! He'd taken the words in Ephesians 5:25 to heart the first time he'd learned them: *"Husbands, love your wives, even as Christ also loved the church, and gave himself for it."* He would die for Natalie if he had to. He'd vowed to protect her at all costs. The sooner he got this murdering creep off the streets, the better he'd feel about his family's safety.

CHAPTER 22: A FAMILY ENVIRONMENT

atalie really didn't expect Aneetra to be at work, but she'd hope to hear from her by late morning, which didn't happen. Her concern about her friend's well-being was fueled when their boss called Natalie into her office later that afternoon. Aneetra's sudden disappearing act was alarming to many in the office. While Alex wasn't the only one inquiring, she was the only one with the authority to pull Natalie aside.

Unlike many of their coworkers, Alex's concern was sincere. She genuinely cared about her employees and Aneetra was undoubtedly *the* most favored. After being friends with Aneetra for several years, Natalie understood why. She was a hard-working woman of integrity. Aneetra's happy-go-lucky spirit was infectious around the office. When she wasn't at work, her presence was missed.

After evasively addressing their boss's concerns by assuring Alex that Aneetra would be okay given a little time, Natalie returned to her cubicle to find a note on her desk from Troy, stating that he and Nate were in the lobby waiting for her to join them for lunch. Someone had to have brought it up for him because, detective or not, he couldn't get through the security doors without an appointment or warrant. She sent him a text saying that she'd be down in a sec. "Mommee!" Nate squealed as he ran and hugged her legs as soon as she stepped off the elevator. He acted like he hadn't seen her a few hours ago.

"Today my birday!"

"I know, honey." Troy followed behind him, giving her a kiss on the cheek. "This is a surprise."

"I know. Chances are I won't be home 'til late tonight and I didn't want to go another evening without spending some time with my two favorite people, especially in light of Nate's personal holiday."

"Daddy takin' me to McDonald's."

Natalie had planned to work through lunch since she'd left early yesterday and was taking Friday off. That only left the rest of today and tomorrow to complete her work and the things she'd taken over for Aneetra during her absence. This lunch was likely to extend past an hour and she'd have to put in leave unless she worked later or came in early. Neither option was viable since she was solely responsible for getting Nate to and from school.

"You guys enjoy. Nice seeing you again, Troy. Don't be a stranger around here." Karen, the receptionist, was smiling a little too much for Natalie's comfort. She wondered how long Troy and Nate had been waiting for her. Karen was nice, in general, but she always seemed overly kind to Troy. No doubt she was the one who'd gone above and beyond her job description to go up to the second floor and leave Troy's note. Natalie wondered if she'd be displaying signs of insecurity, PMS, pettiness, or all of the above if she told Karen that she had one more time to bat her eyes and flash her thirty-twos at Troy in front of her again before she got jacked up.

"C'mon, baby." Troy, who had Nate by the hand, grabbed Natalie's with his free one and the three of them walked out to the car. "You know it's not polite to give people dirty looks, right? I think you visually assaulted her back there."

"She better be glad that's all I gave her pale behind. Blondie better step back."

"You need to calm down and know that I love you. I don't want that woman."

"You don't necessarily have to want her for something to go down. Women know how to be persistent." She was speaking from personal experience.

"Trust that you not only have my heart, but my body as well. You don't see me getting all bent out of shape when Jon flirts with you because I know I got you. He ain't got a chance."

"Oh, aren't we a little cocky?"

"Not cocky, baby, confident."

Either a lot of parents had gotten their little ones out of pre-school and decided to take them to McDonald's, or this was the place where stay-at-home moms hung out. It was packed! Nate, eager to get to the play center, quickly inhaled his food and then he was off.

Natalie and Troy talked about various things and it was clear that they both tried to avoid the topic of Aneetra and Marcus. He knew she was hoping he'd slip and let her in on all the details of yesterday, but Troy was too good at his job to feed her information. If anything, she'd inadvertently done that for him during past conversations about the couple. Thanks to Natalie, he'd known that Marcus had gotten home late Saturday night and left early Sunday morning—the same time frame that Mindy went missing. He'd promised himself that he wouldn't manipulate his relationship with his wife in order to gain additional information about the couple. If Marcus was connected to Mindy Lee's disappearance, Troy would find out through good, old-fashioned detective work. Unsolicited tips from Natalie could be classified as such.

"Nate, wait your turn!" Natalie ordered as she noticed their little one cut in front of another child at the slide.

"That boy doesn't know the meaning of patience because he doesn't have to wait for our attention. Courtesy of being an only child…y'all are sort of spoiled," Troy stated.

"Whatever. If that's the case, then what's your excuse because you persistently push until you get your way at times? Maybe I should make you wait for my attention."

"Naw, you give me good attention for sure." He leaned across the table and whispered, "Why don't you give my lips some attention right now?"

"Sit down, silly." She playfully popped him in the mouth. "This is a family environment. You're trying to have us both arrested for indecent exposure."

"Every time you expose yourself to me, it's decent."

"Finish eating and get your mind out the gutter."

Troy enjoyed the teasing and foreplay, but she was right—this was not the place. Besides, other families were in earshot at nearby tables and things Troy wanted to say to his wife, should not be said in public. "All jokes aside, I think we should both get checked to make sure nothing's wrong. I am getting frustrated that we're having a hard time getting pregnant. I want to give Nate a little brother or sister."

He noticed the tension lines in her forehead. "Maybe it's not meant to be. Besides, he already has a sister."

"I know it's been rough trying, but let's not give up. Corrine is much older than him. He needs someone he can grow up with."

"I don't want to go to the doctor. I'd rather let nature take its course."

"Neither of us is getting any younger. Nature might not exactly be on our side. We've been trying forever and nothing is happening. Before calling it quits, let's see if there's anything medically we can do."

"Like I said, if it's meant to happen, it will. I won't be devastated if it doesn't because *we* aren't the ones who will be home with two children when *we* work late or when *we* suddenly get called on a case."

"Are you implying that I don't do enough with him? I bust my a—butt to make sure that you and Nate have everything you need."

"I know you do and I appreciate that. I'm just saying—"

"Hi, Detective and Mrs. Evans!" rang a strange, but familiar, female voice.

Natalie looked relieved. "Oh, my goodness! How are you?" She embraced Lisa, Robert's wife, and before Troy knew it, Natalie had invited her to sit down with them while her little one ran toward the play area.

Troy didn't appreciate how easily Natalie welcomed Lisa's interruption. Why couldn't she tell her that they were on a family outing or better yet, that they were in the middle of an important conversation! Instead, she sat there talking to her like they were high school buds when they barely even knew each other!

With a light complexion similar to Natalie's and a great figure, Lisa glowed with joy. Much like what Robert had when Troy was at his office on Monday. This couple was amazing. They'd been through the ringer, but both looked so far removed from their troubles. *And the peace of God, which passeth all understanding shall keep your hearts and minds through Christ Jesus.* Maybe there was some truth to that scripture.

"I need to get back to work," Natalie announced, more so to Lisa than to Troy. She'd hardly spoken a word to him the last half hour. "I would really like you guys to come to Nate's party on Saturday."

"Let me check with RJ to make sure he doesn't have anything planned, but otherwise I'd love to come."

They wrapped up their conversation with Lisa inviting Natalie to some ministry meeting Friday night that Natalie said she'd try her best to attend. On the way back to her office, Natalie went on about how good it was to see Lisa. An obvious stall tactic, but to him, their conversation was far from over.

CHAPTER 23: OPERATION

The Avenger paced back and forth nervously. Stupid, stupid boy! Had he minded his own business he would still be alive and things would be going according to plan. The way he cried and begged for his life did tug at the Avenger's heart.

"Please, let me go. I promise not to tell anyone." His face, bright red, was twisted from the pain of his bleeding left leg where he'd been shot during the chase.

The Avenger knelt next to him. "I'm sorry. This is nothing personal. You're simply a casualty of war."

"W-what are you talking about? Please, I don't want to die. I wanna go home."

"What's your name?"

"Ste-Stephen."

The Avenger stood up again. "Do you know Jesus, Stephen?"

"W-h-hat?"

"I want to give you an opportunity to go to heaven before I kill you."

"Heelp! Somebody, please help me!"

A hard kick to the face produced more tears and blood, but it was enough to shut up all that screaming. "Look here, boy, I'm going to ask you this one last time and after that I'll send your soul to hell. Do...you...know... Jesus?"

"Oh, Gawd! Please help me!"

"I hope that's a yes." And with no further delay, Stephen was sent off to meet his Maker.

It wasn't until after Stephen was killed that the Avenger saw the cell phone and heard the 9-1-1 operator repeatedly saying, "hello." How much had the operator overheard? How did the Avenger's upper lip get scratched? Had Mindy done that in her attempt to escape? And what about the item the Avenger was missing? Mindy hadn't somehow grabbed it as initially thought. To the Avenger's knowledge, no one had discovered it. Still, for the first time since this mission began, nervousness set in. Things were much messier than they should have been. It was time to expedite the last and final phase of this mission. So much time and planning had gone into this. Bringing Eric into the plan was genius. He had been such an easy mark. He was so full of himself, so convinced that he saw and heard things from God like none other. From the first moment Eric was noticed, the Avenger knew that he would be a great accomplice.

Initially, he was supposed to be the fall guy, but the Avenger didn't think Evans was convinced of his guilt. Sadly, plan B would have to be executed, but not without the next woman. Information about this one had come by accident. The Avenger didn't have time to do the legwork like with the others. This one was a gamble, but if it paid off, all would be perfect!

When Natalie got back to work, there was still no word from Aneetra. She promised Troy that she wouldn't go by there after work, but she was tempted. She wanted to tell her about the Wise Wives ministry that Lisa had invited her to. She'd love to go this Friday, but would probably have to wait until next month so she could secure a sitter since there was no telling when her husband would be home. Maybe she could ask Corrine.

Troy had some nerve getting an attitude with her about this whole baby thing when she was the one always coordinating her personal activities around Nate and his work schedule. She was glad that Lisa saw them because Natalie knew where the conversation would be headed next—her being a stay-at-home mom. Troy made a decent enough salary for her to do so and they were blessed to have financial abundance, but to completely give up her income would mean a change in their lifestyle. Plus, Natalie had spent most of her life being dependent on men and their money. She was determined to have her own back from now on. She loved and trusted Troy to the utmost, but she still wasn't willing to give up her financial independence for him.

The remainder of Natalie's afternoon went smoothly. Despite her mind being on Aneetra, she was able to get most of her work done. The rest was coming home with her. Elated when 4:30 p.m. hit, Natalie didn't hesitate to get out. She'd thought about stopping at the store to get a small cake for Nate so it could *feel* like his birthday, but quickly changed her mind once she got to his school. Thanks to Troy's surprise earlier, Nate missed his nap at school and so, like the previous evening, Natalie found herself with a cranky toddler on her hands.

Troy wouldn't be home until late and Nate didn't have but another good hour—maybe two at the most—left in him before he clonked out. Thus, it made perfect sense to Natalie that she should pick up something on the way home for dinner. Since Nate had had McDonald's for lunch, she got Burger King. What some would call bad parenting, she termed convenience. After they ate, Natalie played Operation with Nate for about thirty minutes until he started getting on her nerves, whining every time the machine buzzed. She gave him a bath, tucked him in, and within minutes he was asleep.

Somehow Natalie had missed a call from Aneetra. She listened to the voice message. "Um, hi, Natalie…I was wondering if…you know what, never mind, you guys are probably in the middle of doing something for Nate's birthday. I don't want to impose on you. Please disregard this message. You don't have to call me back."

Aneetra should know better than to think she could leave that raggedy message and Natalie would go about her business like nothing ever happened. That's like a judge telling a jury to "strike that last statement" when, in reality, it's never forgotten, only tucked away until deliberation when it's not mentioned, but subconsciously factored in.

"Hey, Nat, you didn't have to call me back."

"Nonsense. What's up?"

"Did Troy tell you about last night?"

"No. He wouldn't tell me anything. He wants to keep his professional life separate from his personal one," she mimicked.

"At least your husband has more integrity than mine. Things have gone from bad to worse. I had to get out of that house. I called earlier to see if the girls and I could crash there for a few days, but we're at Lynn's now. She said we could stay here as long as needed."

Natalie tried to ignore the feelings of jealousy that rose up inside of her because Lynn likely knew all about what happened last night while she was still left in the dark. *It's not about you!* She scolded herself. "I'm so sorry I missed your call. You should have come by anyhow. You guys are more than welcome here."

"Are you sure? I would rather stay there because I can't stand these stupid cats of Lynn's, but I don't want to be an inconvenience. Troy may not want three extra females in the house."

"Girl, come over. There's no telling what time Troy will be home tonight. He won't care." She tried to sound optimistic. When Aneetra stated that she was on her way, Natalie sent Troy a text explaining the situation. He called instead of texting back.

"I was hoping we could finish our discussion when I got home." She played dumb. "What discussion?"

"You said some things earlier that I need you to clarify."

"I'm sorry, okay? We can call the doctor next week. Let's get through Nate's party first." Her words were a quick fix, enough to shut him up. By the time subject came up again, she'd come out and tell him that she was no longer interested in having another child.

"Okay, that's fair. Meantime, I think we should keep practicing."

"C'mon, Troy. This is not the time. Are you cool with Aneetra and the girls coming over or not?"

"*Fine.* I need to go. See you later." He hung up.

CHAPTER 24: UNEXPLAINABLE TRUST

"I feel like I'm in the Twilight Zone," Aneetra cried as she and Natalie sat on the futon in the office near the living room. Lauren and Ashley were sound asleep in the guest room. and by 10 p.m., Troy still was not home. "Did you see the news about the missing girl whose body was found yesterday?"

"No."

"Long story short, the murdered lady was Marcus' mistress and to top it off, she was carrying his child."

"Oh my gosh! Are you serious?" Natalie sat frozen while Aneetra went on to tell her how Troy had come by to ask Marcus about the woman. Marcus had told Aneetra about the affair Monday night after she confronted him, but he'd left out some specifics until questioned by Troy and Jon. That was the first time Aneetra had learned that her husband's girlfriend had been expecting.

"Marcus is a cheater, no doubt, but I don't think he had anything to do with that woman's murder. Then again, I never thought he would cheat on me."

"I know it's not the best of situations, but at least you knew about the affair before Troy and Jon got there. It would have been worse finding out about that *and* the baby at the same time." Tears continuously poured down Aneetra's face. Natalie rubbed her shoulder for reassurance.

"My husband has thrown away sixteen years of marriage for a few good nights with some tricks."

"You think he's slept with more than one woman?"

"I know he's slept with someone else other than the dead lady. He started to tell me, but I couldn't take any more at that time. That's when I left and went to Lynn's."

Natalie was at a loss for words. This seemed so out of Marcus' character. Underneath his quiet nature, was a kind, sometimes silly, God-fearing man whom Natalie had grown to know and love. But the bags under Aneetra's eyes, the flare of her nostrils, and the overall distress of her countenance, told a different story. Marcus Bennett had a dark side. One affair Natalie would consider a mistake, but *two?* He was being whorish. "You should really get checked out to make sure they didn't give him anything to bring home."

"Umph." She stared into space. "I've decided to leave him. Next week, I'm sending the girls to Louisiana with my sister. I plan to work until the end of the summer and then I'm gone, too."

"You're understandably upset, honey, but don't make any rash decisions. Give it some time. The last thing you want is to have your emotions dictating your actions."

"That's easy for you to say. Your husband doesn't have a dead, pregnant mistress and another lover on the side."

"It could be worse; he could have cheated on you with two men. Imagine the thoughts you'd be having then."

Natalie was relieved when Aneetra gave a slight chuckle. She hadn't been sure how well her comments would go over considering the sensitivity of the matter. "You got a point there." Her smile, though fleeting, was refreshing. "I hear what you're saying about not making hasty decisions. I don't know how our marriage will get past this. If that girl hadn't died, I might have never known he cheated or that he had a baby on the way." Aneetra closed her eyes and shook her head as if she could erase the information it now contained. "I feel like such a hypocrite. I mean, I feel bad that the lady is dead. I only hope she had a chance to repent before dying. But, at the same time, I'm relieved because *if* I want to work on my marriage, it will be much easier to do so without her or their illegitimate child. I know that sounds horrible, but it is true."

"Don't beat yourself up. That doesn't make you a bad person; it makes you human. I'm sure I'd feel the same way."

"But it seems so selfish and ungodly."

"It is selfish, but Aneetra, you are one of the most unselfish and godliest women I know. Do you know how many women would say she got what she deserved? But, you haven't. This woman slept with your husband and you're hoping she repented."

"I feel stupid. I have every right to hate him, but I still love him. Even though there's another woman out there and for all I know, she could also be carrying or have had his child, I still love him. Part of me wants to work things out, but I don't know if I can handle anything else he has to confess. Lynn thinks I'd be better off not knowing and simply divorce him."

"Forget what Lynn or anyone else thinks. The only One who can truly guide you is God. He created marriage and I'm sure He's hurting over Marcus' actions, too."

"He sure didn't stop him."

Natalie could relate to her bitterness. There was a point in her own life when she'd questioned why God allowed certain things. She still didn't have answers, but she had an unexplainable trust in His sovereignty. Deep down, she knew Aneetra did as well. Her feelings were in the way of her faith at the time. "Honey, we may not ever know why this all came to light, but our trust in God should not be conditional. He loves you, Nee. I know you know that."

Aneetra grinned slightly. "I do know that I am loved. At least by God, if no one else."

"Oh, don't act like He's the *only* one who loves you. I've been sitting here wiping your tears and snot for over an hour."

"I love you, too, girl."

"By any chance, would you be interested in attending a meeting with me on Friday?" Natalie filled her in on the Wise Wives ministry group Lisa had started shortly after she and her husband had reconciled. "They've been through so much as a couple and God is using them tremendously."

"I don't know that I want to tell all my business to a group of strangers."

"You don't have to. You know I'm not the public sharing type. I think it would be good for us to go to be encouraged."

"Why do you want to go so bad? You and Troy are doing fine."

"It's not only a ministry for broken marriages; it's something that happily married women can benefit from as well."

"Okay, we'll see how I feel come Friday. Right now, I don't want to talk about marriage or Marcus anymore."

"Well then, I'm going to bed because it's after midnight and one of us still has to get up for work in the morning."

"I didn't realize it was so late. Take your butt to bed. I'm all right. Thanks for letting us come over."

"No problem. *Mi casa es su casa.*"

atalie brought the files she'd taken home last night back to work with her this morning. She hadn't even touched them, but surprisingly she'd been able to get more done today than she'd thought. Her mind was more at ease now knowing Aneetra was safe at her house. Nate didn't go to preschool this morning. Aneetra asked if he could hang out with her and the girls for their own personal pre-birthday party celebration. Normally, Natalie would have made him go—especially since she and Troy had already paid their $140 non-refundable fee for the week, but she thought it might be good for Aneetra to be around the little booger. As busy as he was, she wouldn't have time to sit and think about what's happening with Marcus.

Not having to worry about picking up Nate afforded her the ability to work overtime and actually catch up. She and Troy hadn't spoken much since their conversation last night. It was close to 1:30 p.m. when he got home. Natalie was awake lying in bed, but pretended to be sleep to avoid any conflict. Troy was already up and in the basement working when she left. He kissed her, but it was robotic more than passionate. She didn't take it personal. When he worked like that with little sleep it was because an unsolved case was getting to him.

She loved his dedication to his job and she knew he took his vow to protect and serve to heart. He took everything to heart. She knew that man loved her and their son more than anything else on this earth. Troy would do anything in this world for her and she would do anything for him—except give him another baby. She understood the loneliness of being a single child as that was her life, but Troy didn't seem to understand what it would take for her to have another baby. She really would have to give up her career because there was no way she could balance two children with his work schedule.

After spending so much of her adult life depending on men, Natalie liked the independence she experienced. What if she gave up her career and right to her own paycheck and he decided he would cheat on her after sixteen years? Where would she be then? *God has not given you a spirit of fear, but of love, power and a sound mind.* 2 Timothy 1:7 popped in her mind. "You're right," she said aloud, but that didn't override her insecurities. She'd thought Aneetra and Marcus were the near-perfect couple. Marcus seemed to dote on his wife and the girls. If anyone other than Aneetra had told her he was cheating, she would not have been inclined to believe it.

Natalie was in the midst of wrapping up her last account when her cell phone rang. "Hey, Nat, I called to let you know that I'm back in Columbus."

"Hold one second." Moments later she said, "My bad. I needed to put my Bluetooth in so I could keep working."

"What are you doing still at work? It's after six. Did Troy get Nate?"

"No, he's with Aneetra. I'm taking off tomorrow to run around for his party on Saturday. This was a good time for me to catch up on work since I've missed a lot this week."

"Everything okay?"

"Things are cool. I'm glad you had a safe trip. How was Chicago?"

"That city is too busy for me. I wouldn't like to live there, but it was a nice business trip and I got to see a lot of the attractions. I brought Nate back a T-shirt from Navy Pier."

"He will love that. He definitely missed his sissy."

"I missed him, too. I can't wait to see him. I would come by tonight, but I need to unpack. I have to go in the office tomorrow."

"Are you busy tomorrow night? Can you babysit so Aneetra and I can go to a meeting?"

"Brent is coming over tomorrow, but if you really need me, Nate is welcome to come hang with us."

"I don't think that's a good idea. Besides, I was going to ask you to watch Aneetra's girls as well and being in the presence of you and your married lover could spark too many questions."

"Why do you have to be so negative? Brent is a good man."

"Corrine, you're young and you've gotten yourself in a situation that I don't think you really understand. Good men don't cheat on their wives." *But you still believe that Marcus is a good man. What about Lisa's husband?*

"If it makes you feel any better, we don't do it that often. He knows I'm not comfortable with having sex until after he signs his divorce papers."

What about until after you're married! She and Corrine had only ventured on the topic of sex a couple of times in their short history with each other. Corrine admitted to no longer being a virgin, but having only done it with one—now two—men. Natalie was as candid with her grown daughter as she could be without divulging all of her acts of promiscuity. She tried to sympathize with Corrine's feminine needs while being sure to affirm what the Bible says about premarital sex. She wanted Corrine to understand how sacred and intimate a sexual relationship was and the emotional, physical and spiritual consequences that came from disobedience to the Word. "I think you're making a mistake. In fact, I know you are, but if you are determined to walk into a brick wall, I pray that God protects you from getting too many bruises."

"I feel you, Nat, but, I promise everything is cool. He knows I'm not trying to be his side chick."

"What does he tell his wife when he's with you?"

"I don't know. I don't ask because it's not my business. His wife is a trip. If you knew all the stuff he told me about her, you'd agree."

"He can tell you anything, but it doesn't mean it's true. He only wants to get in your pants—"

"He's not like that."

"Whatever. Men lie. As important as marriage is, you should know better. I did my share of dirt, but I didn't have half the witnesses around me as you do. If nothing else you had your parents and uncle Earl and Crystal as positive examples. I had nothing and deep down, I even knew what I was doing was wrong."

"I see this conversation is going nowhere, so I'm out. If you change your mind about tomorrow text me, otherwise I will see you at Nate's party on Saturday." The next thing Natalie heard was dead air on the phone.

Corrine had some nerve hanging up on her! Natalie had half the mind to call and tell her about herself, but she knew her head was as stubborn as a bull's. *Lord, please open her eyes and protect her.*

She was almost finished with her work when her cell phone rang again. She would have ignored it, except it was Aneetra's ringtone. She'd called this morning to say that Nate's package from his grandmother had arrived. Nate was in the background nagging her about going to the park. Natalie hadn't spoken with her since then, but she was sure Nate had to be driving her crazy by now. "Sorry I'm not home yet. I'm logging out now and leaving in a few minutes."

"Hi, Natalie, this is Marcus."

She could have cursed.

All Bennett family members had the same ring tone, but nine-point-ninety-nine times when the chorus of "That's What Friends are For" played on her phone, it was Aneetra. It was always Aneetra! "What's up?"

"I'm sure you know all about the mess I've made of my marriage. I really do love Aneetra and I want to work this out."

"O-kayyy. And you're calling me because?"

"There's one last thing I need to come clean about and I know it's going to crush her. You're her best friend. I want to tell you before I speak with her because she's going to need you, Natalie…much more than she does right now."

Hearing his sniffles and the desperation in his voice prompted Natalie to lend him a sympathetic ear despite not wanting to be in the middle of their issues. She logged off her computer, took a deep breath and said, "Tell me what's up?"

CHAPTER 26: PRECIOUS CASE FILES

Troy woke up Friday morning to his wife kneeling at the foot of the bed, praying. She was asleep when he got home last night. The young boy's murder bothered him as much as the six dead women…bringing the total to seven victims so far. This was getting out of hand. Something had to give. Technically off work until Monday, Troy had no intentions of clocking out mentally. He'd brought as much work home with him as he could and gave strict orders to be phoned if there were any new discoveries. With Nate's party tomorrow, he hoped to have some type of breakthrough today. He'd planned to call Cheryl to see if she could offer additional insight.

Troy heard Aneetra say something to her girls and then the three of them trotted down the stairs. He hadn't been home long enough to assess whether or not they were cramping his style, but he wondered if Aneetra had asked to come over or if she'd been asked. She was cool, though.

"Good morning," Natalie said when she had finished praying. Something was wrong. He saw it on her face.

"Come lay down with me, babe."

"I can't. I need to get going. I have a lot to do today for this party." She began laying her clothes out on the ottoman.

"Natalie, come here, *please*."

His statement was initially meant to be a directive, but he knew better. She didn't respond well to orders. Reluctantly, she came and sat on the edge of the bed. "What's wrong?"

"Marcus called me last night."

"For what? Did he threaten you?"

"No, it's nothing like that. He told me something that Aneetra doesn't know yet. Well, she knows, but not all the details. Basically, that dead lady isn't the one he has had an affair with."

"Why did he call you?"

"Because…" Natalie collapsed on his chest and cried as she shared the details of Marcus' confession with him. "What am I supposed to do now? Aneetra is going to be so hurt. I don't understand how they could do this to her. She has such a good heart."

"I think you need to stay out of it. Don't let on that you know. Marcus' reason for calling you seems bogus to me. It seems like he's trying to use you to break the news to her so he doesn't have to be the one to do so."

"No, he told me he wanted to tell her. He wanted me to be aware because it's going to get real ugly."

"It will." Her tears had caused her hair to mat to her face. He gently pulled the strands from her face. "Be careful, babe. Like I said before, you can be there for Aneetra, but don't be any where around when the two of them are together, especially now that this is about to come out."

"I'm sick of you always thinking the worst of people. These are our friends. Quit treating them like suspects. They need us."

She tried to pull away from him, but Troy held her tight. "Professionally, I have to keep my distance from Marcus until he's completely cleared. Personally, I have nothing against them, but let's be real—they are not *our* friends; they're *your* friends."

"I bet you wouldn't be so distant if it were Elvin and Nicole."

She had to go there. Elvin had been his best friend since they were little. Though he and his wife lived in Chicago, Troy couldn't imagine turning his back on him. He'd hop a flight to Illinois in a minute if he was needed. "I'm sorry for being so insensitive. I love you. I don't want you caught in the middle of anything."

"I won't." She stretched to kiss him. "I hope we never experience this."

"Me, too." He pulled her on top of him. As they began to kiss more passionately, Troy started to untie her robe.

"You do remember that we have guests."

"They are downstairs and as far as I know, Nate is still asleep." She wore a sexy, lace pink bra and panty set. Natalie was fanatic about making sure her undergarments matched and he found that to be quite attractive. Thanks to Corrine's employee discount, he got to see a lot of Victoria's secrets.

"You like?" She smiled teasingly as he traced her outline with his index finger.

"Of course, I do. It'll look much better on the floor, though." He assisted in removing her garments and the two of them had a brief, but very pleasant encounter. He would have loved to savor the moment longer, but the sound of footsteps coming up and down the steps broke his concentration. "How long are they staying?" He tried to sound inquisitive rather than impatient.

"I don't know, but it won't be long…maybe a few more days. Marcus told me that after he speaks with her, he is going to stay at a hotel and let her and the girls have the house until they work something out."

Cool. He could handle that.

"Since you're not working today, can you watch Nate and the

girls so Aneetra and I can go to the Wise Wives meeting that Lisa told me about? I asked Corrine, but she has plans. Plus, she's mad at me."

"Why?"

"I was getting on her about that guy she's dating. So, can you do it?"

"Yeah, that's cool."

"Thanks," she said, getting up and going into the bathroom.

Troy lay feeling uncertain about his commitment. He didn't mind hanging out with Nate, but he didn't know those girls well enough to be left alone with them. He didn't like that at all, but thankfully they were old enough to entertain themselves.

He recognized the ring tone when Nat's phone went off. "Babe, Corrine's calling you."

"Will you get it? I'm on the toilet."

Too much information! He hopped out of bed butt naked, tracing the sound to her purse. Forget scavenger hunting; Troy dumped the whole thing on the bed, sorting through the pile of mess though the phone had stopped ringing. Amongst the rubbish was a small, plastic and round compact, he desperately hoped was a mirror.

"What did she want?"

He'd heard Natalie, but then again he didn't. He was in a daze. The discovery explained a lot and yet nothing at all.

"Honey, what did she…"

When Troy looked up, Natalie was standing in front of him. Her eyes going from him to the pack of little green pills he held in his shaking hands. Trying very hard to control his anger, Troy spoke extremely slowly, taking a breath between each of his words. "When did you start taking birth control pills again?"

"I… I never stopped."

"You mean to tell me that for nearly a year, I've thought we were having trouble conceiving and you weren't even trying! This is what you call letting nature take its course!"

"Please lower your voice. We have guests in our home."

Troy used as least three expletives to explain that he didn't give a care who was in the house. *"How could you lie and make a fool of me all this time!"*

"Everything is all about *you* and what *you* want. What about me? *I don't want another child!"*

"All we've ever talked about was filling this house with kids."

"That's all *you've* ever talked about."

"Oh, so it was solely my decision to build this four-bedroom house?"

"I think it'll be better if we both calm down and talk about this later."

As she began to walk toward the bathroom, Troy's anger soared. He grabbed her arm. "We're talking about this now!"

"Get off of me!" She jerked free, pushing him in his chest. "Touch me again and you'll be living in this house alone with nothing but your precious case files!"

Troy hadn't meant to grab her, but at the same time he knew he hadn't harmed her. "Don't you dare threaten to take my son away from me!"

"It's not like you have had much of a hand in raising him. I might as well be a single mother as crazy as your work schedule is. You don't have to check with me before making plans, but I can't even attend a ministry meeting without first asking if you're available to keep him. You don't ask if I'm going to be home before doing anything. You assume I am. I love Nate and I don't mind being there for him, but I don't think I can do this again."

"What more do you want from me? I work so I can provide a home for you guys, so you don't have to worry about anything. Now all of a sudden, I'm a bad father!"

"I work, too!"

"That's your choice! We wouldn't be rich, but we could live comfortably on my income!"

"Yeah, well, I don't want to rely solely on *your* income!" she said before storming to their bathroom and slamming the door.

Troy stood there, the draft in the room finally catching up to him. Hastily, he threw on some clothes and left for an extremely long jog.

CHAPTER 27: THE RING LEADER

The mission was to make examples of seven women in hopes that others would take note and change their ways. Biblically, seven represented the number of completion and the Avenger had been chosen by God for this special assignment. The women were sinful beings, living contrary to the Word. They'd been given time to repent on their own before being taken. It was their lack of contrition that forced their fate. The seventh woman had already been selected, but had God spared the life of Cynthia Adams, who was scheduled to be next, in favor of someone else?

The Avenger thought long and hard about the next target. This would be spontaneous, but if all worked out, it would be a sweet victory. Was it worth the risk? All the others had been watched for months, some years, before any action was taken. Routines, work schedules, and daily activities were all recorded to a tee.

With Mindy's death, the Avenger knew that Evans would try even harder to connect the dots. What better way to score a home run on him than to blindside him with this next move! "Ha!" Adrenaline soared through the Avenger's veins. The mission would end with Cynthia Adams being replaced.

Overall, Troy's morning run had done little to calm him. He was still very much ticked by all Natalie had done and said. She had a lot of nerve, deceiving him all this time and then hurling false accusations about him being a bad father. Yes, his job took up time, but he went out of his way to balance his home and work responsibilities. Didn't he put off working last Sunday morning to keep Nate when she was upset before church? Didn't he also delay work to take her and Nate out Wednesday? Even though there was a serial killer running rampant, he took off the entire weekend for his son's birthday! Technically, he could still be called in if the killer struck again, but the point was that he'd made an effort to put his family first and his wife was too stubborn to see that!

After showering, he tried to unwind further by toggling between games of Madden NFL and Call of Duty on his Xbox. It was impossible for him to completely take his mind off of work. Unfortunately, the only thing that could be heard from the young boy's 9-1-1 call was the gunshots that ended his life. The whole situation was so sad. The boy was an honor student, preparing for his junior year of high school with an ultimate goal of getting into MIT. The killer obviously saw him as a threat, but why not Eric?

Troy knew that Freeman was innocent of Mindy Lee's murder, but what about the others? Could there be two killers? Was the Lee girl killed by Freeman's partner to throw them off? If Freeman was truly innocent of the other murders, he didn't understand why he wasn't coming clean with all he knew. Was the killer blackmailing him? Was the killer a friend or family member? The whole thing about receiving messages from God was a bunch of bologna. Still, Freeman was getting his information from somewhere. Once that link was discovered, the case was sure to be blown wide open.

With thoughts of the case taking over, Troy decided to check in with Jon.

"Evans, what's up, man?"

"Any new leads?"

"I knew you wouldn't be able to go the entire weekend without calling. I do have some very bad news: there's been nothing conclusive found from the Lee scene."

"Are you serious?" Troy spat out so many curse words that he probably invented a few. "How can a guy kill so many people and not leave a trace of evidence?"

"We're dealing with a very smart person. Plus, the rain didn't help. Some things probably got washed away. The examiner found that Mindy's hands were soaked in bleach at some point. She probably scratched the killer and he wanted to wash the evidence. The good news is that we still found some trace amounts of blood and we believe it's enough to get a DNA profile. In the meantime, I'm working on a court order so we can get DNA samples from Bennett and Freeman.

"Oh, by the way, I found out that Marcus' orders were only for two weeks. He'd told his wife that he was gone for a month because prior to leaving, he was with Mindy. He'll probably submit a sample voluntarily since he's got enough drama to deal with. Freeman will be hit or miss, depending on his mood. Freeman's connected somehow, but I honestly don't think he or Marcus is our guy."

"I get that feeling, too, but we have to rule them out for sure."

"Chances are, we're looking for a white male just like Ch—uh, Agent Hunter said. Statistically most serial killers are white."

"Don't remind me. It's an embarrassment to my race."

"Dude, sometimes, *you* are an embarrassment to your race," Troy teased. "By the way, how is the chat room investigation going?"

"So far, we haven't been able to connect any of the other victims to the site Marcus told us about, but we're still looking."

"Call me if you hear anything. Meantime, send me what you have so I can go over the stuff this weekend."

"I would say no, but you'll come get everything yourself. Promise that you won't work all weekend. Enjoy your son's party, man. I got your back. You don't know how much I wish I could be there for my son's special occasions."

"I hear you. Are you coming by tomorrow?"

"Uh, no. I, um, I have some things to take care of."

"Anything to do with the cat?"

"Oh, um, naw. I'm not worried about that little gray thing."

"I thought you said it was orange and black?"

"Yeah it is. In fact it has several colors. But, hey man, I have to go. I'll get this info to you and we'll talk later."

Just as Troy hung up with Jon, his mom called. "Hey, Mama, I'm so sorry that I didn't call you back the other day. I completely forgot." Acknowledging his negligence was a pre-emptive strike in attempt to avoid an earful.

"At least I was able to get a hold of you now. How are you? Natalie said that you've been workin' on a big case."

"All my cases are big to me."

"I see, 'cuz apparently, you were too busy to call your mother, but that's okay. I still love you, son."

"I would hope so, Mama."

"Oh, boy, hush with your smart mouth," she said lovingly. "Hey, I saw Lilly the other day for the first time in years. She said Elvin and his family were leavin' for vacation this week. I didn't know his boys were so old. I think she said they were what, um, fourteen and eleven?"

"I couldn't tell you for sure, but that sounds about right." Troy didn't want to admit that he'd spoken to Elvin a few days ago because then he'd be given a guilt trip about being available to talk to his friend and not his mama.

"She looked so good. My heart still goes out to her about Elana.

I'm sure it's tough for any parent to lose a child, but it has to be so hard not knowin' what happened after all these years."

The disappearance of Elvin's sister when they were younger was something Troy didn't like to talk about. He felt partly responsible. "So, how are you, Mama?"

"I'm all right, tryin' to cope with this Texas heat. It was one hundred and ten degrees today."

"You've lived in Houston all of your life, you should be used to it by now."

"I don't think I ever will. I like it better here in the winter, though. Y'all comin' down here again for Christmas, right? It's too cold up there in December for me."

"I don't know. We'll see… How are Tracy and the kids?"

"They are fine. Tracy's getting ready to move out. She and Al are gettin' back together."

Troy rolled his eyes. His brother-in-law and father were two of a kind. Al and Tracy had been miserably married for nearly a decade and there was nothing but abuse, adultery, and an unstable environment for their children.

"Your dad and I are happy to have the house to ourselves again. He moved backed in a few weeks ago. By the way, he says, hi."

"Okay." Troy's father was a drunk, cheating scum bag. Troy swore to himself that he would hang up if his mom put that man on the phone. If they were still together come December, his family would definitely not be in Houston. However, with Christmas still over five months away, history put the odds in favor of them being separated by then. Ever since Troy could remember, his father had kept another house furnished that served as an alternate dwelling whenever he and Troy's mother broke up, which was quite often. "Mama, I need to go. I have some work to finish."

"You're always workin'."

At least I'm not an abusive drunk.

"Oh, before you go, did y'all get Nate's package?"

"Yes, I'm sorry. It came yesterday. We'll have him call you after he opens it tomorrow."

"Good. Tell him and Natalie I said hi. I love you guys."

"We love you, too, Mama."

"Your father wants to—"

"I have to go. See you later." The thundering herd of elephants followed by a loud thump and Nate's cry captured his attention. He and Aneetra made it to the living room at the same time to investigate.

"What happened?" they asked in unison. Natalie was out running errands and had kept Nate home with Aneetra and her girls for the second day in a row. If she felt so overwhelmed, she should have sent his butt to school instead of messing up the boy's routine so he could run wild around the house.

"Her made me fall." Nate pointed at Lauren, Aneetra's oldest, while reaching for Troy to pick him up. There was nothing broken and there was no blood. Troy ignored the request. His son would not grow up to be soft.

"It was an accident. We were playing tag and I accidently tripped him."

Aneetra eyed her suspiciously. He didn't know the girls well, but Lauren was at the pre-teen stage and sometimes it seemed like the younger kids really got on her nerves.

"It's true, Mommy." Ashley spoke up. "Lauren didn't mean to do it."

"Y'all know better than to be running around the house anyhow. You don't do that at home so I don't know what makes you think you can do it here."

"Nate knows better, too, don't you, man?"

With an expression mixed with guilt and pain, he slowly nodded his head.

"Lauren and Ashley, y'all better get somewhere and sit down. If something gets broke around here, it's going to be your butts."

"And yours, too," Troy said to Nate. "Why don't y'all go outside? There's plenty of space to run around in the back yard."

"Oh, can we, Mommy?" begged Ashley.

"I don't care."

Nate was likely the ring leader in this in-house game of tag they were planning because he was first to take off. "C'mon, guys!" he yelled, running out the living room, through the kitchen to the back door. Lauren and Ashley took off behind him.

"Walk!" shouted Aneetra. She turned to Troy. "I bet you are ready to kick us out, huh?"

"Y'all aren't bothering me."

"I appreciate you guys opening your home to us. We'll be out by Sunday, Monday morning at the latest."

"Not a problem." Hearing the garage door open, he knew Natalie was home and he wanted to be back in his man cave before she walked in. He was sure that Aneetra was aware of some kind of tension between them. She gave him a funny look when he said, "I need to get back to something," and jetted down the stairs. Moments later, he heard Natalie's footsteps walking across the house. He was glad that she didn't bother coming down to say hi. He was not ready to face her. Apparently she was just as mad at him as he was her, but for what, he hadn't a clue. He hadn't done anything but trust her and she'd made a fool of him for an entire year. She owed him an explanation, though none would really be good enough. The least she could do was apologize, but she was too stubborn for that!

Troy took the opportunity to get his mind off of Natalie by calling Cheryl.

"Agent Hunter." Her stern, low voice intimidated him for some reason.

"Hi, this is Troy."

"Oh, hey, Troy." Her pitch rose several octaves. "I didn't pay attention to the caller ID."

"Is this a bad time?"

"Not at all, what can I do for you?"

"I was calling to touch base since I neglected to respond to your text."

"No problem. Any luck in finding this creep?"

"Nothing." Troy shared with her the details of what went on in the woods in Hocking County and what Jon had told him about the evidence.

"Being forced to break his M.O. could turn out to be a blessing in disguise. I wouldn't be surprised if evidence was left at the scene. If not this one, then most likely the next. The killer has been so methodical and now he has to reinvent his whole strategy. There's a good chance he'll make a mistake as he attempts to regain control."

Troy didn't want anyone else to die before catching this guy. He also knew that sometimes it was clues from the last victim who helped police find the perpetrator. Somehow he and Cheryl started talking about the good old days and eventually Troy was reminded that he'd broken her heart because she was ready to settle down and he wasn't.

"I was young then. My priorities weren't to start a family."

"Understandable. If I would have been more patient, things could possibly be different. I got married about a year after we split. The ink never had a chance to dry before he started cheating on me. A few years later he died in a car crash."

"Sorry to hear that."

"I was so depressed. It was hard for me to admit that I loved the idea of being married more than I loved him. He was a rebound. After that I focused on my career and now I sort of regret not having kids. I love my job, but I think I could have been happy just being a wife and mother."

"Man, I wish you could talk some sense into my wife." Troy found himself sharing his frustration about Natalie not wanting more children, including the birth control discovery. "I don't understand the change of heart. My work schedule was crazy when we were dating, so she knew what she was getting into. I try very hard to balance work and family. I even passed up an opportunity to be on SWAT."

"That's too bad. I remember you used to talk about that being your ultimate dream back in the day. Do you regret it?"

"Not really. It is one of the sweetest gigs on the force, but it can also be the most demanding. I'm pissed because Natalie doesn't recognize any of the sacrifices I've made for us. She acts like everything is all on her. There's no reason we can't have more children."

"At least you guys have one child, but I understand your point. Hopefully she'll come around before it's too late because the clock does not turn backwards. My forty-four-year-old eggs have about dried up."

"Wow. I forgot that you were older than me. You look great, though."

"Thanks. I do my best to stay in shape, but you're also a pleasure to look at. You have got to be a distraction for female officers."

"I wouldn't say all of that."

"I would. I had a hard time staying focused when I saw you in that room."

"I couldn't tell. I thought you were going to bite my head off when I questioned something you'd said."

"I'm sorry. I know I can come off very abrasive sometimes, but you, better than anyone, should know that I'm as soft as pudding." There was enough seduction in her voice that Troy felt uneasy. Perhaps it was not her, but the smile he'd formed as he recalled a memory from their time together. "Hey, are you free this evening? Let's meet for coffee. We can discuss the case further and I can also prove to you that I'm not an ogre."

"Tonight's not good."

"Maybe another time."

"Yeah, maybe. Um, I should probably get off here."

"Me, too. It was good talking to you. Good luck with the case and please don't hesitate to call me about anything."

"Thanks, Cheryl. You take care." When they hung up, Troy had a hard time understanding why he had butterflies.

CHAPTER 28: PLAIN OLD COMMON SENSE

orrine got to work that morning, surprised to learn that Brent wasn't coming in. The director said that he'd taken a personal day. No one in the office knew of their relationship. No one could know about them, as it would complicate matters for sure. Hurt that he didn't inform her, she texted him to make sure everything was okay. He responded saying that his son was sick and that he'd have to cancel their plans for that evening.

Corrine tried calling Natalie to tell her that she could keep Nate if she still needed a sitter. When Natalie didn't answer, Corrine had second thoughts, remembering that Nate came as a package deal and didn't leave a message. She had nothing against Aneetra's girls, but it took a lot of energy just to keep up with Nate. She wasn't eager to add two more children to the mix, having gotten back from her trip last night. She'd been looking forward to a relaxing evening with Brent.

During lunch, she went out to her car and called to talk to her mom. After finishing the call, she listened to the radio while browsing through Facebook. She updated her status to *Home sweet home! Chillaxin' by my lonesome tonight.* ☹ She also accepted a friend request from one of Troy's acquaintances before noticing that Brent had unfriended her. She sent him a text asking what was up with that and he called her back.

"Hey, sweetness." His voice was low. "I'm sorry. Hannah figured out the password to my account and I didn't want her to stumble across anything that could give you away. I'm only trying to protect you. I'll change the password and send you another request in a week or so. Give her time to quit snooping."

"I hate all this sneaking around."

"I do, too. I'm so sorry about having to cancel on you tonight. My son is really sick. His temperature was over a hundred."

"I hope he feels better. Why'd you have to stay home if Hannah's there all day?"

"She's useless; been passed out drunk since early this morning. Honey, I have to go. I'll try and call you later this weekend, okay?"

Brent hung up before she could say anything else. He was probably whispering so his son could rest. She hoped he didn't think she was being insensitive by inquiring about Hannah. It had been so nice to spend time with him in Chicago. To keep Hannah from calling so often, he'd finally told her that his phone battery was dead and that he'd forgotten his charger. She'd been glad to have Brent to herself without the interruption. She commended him for being so dedicated to his children. It had to be hard to be stuck in a marriage for his children's safety. Corrine looked forward to meeting them one day. Hopefully they would accept her. She'd certainly make a better stepmother than Hannah had been a mom.

The day seemed to drag by since there were no secret instant messages or flirtatious looks shared with Brent all day. Later that evening, Corrine found herself dozing on her sofa while watching television. Her last memory of the clock was 7:43 p.m. Several hours later she was awakened by her cell phone and instantly perked up when Brent's number flashed across the screen. "Hey, babe…"

Click.

After several tries to reach him, she gave up.

Moments later he was calling her again. "What happened?"

"Give me my phone, Hannah," she heard Brent say.

"Are you sleeping with her?"

"No, not at all."

"Let's hear what she has to say. Hello?" Her voice was a mixture of anger and pain. "Are you screwing my husband?"

Corrine froze. She wanted to hang up, but she couldn't. It pained her to hear Brent in the background dismissing her so easily. Why wasn't he standing up for their relationship? If he'd take the kids and leave, she'd help him with them! "Give me the phone!"

It sounded like Brent had reached for it but was unsuccessful. After several moments of tussling, the phone dropped.

"How come her number is all over our phone bill?"

"We work together."

Though distant, their voices could still be heard. It seemed like their argument went on forever. Tears burned Corrine's cheeks as she listened to Brent continuously declare his love for Hannah and swear that Corrine meant nothing to him, even calling her a tramp.

"You're a liar!"

"No, baby, I mean it."

"Just like you did with all the others, right?" Hannah broke down in tears. "You've cheated on me more times than I can count. I can't take it anymore."

"I'm sorry, baby, please give me another chance. I—"

Corrine couldn't stand to hear another word. She hung up, feeling every knife that Brent's words had put through her heart. She'd gone against her morals, her faith, and plain old common sense believing in a relationship that had been a lie. She felt like such a fool. How would she face him at work on Monday?

Natalie had been right! Why didn't she listen? She wanted to call her, but Corrine wasn't ready to hear "I told you so." Brent was calling back. Maybe it was Hannah. She didn't answer. How'd she get in the middle of this? She couldn't breathe. She had to get out of the apartment. The walls were starting to enclose her. Slipping on her Crocs, she went for a walk, leaving her ringing cell phone behind.

CHAPTER 29: THE S WORD

Troy regained consciousness by the ringing of his cell phone. It was Cheryl. "I'm sorry; did I wake you?"

"Yeah. What's up?" he said, searching for the remote control so he could turn his game console off. The last thing he remembered was lying on the couch to play Madden. After that everything was a blur.

"I thought of something else I wanted to share."

It was after seven. "Let me call you back in a few. I need to check on something." Troy soon learned that the house was empty. *What happened to Natalie's meeting?* She didn't answer when he called. After leaving a message, he dialed Cheryl. "My bad. I was supposed to watch my son while my wife went somewhere, but she's gone. She must've found a sitter."

"Well, do you want to take me up on my earlier offer about getting coffee?"

"Sure, why not?"

"I stay out west; what about you?"

"Gahanna."

"Dang, why do you have to be on the other side of town. You want to meet at Starbucks on High? Not the one on campus, but further downtown?"

"Yeah, that's cool." Troy left the house about ten minutes after they'd hung up. Cheryl was already seated when he arrived. "I see you still have a lead foot."

"Only when I'm anxious." She had on a fiery-red, wide-strapped sundress that showed off the distinct, yet feminine lines accentuating her arm muscles.

"So what did you want to tell me?"

"I think the person you're looking for feels rejected by these women for some reason. All of them were single—"

"All of them, except the first one. She was married."

"Sometimes we find variations between the first victim and the others because the killer is getting started. I think there may be a personal vendetta against these women or rather these *types* of women. The killer might also be unattractive and could possibly feel shunned. The lack of any viable evidence at the scenes makes me think he's a perfectionist." Cheryl went on to share additional insight—someone divorced or widowed with no kids. "Find the common denominator with these women and you will find the killer."

What did she think he'd been trying to do all this time?

"I hope you don't mind me keeping up with the case. I'm in no way doubting your abilities or trying to step on your toes. I simply want to help an old friend out."

"I appreciate it."

After about an hour, Troy knew it was time to go when Cheryl started with her remember-the-time moments. "I will never forget that weekend you, Elvin, Nikki, and I went to Cedar Point and you spent seventy-five dollars to win that bear for me because Elvin had won one for Nicole."

"Testosterone gets in the way of common sense sometimes."

"I still have that. It sits in my spare bedroom right next to the first Cabbage Patch doll I ever got."

"You have issues."

When she laughed, that dimple in her chin called out for his attention. "Don't we all? How are Elvin and Nicole anyway? They live in Chicago, right?"

"Yep. I spoke with him the other day. They're good. They have two boys."

"That's great. The next time you talk to them, tell them I said hi. Lately, I've been thinking a lot about what could have been with us. I know you're married and I don't mean any disrespect to your wife, I'm being honest."

"As I remember, you had a knack for keeping it real."

"There is something I never told you before. You were my first."

Troy nearly choked on his drink. "I don't believe that. A girl doesn't give up her virginity to a guy she met only hours earlier."

"She does if she had come to the party intending to get laid. I was twenty-five and tired of being so inexperienced. I'd been to third base several times, but no one had ever scored a home run."

He would have never knowingly been a girl's first—too much emotional baggage involved. He was a player back then, but a smart one. Her reaction the night they broke up nearly twenty years ago now made more sense. "I'm sorry, I didn't know."

"Don't be sorry." She laughed. "I know it was dumb of me to plan to sleep with someone that night, but I don't regret it. Besides, it's not like I haven't been with other men since. I wasn't a slut or anything like that. Do you have any memories of me—our time together?"

"Nope." He refused to disclose those details suddenly brought back to his memory. It had only been sex—nothing like making love to his wife. Troy was extremely uncomfortable and stared at the brown table top, trying to think of a way to end this.

"That's too bad. Though I've been with other men, none have

come close to matching your ability. As I recall, you had one heck of a weapon. I'm sure like fine wine, it has gotten much better with age. Your wife is one lucky woman." She touched his hand and he jumped.

"Um, I need to get going. Thanks again for helping with the case. You have a good night." He rushed out of there before Cheryl could object, unable to understand why, once again, he had butterflies.

"Natalie and Aneetra, I'd like to thank both of you for coming," said Lisa. "The purpose of Wise Wives is to uplift, support, and encourage each other in our marriages. While this is a safe place to vent about any marital issues you want to share, we don't tear down our husbands. They are all flawed, as we are, but we are to celebrate what God is doing in them and our marriages. You may see different faces from time to time as women come and go, but my goal is truly to provide a safe-haven for women to share and encourage each other with our testimonies. What's said in Wise Wives is expected to stay here. The group is about a year and a half old and we haven't had any issues with confidentiality so far, but should any woman violate our trust, she won't be allowed to join us again."

"We'll still pray for her and her marriage," another lady chimed in, "but we won't tell her our business."

The women laughed and Lisa said, "Since you all are new, we'll start by introducing ourselves and telling how long we've been married. I'm sure everyone knows my name, but I'll say it any way. I'm Lisa. Saying how long RJ and I have been married is a little more complicated than it should be. I never know if I should go by the date of our first marriage, what seems like centuries ago, or our remarriage within the last two years."

"She likes to make things more complicated than they need to be," teased Angela, a short heavyset lady, who went next, followed by the other ladies and ending with Natalie and Aneetra, who shared the basics very matter-of-factly. Prior to the meeting, Aneetra had shared with Natalie her mixed emotions about wanting to remain married. After the meeting Natalie was dropping Aneetra off at her house so she and Marcus could talk. Natalie suspected that he'd be making his big confession tonight.

Natalie wasn't sure if coming tonight was a good idea. Her enthusiasm about the ministry faded after her argument with Troy this morning. His actions after that added fuel to the fire. She was too upset to celebrate him as Lisa had instructed. He knew she wanted to come to the meeting tonight and had agreed to keep the kids, but he did not come up from the basement all day. She refused to beg him to watch *his* son so she left Lisa a message saying that she and Aneetra wouldn't be able to come because they didn't have a sitter. Lisa called back and stated that Robert would watch the kids.

"No, that's okay," Natalie had replied. "Neither Aneetra nor I want to impose. We'll plan better next month."

"Girl, you won't be imposing. Sometimes RJ takes Chandler out during the meetings, but they aren't going anywhere tonight. Your friend's girls and Nate are both welcome to hang in the basement with them. It will give Chandler and Nate a chance to play together before his party tomorrow. How old are your friend's daughters?"

"Twelve and eight."

"I'll rent some movies for them so they won't be bored because I know they won't want to play with Chandler's stuff."

"I don't know…"

"Oh, c'mon, Natalie. I promise it's not a problem. I would really like you to come."

"Let me talk to Aneetra and see what she thinks. If she agrees, we'll be there." Aneetra wasn't sold on the idea of having her daughters hang in the basement with a woman's husband whom she had never laid eyes on. She'd said she would call Lynn and see if they could go over there, but thankfully Natalie had been able to convince her that Robert and his wife were good people. Thus, all five of them piled up in Natalie's tweener and headed to the two-story suburban home of the Hamptons.

The living room was spacious. Natalie and Aneetra were the only two women seated on the cream, plush sofa. It was so soft, definitely good for napping. After the long day she'd had, she could use one of those right now.

"Today, we'll begin our discussion on submission. Let's start by reading Ephesians 5:22-24. *'Wives, submit yourselves unto your own husbands, as unto the Lord. For the husband is the head of the wife, even as Christ is the head of the church; and he is the savior of the body. Therefore as the church is subject unto Christ, so let the wives be to their own husbands in everything.'"*

"I don't know if I'm ready for this," one of the women said. "The scripture makes it sound so easy, but it's hard, especially in my case because I disagree with my husband's leadership. We'll be here forever if you think you can convince me otherwise."

"I knew this would be deep and that's why we'll be talking about this for several months. Don't worry, Monica, I'm sure you're not the only one who has a problem with the 'S' word. Some men like to abuse it and some women think that submitting to their husbands means that they must become doormats."

"I don't understand why Paul says we have to be subject to our husbands in *everything*. Marriage is a partnership," Angela said. "How can we be *partners* if one person is in charge? If he says jump, am I supposed to be like 'one leg or two'?"

"I think it's important to differentiate between control and leadership. What you're describing is control. Leadership is providing guidance and direction. Verse twenty-one actually says that we should submit to one another out of respect for Christ, so you're right that marriage is a partnership. Husbands and wives are accountable to each other and to God. Even with mutual accountability, our husbands are the heads of our households, or at least they should be. If we would read verse twenty-five, we learn that our husbands are required to love us to the point that they would be willing to die for us. How many of you have some type of leadership role, be it at your church, on your job, or wherever?" Nearly every woman's hand went up. "Without considering your leadership role with your kids or anyone else in your family, how many of you would be willing to die for those that you lead?" All hands went down. "We think we got the short end of the stick because of the word *submission*, but leadership actually carries a lot of weight. Whenever we fail to submit, there will always be conflict. But, if our husbands aren't doing what they are supposed to do and things go awry in our homes, God holds them accountable."

Much of what was said during the meeting went into one of Natalie's ears and out of the other. There's no way she was supposed to submit to Troy's desire and have a baby when she was the one making all the sacrifices for Nate. *She* got Nate up for school every morning; *she* picked him up on time; *she* made dinner, *she* did everything while he filled in whenever he was available. She rarely got to go to her poetry writing classes anymore since having Nate. Nate took over her free time. She loved him to death and couldn't imagine life without him, but she didn't want to do this all over again. How selfish of Troy not to take any of that into consideration.

"Does anyone have anything to add before we close?" Lisa looked around the room, noticing that no one said anything. "Okay, well Natalie and Aneetra, we thank you both again for coming. We hope to see you again. Let's pray: Father God, I thank You for being in the midst of our meeting. I ask that You bless every woman present tonight, their spouses, and their children. Lord, marriage is not always a walk in the park, but if we walk with You, we know we are headed in the right direction. Help us to swallow our pride and submit to our husbands. Help them to lead according to Your word. Please give everyone here a desire to fight for her marriage. Do not let the enemy destroy these unions You have created. If anyone here is on the brink of divorce, I ask for a spirit of reconciliation. You did it for RJ and me. Help us to share our testimony so we may be a witness to others about Your goodness. In the name of Jesus I pray, Amen."

When the meeting was over, Aneetra volunteered to go get the kids from the basement. Natalie knew it was to avoid mingling with everyone. If Aneetra hadn't jumped at the chance, she would have herself. Did these ladies not realize that she had shared everything she wanted to when she said, "I'm Natalie Evans. My husband and I are one month shy of our fourth anniversary." Now there were questions like, "What do you do? What does your husband do? How many kids do you have?" She was courteous though they were really working her nerves. Lisa was a life-saver.

"Ladies, chill! Leave Natalie something to talk about next month if she decides to join us."

Soon, everyone left and Natalie and Lisa waited for Aneetra and the kids.

"Thanks for inviting me, us. It was good."

"Really? You didn't seem like you were into it much."

"I'm sorry. My mind is a bit preoccupied, but it was nice. Everything was cool, except the interrogation."

"Girl, I'm sorry about that. We're such an intimate group that sometimes the ladies don't realize they're being invasive, but they didn't mean any harm."

"It's okay. I think it's more me and my reclusiveness than anything else."

"You don't have to share anything you're uncomfortable with. Do you think Aneetra enjoyed it?"

"It's hard to say. She's going through a lot right now."

"I can tell. I'll be praying for her." As she finished speaking, everyone was coming up the stairs.

"Mommy, him comin' to my birday party."

"I know. Tell Mr. Robert thank you for letting you hang out with them and tell Chandler that you will see him tomorrow."

"Do you have everything all set?" asked Lisa.

"No. I'm starting to think it would have been easier to have the party somewhere else than at the house."

"Lisa and I could come early and help out."

"Oh, no! I wouldn't dare ask that of you guys. Between Troy, my daughter, and me, we should have it all covered."

"Plus, I'll be there," said Aneetra.

"You didn't ask, we volunteered. Besides, RJ and I don't have anything else going on tomorrow."

"Y'all are welcome to come early, but I'm not putting you guys to work. That's tacky."

Lisa playfully rolled her eyes. "Whatever, girl. We'll see you tomorrow."

Natalie felt a twinge of jealousy at how freely Robert made himself available for his family. She hoped she could still count on Troy or Corrine since both were upset with her. She never did find out what Corrine had called for earlier. Everyone exchanged good-byes and Natalie and crew took off.

"You girls are going home with Aunt Natalie. Daddy and I are going to talk about some things. I'll be over there later," Aneetra said when Natalie was pulling into her driveway. "Thanks, Nat. Don't wait up for me. I have a feeling this may take a while."

Natalie waited until she was safely inside before pulling away. *God, please be with her!*

CHAPTER 30: A VERY CHILLY FOREST

Troy was still barricaded in the basement when Natalie got home last night. She didn't bother speaking to him, even after getting the message that he had fallen asleep downstairs. She went to bed. Apparently he'd been in their bedroom sometime between the night and 8:48 a.m. when she woke up this morning because his side of the bed had been disturbed and there was a note on the pillow. *In the basement. Let me know when you need me.*

"*Ooo!*" She crumpled up the note and threw it on the floor. How childish! What man avoids speaking to his wife for so long over a stupid argument about birth control pills? He wants to have another child, but she already had three: Corrine, Nate, and his immature-acting behind. *Let me know when you need me.* She wouldn't give him the satisfaction of *needing* him. She practically raised Nate by herself. Surely she could handle setting up for his third birthday party without his help.

Natalie called Corrine. "Hey, what's up? I saw you called yesterday morning. Sorry I forgot to get back with you. I texted you last night and you never responded. Are you still coming over early today? The party starts at one. The sooner you get here, the better. I hope you're still not trippin' from the other night. I don't support this relationship you're in, but I will love you through anything.

Call me. Actually, forget calling, just get your butt over here because I need you." She then sent Aneetra a quick text asking if she was okay because she hadn't heard anything from her all night, either.

Natalie jumped out of bed, checked to make sure that Nate and the girls were occupied before jumping in the shower. She was thankful that Lauren and Ashley were there. At least they would be able to keep an eye on Nate while she got things together.

She rushed to her cell after hearing the text alert. It wasn't Aneetra or Corrine as she had thought; it was Lisa. *We'll be there by 11. Cool?* Natalie replied. She was thankful for their insistence. She would take all the help she could get—except from Troy.

It was close to ten by the time Natalie had finished getting herself together. Hearing the kids downstairs, she rushed to see what was going on. She was surprised to see Aneetra at the table eating pancakes with the kids.

"Hey, sleepy head, I figured you'd be up before now. Grab a plate and join us, well, me, because they're almost done."

"Mommy, is my birday party today?"

"Yes, honey." She kissed him on the top of his head.

"Yay! Aunt Nee Nee, is them comin' to my birday party?"

"It's *are they* and yes, sweetheart, they will be here."

"Mommy, is Sissy comin' to my birday party?"

"*Yes.*"

"Is Austin comin' to my birday party?"

He inquired about several other kids in his preschool before Natalie put a stop to it. "Wait and see, okay? Let the girls take you to wash your hands and face and then I want you to be on your best behavior or no one is coming to your birthday party."

"'Kay. C'mon, girls. We gotta be good for my birday party." All the kids took off.

"No running!" shouted Aneetra. She turned back to Natalie. "Troy and I had to get on them yesterday about running through the house."

"Umph." Natalie did not want to hear anything about Troy. "How'd things go last night?"

Aneetra shook her head. "Good and bad. We talked for a long time."

"I was up until after two waiting for you."

"I told you not to. I stayed home last night. I got here while you were in the shower."

"Things went *that* good?"

"Naw, it wasn't even like that. He held me while I cried myself to sleep. He told me that you know."

"Know what?" Natalie had to make sure that they were on the same page.

"That Marcus slept with Lynn a year ago and she's been trying to get with him again ever since. He told me that she even had the nerve to get mad at him for not telling her about Mindy."

"Have you spoken with her?"

"No. I honestly have nothing to say to her. I could ask her why and all the other questions going through my mind, but it won't do any good. I need some time to myself. Marcus claims he's made arrangements at a hotel and on Monday the girls are going to my sister's for the rest of the summer."

"Are you still thinking about moving there?"

"I don't know what I'm going to do. I know I need time to sort this all out. I'm hurting so much right now. I feel like I need that cruise more than ever, but there's no way I'm going with Lynn. She was my maid of honor. She's my girls' godmother for good-ness' sake. If I can't trust her, who can I trust?"

As tears pooled in Aneetra's eyes, Natalie wanted to reassure her by saying, "You can trust me," but she hesitated. Aneetra knew about what she'd done to her previous so-called best friend. If her deceitfulness had been exposed, she would have slept with her friend's husband. She reached out for Aneetra's hand. "I'm sorry this happened to you."

"I didn't mean to sound so harsh." She wiped her face. "I saw how you looked when I said that. I do have trust issues right now, but it's mainly with Marcus and Lynn. Thank you for being so candid with me about your past. I don't see my relationship with Lynn picking up where it left off, but maybe she can learn from this and be a blessing to someone else as you are to me."

Natalie leaned over and hugged her tight. "I wish I had the words to say to make you feel better, but the only thing I can think to say is that I love you."

"I love you, too. Now, we better quit all this mushy stuff and get ready for Nate's party. What should we do first?"

"Don't you worry about it, I know you have a lot on your mind. I can handle things."

"Girl, I have been crying all week. I'm sure there will be plenty more tears later, but right now, I'm at your service. Nate is my godson and he's been looking forward to his 'birday' party. There's no way, I'm going to sulk and feel sorry for myself today. Hurry up and finish your food. It's almost party time."

Troy thought he'd have the up-to-date info about Mindy Lee's case, but Jon had sent the email yesterday without the attachment. Not surprising for the non-technical savvy detective who was the worst text messenger that Troy had ever encountered. Jon's texts were always extra long because he spelled out all the words instead of using abbreviations like the rest of the world. Troy left a voice message telling Jon that he needed to resend the info, but so far hadn't heard back. Thankfully, Troy at least had photos he'd taken of the scene on his cell and was able to print and study those.

These latest string of murders gnawed at every inch of his being and he'd worked nonstop laying out each case in the order that they had appeared. Where were the women being held until they were murdered?

When Troy looked at his watch and saw that it was a quarter after twelve, he knew the tension between him and Natalie would be turned up several notches. Natalie hadn't come to get him to set up for Nate's party. He ran upstairs, surprised to see Robert and Lisa sitting at the kitchen table blowing up balloons.

"There's the man of the house."

Natalie and Aneetra were decorating the kitchen with fake spider webs. Troy hoped he was the only one who saw Natalie pucker her lips at Robert's greeting. "What's up, man?" The two exchanged a typical male handshake before he and Lisa greeted each other. "I didn't know you guys were here already."

"When Natalie was at the house last night we told her we'd come early to help decorate."

"Aneetra and I went to the Wise Wives ministry meeting that Lisa invited me to. Remember, I asked you if you could keep the kids, you said yes, but never came up from the basement, so we took them with us and *Robert* watched them all."

He could see all the children running around out back. "I'm sorry, I fell asleep." He turned to Robert and Lisa. "My bad, guys."

"RJ usually has Chandler anyhow, so it wasn't a problem."

"Thank you. I feel bad that y'all have been up here decorating. I was working on a case and lost track of time."

"You're *always* working on a case." Natalie didn't even attempt to sound cordial.

Robert tried to make light of things. "That's what we do. The Bible says that if a man don't work, he don't eat."

"Then we have an abundance of food around here," Natalie snapped.

"Natalie, is there anything else that needs to be done?" He'd been willing to put their issues aside today for Nate's sake, but apparently she hadn't taken her big girl pill.

With a sarcastically sweet tone, she replied, "No, we've taken care of everything. You may go back to work on your day off and I'll let you know when the party starts."

Aneetra gave Natalie a "you're trippin'" glance while Robert and Lisa looked at each other. If Natalie's intent was to anger him all over again, she'd succeeded. Why couldn't she appreciate the fact that he cared about his job? Before her, he was dedicated to his work for the sole purpose of protecting society. Now it wasn't only society's well-being that concerned him, it was hers and Nate's. Every creep he helped put behind bars was one less monster he had to worry about and the better he felt about his family's safety. He didn't think it was appropriate for them to spar like this in front of guests, but he'd had enough of her attitude. "I *said* I'm sorry. If my apology isn't good enough, then there's nothing else I can do. At least I didn't lie to you about what I was doing. I don't appreciate your disrespect or how you're trying to make it seem like I'm so involved in my work that I ignore you."

"And I don't ap—"

"*Troy*, why don't you and Robert go do whatever it is men do while waiting for a three-year-old's birthday party to start? I'll handle this one and I promise she'll have a better attitude by one o'clock." Aneetra stepped in.

This time it was Natalie who gave Aneetra the look and Robert nodded toward the basement.

"I'm sorry you had to witness that, man," Troy said to him once they were down there.

"That's okay. I know that marriage isn't always a walk in the park."

"Yeah, well, currently I feel we're going through a very chilly forest."

"You need a big dose of act right." Aneetra wasted no time laying into Natalie.

"Whatever. I'm sick of him not having his priorities straight."

"Girl, you know how focused your husband is. It wouldn't have hurt you to gently remind him and I believe he would have dropped everything for you. You're being petty and you were wrong for calling him out like that."

If Natalie could have slapped Aneetra, she would have. She had some nerve siding with Troy after Natalie had had her back the whole week with the Marcus situation. *Traitor!* "Lisa, what do you think? Would you be upset if Robert worked all the time and you basically felt like a single mother?"

"I was a single mother for several years when RJ and I were divorced. Our daughter was a teenager at the time. Imagine how fun that was."

"So, you get what I'm saying, right?"

"I can understand your frustration, but if I can be honest, I don't think you handled things appropriately. Men have fragile egos. He felt disrespected."

"But—"

"But nothing! Lisa's being politically correct. I have too much on my mind to be beating around the bush. Yes, you had a right to be upset with Troy, but it's not that serious. Even if it was, you should've never addressed him publicly. Put yourself in his shoes. How would you like it if he fronted on you?"

"But—"

"Swallow your pride and admit you were wrong. You were wrong now and yesterday morning."

"What did I do yesterday morning?" Aneetra didn't respond, but it became painfully obvious that she'd overheard their argument about the birth control pills.

"You...were...wrong," she repeated, trying to keep from bringing up the specifics of the argument in front of Lisa.

Natalie wasn't even sure why she was so mad at Troy. He did work a lot, but she'd never felt neglected. She did feel overwhelmed from time to time when it came to taking care of Nate. His pressing for another child without considering the extra burden it would put on her infuriated her. Not babysitting last night and failing to decorate were cover issues for the emotional distress she was under thinking about the whole baby thing.

"I'd trade a cheating husband for an overworking one any day. At least you know he loves you and you don't have a thousand questions and insecurities running through your mind. Trust and honesty are so important in a relationship," Aneetra continued.

"She's telling the truth. When men cheat, it can send a woman's self-esteem completely downhill. We want our husbands to love us and when they stray, it can be hard to believe that they ever did. But thank God for restoration. Marriages can survive after adultery. In my case, they can survive after divorce." Lisa's comments seemed more directed toward Aneetra than Natalie. "There's nothing too hard for the Lord to work out if He's given the chance."

It started thundering. "I hope the rain holds off for a few more hours," said Natalie.

"I doubt it will. We should move everything inside in case it starts pouring. Better safe than sorry," Aneetra responded.

Natalie hated having to redo things at the last minute. Even more frustrating was that Corrine was taking her sweet time getting there when they could really use her right now! Natalie didn't try to leave Troy out this time. She called him up and asked if he and Robert could move the living room furniture and set Nate's inflatable playhouse inside. The tension between them was still thick, but he agreed without complaint. Thank the Lord they had a nice-sized space because there was plenty of room left over for the adults to sit.

Natalie would have preferred to move the things in the basement, but she knew Troy would object to a dozen kids running around his sixty-five-inch flat-screen and all of his other toys. She wasn't too crazy about her Ikea furniture and decorations being in jeopardy either. The women helped make sure the room was kid-friendly so no valuables would be in reach.

"Thank you all so much. I—*we*—would have never gotten this together without your help." She smiled, winking at Troy who stared at her coldly.

"No problem," replied Lisa. "It's a good thing we did this. Look."

Slight drops of rain had started to fall. Natalie stepped aside to call Corrine while Lisa ushered the kids into the house and Aneetra let in Nate's play grandparents, Sylvia and Richard, who were followed by an influx of others.

CHAPTER 32: A POSITIVE SIGN

The ferocious sounds of thunder and lightning had no effect on Nate or the remaining guests. The Evans household was busy! Kids running around laughing and playing; men engaged in conversations about sports; women exchanging tips about hair, beauty and telling once upon a time stories about their children—everything should have been perfect. But two and a half hours into the party, there was still no word from Corrine. Natalie pressed her head against the living room window. Every time she saw shining headlights coming down the road, a glimmer of excitement stirred in her spirit only to be equaled with a mountain of despair when the vehicle failed to stop at her home.

The splatter of rain against the window pane was symbolic of the tears she cried inside. With all his friends, presents, and the sugar rush he was on, Nate had stopped asking for Corrine, but the questions continued in Natalie's mind. Though Aneetra had encouraged her to not worry, she couldn't help it. Corrine would never abandon Nate. She'd be there for him even if she was still mad at Natalie.

"You okay?" Troy had come up behind her. That's the most he'd said to her since the party had started.

"Sort of. I know I have a lot of explaining to do."

"This isn't the time or place."

"I know. For the record, I want to say I'm sorry—for everything."

His pain was still very apparent through his forced smile. "You still haven't heard from Corrine?"

"No. I think something's wrong. I should go over there."

"Okay. I'll ask Aneetra to take charge of things and I'll go with you."

"No. One of us needs to be here. The other parents don't know her like that."

"Well, I don't want you riding by yourself. Sylvia, will you come here, please?"

Having inquired about Corrine several times earlier also, Sylvia was more than eager to oblige. Aneetra stayed behind to pick up Natalie's slack as hostess. Sylvia drove so Natalie wouldn't have to ask guests to move their cars to get hers out the garage. "I spoke with Toni this morning. She said that Corrine recently got back from Chicago."

"Yep. On Thursday. I haven't spoken to her since then."

"Toni talked to her yesterday morning, so don't worry, honey, I'm sure she's fine." Sylvia's words, though meant to be reassuring, were not comforting. Though Natalie didn't particularly like the fact that her godmother had hooked up with her mom's boyfriend after she died, she had to admit that Sylvia had always been there when needed. She'd grown up with Natalie's family in Mississippi and was the one who'd introduced Natalie's parents to each other. When she and her mom first moved to Ohio, they stayed at Sylvia's home.

"Nate is so funny. The last time we had him over, he and Richard were play boxing and I told Richard not to be too rough with him. Richard said something smart like, 'Stop overreacting.' Nate said, 'Pap, no talkin' back to Nani, 'cuz her might spank you,' then he looked at me and said, 'Nani, stop it. But I not talkin' back, okay?'"

She chuckled lightly. "He is such a smart and well-mannered child. You and Troy should be proud of yourselves."

"Thank you." Sylvia tried to act normal like this was some joy ride, but she wasn't as calm as she appeared. The way she raced through the wet streets, her Audi nearly hydroplaning, gave way to her worries. They were almost to Corrine's place.

"Her car is here." Sylvia was the first to notice the silver Eclipse parked outside. "That's a positive sign. Maybe she overslept. I know it's after four, but she had a busy week. Sometimes our bodies are more exhausted than we think."

Natalie still wasn't convinced. Sylvia hadn't yet put the car in park when Natalie jumped out, leaving both Sylvia and her umbrella behind. *"Wait fo—"* was all she heard as she ran through puddles into the building and to apartment 2B.

"Corrine!" She banged on the door nonstop. Water from her wet hair and clothes slowly pooled at her feet. *Crap!* She'd left her keys at the house. She'd had a spare to Corrine's apartment.

"Should we call the police to let us in?" Sylvia had made her way there.

"No. It may take too long. Stay here. I'll be back." Natalie ran down the stairs to the rental office and frantically pleaded with the property manager to open the door.

"I really shouldn't be doing this, but—"

"Thank you so much," Sylvia answered while Natalie burst through.

There was nothing out of place in the living room. Corrine's purse and cell phone lay on her coffee table; Nate's birthday present wrapped, taking over the small dinette on which it sat. "Corrine!" she called out several times with no response, searching every room of the apartment.

"Is everything okay?" Robert asked Troy after Natalie took off. He explained the reason for Natalie's departure.

"I hope her daughter is all right."

"I'm sure there is a simple explanation for all of this." Troy didn't feel as peaceful as he tried to sound.

About thirty minutes later, his false sense of security came to an end when Natalie called in a panic. "She's gone! Her car was outside, but she wasn't answering so I went to the office and had the lady come open the door and we came in and her purse and cell phone are still here and I thought she was maybe in there passed out or something but she wasn't. She's nowhere to be found and her car is still outside. I'm scared and I don't know what to do!"

"Okay, baby, try and calm down. I'll call this in on my way over."

"Please hurry!"

"That was Natalie, wasn't it? What's wrong?" Aneetra inquired.

He quickly filled her in on the details. Richard and Robert were also standing nearby. "I wish I could go with you."

"I know, Aneetra, but someone has to stay here with Nate and see these guests out. I need to figure out who's all parked in the driveway and have them move their cars."

"That could take forever. We parked on the street. I can take you; I'm sure Lisa won't mind. She can help with everything."

"I'll be here, too," Richard added.

"I need to give some type of explanation to these parents."

"Just go, Troy. Between Richard, Lisa, and me, we have everything under control."

Troy almost wished he'd driven because it may have been easier
than having to give Robert directions. He was trying to multi-task
and they'd missed a turn. The rain was starting to dissipate, but it
hadn't stopped. Troy was unable to call in a missing person report
because he didn't know Corrine's address by heart. He called
Natalie back for the information and learned that she'd already
called. "At the next light turn left and then her apartment complex
will be about halfway down the street on the right," he instructed
Robert, figuring he'd bought himself enough time to put in a quick
call to Jon. "Hey, Knight, this is Troy. If you get this message, give
me a call. It's urgent. I want you to meet me at Corrine's place. I
think something has happened to her."

He hung up as Robert was turning into the division. "Go ahead
and park anywhere."

Natalie was already talking to officers when Troy and Robert
made it to Corrine's apartment. Troy hugged her and had Sylvia
take her aside while he spoke with the officers alone. "Have you
found anything?"

"No, sir, not yet," one of the men spoke. Due to the circumstances of recent missing women cases, the standard protocol was
to now search each victim's home and other property for signs
that the case was related to the others. If not, it would be handled
a little differently. Troy prayed that nothing would be found.

He went to the couch where Sylvia and Robert were sitting on
either side of Natalie who rocked back and forth anxiously. He
knelt before his wife. "Has she been taken by that man who's been
killing all these women?" she asked.

Troy hadn't seen her cry like this since her grandmother died.
He wanted to tell her no, but at this point he wasn't sure and
while he didn't want to worry her, he wouldn't lie to her either.

He pulled her cupped hands away from her mouth and pushed her wet hair from her face. "I honestly don't know." She cried harder and he brought her into his arms. "I promise you that I will do everything in my power to find Corrine. In the meantime, I'm going to have Sylvia take you home."

"*Nooo!* I need to stay here. What if she comes back?"

"Then I will call you. Better yet, I'll bring her to you. But, right now there's nothing else for you to do. Trust that I got this." She nodded her head.

"You can take off, too. I'll get a ride home," he said to Robert.

"I don't mind waiting for a while as long as I'm not going to be in your way."

Troy heard him, but didn't respond. His attention had been grabbed by the wooden cross lying next to a stack of mail on Corrine's coffee table. "Don't touch anything." The officers were now in the hall talking to neighbors. He got a pair of gloves from them and bagged the cross, knowing its significance. It was the calling card that the killer had always left behind. Like before, the letters WOS had been engraved on the stem. He sorted through the stack of mail, coming to a blank unsealed envelope. Robert said something else to him, but all outside noises had been blocked. A warm sensation fell over his body and he could feel the rhythmic beat of his heart pumping as he slowly pulled the contents from the envelope. There was a typed note: WITHOUT THE SHEDDING OF BLOOD, THERE IS NO REMISSION OF SIN. THEY HAD TO DIE SO THAT OTHERS WILL COME TO REPENTANCE. GOD WILL NOT BE MOCKED BY SIN! THE WAGES OF SIN IS DEATH! SOON MY MISSION WILL BE COMPLETE AND SOULS WILL BE SAVED. *Corrine Shepherd* WILL BE THE LAST DEATH. Troy's throat tightened and he struggled to breathe. If he didn't find Corrine soon, she'd never be found alive.

CHAPTER 34: AN AWESOME GOD

The Avenger watched as Corrine slowly came to. Due to the impromptu nature of this one, extra precaution had been taken. Normally, the Avenger had been good at giving the victims enough tranquilizers to keep them out for a few hours, but Corrine had apparently been overdosed.

When the Avenger had finally decided to replace the other lady with Corrine, not knowing Corrine's schedule had posed a major problem. Corrine made things a little easier with her Facebook post yesterday, allowing the Avenger to know she'd be home alone. The real issue had been how to get inside her building and get her into the car without anyone else noticing. The Avenger drove around for hours scoping out the complex and checking for security cameras. When Corrine was observed walking alone so late at night, the Avenger knew it had been a clear sign from God that she was the one.

"Wh-where am I?" She tugged on the guard rail that her left hand was attached to. "*Heeelp!*" The Avenger could not help but laugh. Corrine suddenly became aware that she wasn't alone. "*You?* Why are you doing this to me!"

"I think the better question is why have you done this to yourself? Your own actions have brought you here. My assignment is to get your soul right before sending you to God so you don't die in your sin."

"You crazy b—"

"Shh! That's not a nice way to start off our time together and that speech is especially not becoming for a Christian woman. Oh, but you haven't been living like a Christian, have you? At least not from what your stepfather says." Corrine looked horrified as the Avenger laughed wickedly. "Yes, that's right, sweetheart. I know your secret. You are an adulterer and I've been commissioned to save you from yourself. I recommend that you start making a list of any unconfessed sin. Like the thief who was forgiven right before he was crucified with Jesus, you can also spend eternity in Heaven if you repent. I'm curious to know…have you ever played on Troy's pogo stick?"

Corrine had the nerve to look offended. "No, you idiot! He's married to my mom."

"And the guy you're sleeping with is married to someone. People don't hold their vows sacred anymore. I'm putting a stop to that. When the world learns of my mission, order will be restored. What happened to me will never happen to anyone else!"

"I didn't do anything to you!" She cried, grunting as she tugged again on her cuffed arm.

"But you have sinned and in Romans 6:23, Paul tells us that the wages of sin is death. Do you know the rest of that scripture?" She nodded yes. "Say it!"

"But the gift of God is eternal life through Jesus Christ our Lord."

"Vare-ree good! Sin is destructive to all of mankind and God is not going to allow it to go on forever. I have a divine assignment to show you the error of your ways, but if your soul gets right, you'll spend eternity with Jesus. What I am doing right now may seem like a bad thing, but you'll be thankful later."

"P-p-please let me go. I'm sorry for everything I've done wrong.

I swear I'm not even dating that guy anymore. I've already learned my lesson! I promise I will never date another married man again."

The Avenger smiled. "I can tell already that there is hope for you. The others didn't cave so easily. I'm inclined to believe you, but unfortunately, our justice system is so screwed up. Adultery isn't against the law, but righteous kidnappings are." The cops had been left a note explaining why the women had to die with the assurance that there would be no more killings, but they were likely too carnal-minded to appreciate this special assignment. "Because of the legality of things, I could never let you go. I have to kill you. Don't worry. It's not as horrible as it sounds. You'll be absent in the body, but present with the Lord."

Corrine's head sunk and she sobbed. "I need to get going, but I'll be back soon. In the meantime, you should start reading the Word. It's a soul-saver." The Avenger walked away, smiling. Soon, the voice of God would be heard, saying, "Well done, my good and faithful servant."

It was almost 5:00 p.m. The rain had completely stopped by now, but the sun failed to come back out. Natalie was thankful that the guests were gone by the time she'd returned home. She took two extra-strength ibuprofen pills for her splitting headache. Sylvia and Richard asked if she needed them to stay, but she said no. "Call us the moment you hear anything," Sylvia said before leaving.

Aneetra's girls had gotten bored with the little kids way before Natalie left and the last she knew, they were in the basement playing video games. Now that his friends were gone, with the exception of Chandler, who was fast asleep on the love seat, Nate began acting out. He cried because Chandler wasn't playing with him anymore. "I think someone also needs to take a nap," Aneetra said.

"I not wanna take a nap."

"Too bad."

"Nooo!" He ran to Natalie who sat frozen on the couch.

Any other time Natalie would have backed Aneetra up without hesitation. Even if she thought Aneetra was wrong, she would have made Nate obey and said something to the effect of "Don't tell Aunt Nee Nee no!" But she couldn't say anything. One of her babies was missing and the other wanted her affection. She couldn't deny him that. Corrine had needed to talk to her and she had driven her away. As ornery as Nate was being, she didn't have the heart to correct him. She needed him and she held him tight as she wailed.

"Why you cryin', Mommy?"

"C'mon, honey." Aneetra pried him from her arms. He continued to question Natalie's behavior and when Aneetra had finally gotten him up the stairs, Natalie heard him ask for his "Sissy" and that made her cry even harder.

Lisa came and sat next to her. She didn't say a word, she gently rubbed her back. Natalie felt helpless. Shouldn't she be getting fliers printed with Corrine's name and picture? Shouldn't she be going door-to-door in her daughter's neighborhood seeking information? She should be doing something, *anything* to help, so why was she paralyzed?

Natalie wanted to tell Lisa that she appreciated all of her help this weekend and how she knew that Lisa understood what she was going through, but she couldn't speak. Words in her mind could not find their way out of her mouth. When the doorbell rang, Lisa got up to answer. It was Robert. "Are you ready or do you want me to take Chandler and come back to get you later?" Natalie could feel him staring at her.

"Um... I'm not really sure."

"You don't have to stay. I'm all right." Natalie managed to get past the lump in her throat.

"Troy told me to let you know that Jon is bringing him home." It was his unspoken words that panged Natalie. Robert was basically saying that he'd been sent home so the officers could process the place. No civilians allowed.

"Are you sure you don't need me to stay?" asked Lisa.

Natalie nodded. "Thank you."

"Not a problem." Lisa gave her a hug followed by Robert who then scooped Chandler off the love seat. "I'll call you tomorrow to check on things, if that's okay."

When they were gone, Natalie pulled herself up the stairs to her room, plopped on top of her comforter, and bit her pillow while she screamed. Would this monster kill her daughter like he'd done the other women? *God, please keep Corrine safe.*

"Knock, knock..." Aneetra walked into the bedroom some time later. "Oh, honey!" She came over to Natalie who was now on her back, staring at the ceiling. "It's going to be all right."

"What if he kills her?"

"Shh...you'll worry yourself to death thinking like that. Troy won't rest until he finds her and I'll be by your side every step of the way. Don't you worry about anything, not even Nate...I'll take care of him."

"What about your situation?"

"I'll deal with what's going on between Marcus and me when this is all over. Our mess isn't going anywhere. Right now what's happening with you is more critical. I'll be all right for the time being."

"I love you, Nee."

"And I love you."

There was a time when Natalie wouldn't tell anyone she loved them because she didn't want the risk of exposing her feelings and subjecting herself to pain. Now, she'd let down those emotional barriers and freely expressed her love to those dear to her heart without reservation. Or so she thought. Had she done enough to show Corrine that she loved her? What about Troy? She'd crushed his spirit with her actions. Nate, Troy, and Corrine were the most important to her. What if Troy never forgave her? What if she never saw Corrine again? Everything was falling apart.

Aneetra continued to hold her. "I'm always here for you. I'm going to check on the girls. I'll be back."

Unable to say anything, Natalie nodded. With all that she was going through, Aneetra was unselfishly amazing. She silently thanked God for Aneetra and everyone else, especially Troy. When bad thoughts ran through her mind about Corrine getting hurt, she refused to let them run wild. Instead, she forced herself to think of things that were true, honest, just, pure, lovely, and of a good report as instructed in Philippians 4:8. So many wonderful memories of Corrine over the years, so many testimonies of an awesome God. These were the things that Natalie kept on her mind while the ibuprofen kicked in and she drifted off to sleep.

CHAPTER 35: SENTIMENTAL STUFF

"Okay, I'll be home soon," Troy said to Aneetra, sitting in Jon's truck, waiting for him. Troy was no longer lead detective on the case due to his relationship with Corrine, but his Superior was crazy if he thought Troy would stop working this all together. He'd known he would have to officially step back, but he'd hoped to at least stay on through the night until the initial processing was complete. It didn't help his case when Troy shoved one of the officers for picking up potential evidence without wearing gloves. Though he was a rookie, CPD officers endured six months of intense hands-on training. His status was no excuse as far as Troy was concerned. Jon was quick to pull Troy into the hall. He had more strength for a short man than Troy had ever given him credit for.

"Man, you have to chill," he said. "Your emotions are getting in the way of your judgment and if you keep this up, you will jeopardize the integrity of this case."

"Don't talk to me about integrity when you've been lying to me about a cat."

Jon kept a straight face. "You need to chill. Do not go back in there," he'd said sternly. It was shortly after that encounter when Troy received a call from their Superior telling him to leave the premises.

Without his own ride, Troy couldn't exactly go anywhere. He sat in Jon's truck going stir crazy. Television crews had arrived. Reporters tried hard to piece together a story. Troy reclined his seat as far back as it would go, thankful that Jon's tinted windows help hide him from the crowd. He felt useless as time passed. Since the case files were inaccessible, he recalled what information he could. They had yet to figure out the vices of Myesha Turner and the first victim, Lolita Gordon. Her husband hadn't called at all this week. Perhaps he was losing faith in Troy's ability to solve this case. Troy began to lose faith in himself as well.

Saw the news. He's more likely 2make a mistake this time. Don't give up! I'm here 4u if u need me! Call me any time day or night.

Cheryl's text came unexpectedly. Troy started to respond, but stopped short when his conversation with Robert earlier that day came to mind.

They hadn't been too long in the basement when Cheryl had called to see how things were going. "Fine. Nothing new has come to light," he'd said. Cheryl had also apologized for her comments last night, stating that she hadn't meant to upset him. "I wasn't mad. It was awkward though. I didn't know things had gone down like they did." He noticed Robert staring at him oddly. "Um, I need to let you go. My son is having a birthday party today and I have company right now. Thanks for calling."

"Everything all right, man?" inquired Robert.

"Oh, yeah. That was an FBI agent. She wanted to know how things were going with the case."

"I didn't think the FBI would get involved unless it was a federal case."

"They don't. She's an old friend of mine who was asked to come in and do a profile. She's been keeping up with the case since then."

"Be careful, man," was all Robert said, but Troy felt the need to continue explaining that they were friends and how she was only trying to help and that he'd gained a lot of insight from her. "I didn't mean to put you on the defensive. All I'm saying is that you have to keep your ears and eyes open at all times. Things might seem innocent, but it could be a set up. The enemy would love to see you stumble and he has a bit of an opening right now with the tension between you and Natalie. His job is to kill, steal, and destroy. He would love to ruin your marriage."

"I would never cheat on Natalie. I don't care how mad she makes me."

"I said the same thing. The best way to ensure it doesn't happen is not to play with fire. If you ever find yourself thinking about this person more than you should, getting butterflies around them, or sharing details of your marital problems, these are all warning signs that you're headed for trouble. James says to resist the devil and he will flee."

"Cheryl is hardly the devil."

"But she can be used by him. Any of us can if we're not careful. Man, I'm not trying to preach to you, but I'm being real. Be careful, that's all I'm saying." By then Troy was relieved when Natalie called for them to help rearrange things.

Troy now sat in Jon's truck, spending an unusual amount of time contemplating whether or not to respond to Cheryl. This was crazy. Corrine's missing and he's stressing over a text! No matter how good things had been with him and Cheryl back in the day or how mad he was at Natalie about the pills, he loved her and no other woman was going to come between them. Cheryl had already provided the services requested for the case and thus no further communication was necessary. *Delete.*

"How's Natalie holding up?" Jon came out after what seemed like forever to Troy.

"Aneetra said she took some medicine when she got home and has been sleeping ever since."

"Rest is probably the best thing for her right now. I pray God sheds light on the identity of this killer and that Corrine is not harmed."

"We need evidence more than prayer. God has watched while six women and a young teenage boy were murdered by this monster and hasn't done a thing." Troy felt his heart re-hardening. Why wasn't He putting a stop to this?

Jon started the car, but didn't move. "What was your breaking point?"

"Huh?"

"What case was it that started this bitterness? I've seen police officers do one of two things: get closer to God through this job or start to hate Him."

"I don't hate Him, but I don't understand Him. I'm not even sure I believed in God until several years ago when Mitch Denson was killed during a routine traffic stop. I knew how loose his beliefs about God were because I felt the same way. But, when he died, it scared me and I didn't want to play Russian roulette with my soul. When I first started to seek God, everything was wonderful. I prayed on the way to each crime scene. I even told family members of victims that I would be praying for them. I'll never forget when Loraine Andrews' two young sons were shot and killed by their father because he didn't want her to get full custody. At the trial I said to her, 'I pray that God comforts you.' She broke down crying in my arms, asking why God had let this happen to her kids. I didn't have an answer for her because, honestly, I had wondered the same thing myself. She'd trusted Him and her children ended up dead. After that incident, the more bad stuff I started to see happening to Christians, the more I felt like if God is there, He doesn't care." Troy amazed himself by speaking his frustrations so candidly. Jon remained silent. The gentle sound of the humming truck filled the air. *"Well?* Are you going to say something?"

"Loraine's question was normal considering what she was going through at the time. But, she now runs a non-profit organization called Rejoice that provides support services for parents of murdered children. Anyone can praise God when life is going great, but it takes a deeper level of faith to trust Him when your world has been turned upside down. I've been there. Until Belinda said she was having an affair, I thought we'd had a good marriage. Now, I'm living without my son and she's married to the guy she cheated on me with. I'm left by myself with my elderly mother whose Alzheimer's and dementia have spiraled so out of control that she's become violent. I've been wrestling with whether or not to put her in a home and I finally did it this morning."

"So she's been the one scratching you up and not a cat?"

"Yes. I'm sorry I lied to you, man. I wasn't ready to talk about it."

"I understand. You've also proved my point about God sitting back and watching people's lives get destroyed."

"This last year has indeed been rough. I could be mad at God if I wanted to be, but I am not. I know I wouldn't have been able to make it through the divorce or this ordeal with my mom without Him. His word gives me strength. It seems like you're more upset with God about what happens in people's lives than they are. They *still* trust Him. I know I do."

Troy thought about Robert and Lisa and how neither of them seemed to hold a grudge against God for all they'd been through.

Even Natalie was not bitter about her childhood experiences. "Man, I don't know what I will do if something happens to Corrine. Natalie won't be able to handle it."

"Either way this turns out, Natalie will need you. Sometimes I wonder if *you* will be able to handle things. I hope you can look past the offense of my words and hear what I'm saying. You need to step up, man. All this swearing and losing your temper is not representative of a godly man. What happened in there was out of line. Don't get me wrong, I understand you being upset and I would've been, too, but dude your mouth is getting real foul. It's to the point that I hate being around you when you're cursing. It's worse than before you claimed salvation. I truly pray that we find Corrine before it's too late. If for some reason we don't, remember *you* are the head of the household and the way you respond to God might have an impact on how Natalie handles this situation. I know she's a strong believer, but even the best of us can give into fear and feelings every now and then. You are her covering. Don't leave her unprotected because you're having this pissing match with God. It's not worth it and you can find yourself like me, having lost everything."

Troy was surprised to find a tear rolling down Jon's plump face. When Natalie cried, he held her, but he didn't know what to say or do in this situation. It was awkward. In the eighteen years he'd been with the Columbus PD, he'd never seen an officer cry except at a funeral of another officer. Troy had feelings of sorrow when investigating horrific crime scenes, but he'd never displayed his emotions. Cops didn't do that—at least not in front of other cops. "Um…you ready to go, man? The truck's been running for a while."

Jon wiped his face and chuckled. "You're something else, Evans, but I love you, man."

"Yeah, whatever, you're all right, too. I heard what you said and I appreciate your honesty. I'm sorry to hear about your mom and my heart goes out to you about Belinda because I know you still love her. But, man, please stop all this sentimental stuff because you're making me feel uncomfortable."

Still smiling, Jon said, "What would I do without you?" before driving away.

CHAPTER 36: A VALIANT EFFORT

When Troy walked in the house, Aneetra was standing next to the open dishwasher panel, eyes glued to the small kitchen flat-screen.

"Another woman has gone missing. Twenty-three-year-old Corrine Shepherd was last seen Friday afternoon when she left work. Sources tell us that loved ones became concerned when she failed to show up at a family event earlier today and that's when police went to her home and found evidence that, they believe, ties her to the same person who has killed six women and a teenage boy so far. We learned that Shepherd is the stepdaughter of Detective Troy Evans, who has led this entire investigation from the beginning until hours ago. CPD declined to comment about why he was forced to step down and Detective Evans could not be reached."

"We also don't know what evidence was found in Shepherd's apartment, but if you recall, it was nearly two months ago when the first victim, Lolita Gordon, disappeared. Her body was discovered several days later with a copy of the Bible placed on her chest. Since then, the suspect has been coined the Bible Butcher and thanks to an FBI profile, detectives believe they are looking for a white male in his late thirties or early forties, but they don't have any real clues to go on."

"If you have any information regarding this case, please call 614-555-TIPS. Remember, you can remain anonymous and your tip could help put away this creep for good."

"I hope Natalie isn't watching this."

Aneetra jumped, quickly using the remote to turn it off. "Hey. I didn't hear you come in. I checked on her about a half hour ago and she was still sleeping."

Troy was relieved. He did not want her to hear he'd been taken off the case like that. Aneetra had done a spectacular job cleaning up the place. "I would have taken care of this, but thank you."

"No problem. You and Natalie have enough on your minds. You mind me asking what happened?" Troy filled her in on his altercation with another officer. "Honestly, I think it's best that you're not the lead on this because you're too emotionally involved. But, it doesn't mean you can't work it behind the scenes, which I know you will do."

"You're right. It's frustrating not to have a single clue." He plopped down at the island across from her.

"I don't know if you guys still consider Marcus a suspect, but I don't think he's behind this. I was with him all last night until this morning. Plus, he doesn't fit the profile."

"I know. He didn't really have an alibi for Mindy Lee, but he was gone on assignment when at least two of the murders took place so he should be cleared. Sorry all of this had to be brought to light. I know it's been a rough week for you."

Aneetra nodded. "Thanks again for letting the girls and me stay. We'll be out of your way tomorrow. If you guys don't mind, I'll take Nate with me so y'all can focus on finding Corrine without having to tend to him. I'll be able to take him to and from school."

"Thanks. I appreciate it." Natalie had already filled Troy in on the soon-to-be living arrangements between Aneetra and Marcus so he felt more at ease about Nate going with her since Marcus would be gone. "How's he been?"

"Okay. He's been asking for Corrine and he's been getting a little whiny. It's almost like he senses something is wrong."

"I'm sure he does." Troy stared at the granite counter, thinking about Jon's words: *The way you respond to God might have an impact on the way Natalie handles this situation...You are her covering. Don't leave her unprotected...* "Are you upset with God about what happened with Marcus?"

Aneetra didn't respond right away. She put up the last glass, closed the dishwasher, and sat on the other side of the island. "At first I was mad because I felt like my marriage should have been exempt from this stuff. I'm not blaming myself for Marcus' actions, but I know there are things that I could and should have done differently. Sometimes I think I took him for granted. Don't get me wrong, I'm still very angry with Marcus, but I've been trying to put myself in his shoes as well. I questioned God, but not to the point where I'm willing to turn away from Him. He's been good to me."

"He let your husband get another woman pregnant and sleep with one of your best friends and you *still* say He's been good?" She seemed surprised that Troy knew about the other lady and he felt like a dummy for mentioning it. "I'm sorry. I shouldn't have gone there. For the record, Natalie wasn't trying to betray your confidence. She was upset that Marcus had told her and—oh gosh, am I talking too much? Did you even know that Marcus had told her? She's going to kill me."

"Relax. You're cool and to answer your question, *yes*, I can still say that God has been good to me, despite all of it. When I look over my entire life, the good has outweighed the bad. I don't serve God because He gives me stuff. I serve Him because He is. Marcus' affairs doesn't change who I believe God is."

Wow. "I'm impressed with your faith."

"Don't be. You happened to catch me at a time when I'm in good spirits. I cling to Romans 10:17, which says that faith comes by hearing and hearing by the Word of God. My feelings are flaky, but my faith is firm and that's only because I've been burying myself in the Word."

"I've been the exact opposite. My buddy recently told me that I need to get it together. I'm worried about how this thing with Corrine will affect Natalie, especially if we don't…" He couldn't bring himself to say it.

Aneetra reached across the island and patted his hand. "No matter what happens, God is good. Until we get proof otherwise, let's believe that she will be found alive. It only takes a mustard seed of faith for God to move mountains."

With those words, Aneetra got up and went upstairs. Troy was so emotionally overwhelmed that he put his hands over his face and before he knew it, he was crying. *Danggit, Jon!* He was hurting and everything came at him at once—his feelings about Natalie's betrayal, the frustration over the case in general, and the horrific thoughts of never finding Corrine. Like fluid being drained from a swollen knee, he felt pressure being released with every tear that dropped. His pride urged him to stop. Someone might walk down the stairs any moment and see him, but he didn't care. He was supposed to keep his family safe, but because he hadn't been able wrap things up the killer had a chance to harm them. Now that he'd been taken off the case, there was only so much information that he had access to. No matter how many cases he'd closed during his career, this one would make or break him.

God, I'm sorry I've been so distant. Thank you for Your patience with me. Your Word says that I am to love Natalie as You loved the church and gave yourself for it. I would give my life to protect Natalie from the evils of this world. If Corrine doesn't make it, I don't know what will happen. Maybe Natalie could take it. Perhaps it's seeing the pain in her eyes that will remind me that I failed her is what I can't take. I give up and acknowledge that You are in control of everything. I want Corrine to be found alive, but if she isn't, I declare from this day forward that I will serve You without reservation. I want to be the man of God that my wife needs. I repent of my wrongs and I ask that Your guidance and wisdom lead me from here on out.

Troy cried so hard that his tears pooled underneath him. So many had had died and the police were no closer to catching this perp than they were when the first killing took place. The odds of finding Corrine alive were slim to none. *"All it takes is a mustard seed of faith…"* That's all he had. Hopefully that would be good enough.

Natalie stopped in the middle of the staircase when she observed Troy sitting in the kitchen crying. Had he found Corrine's body? She wanted to go down and demand answers, but her feet wouldn't move. She didn't feel Corrine was dead and yet she feared hearing those dreadful words. She didn't want anything to interfere with her hope and so she tiptoed back up the stairs, got in bed, and calmed her nerves via prayer.

Her heart raced when Troy came into the room and called her name. *Oh no!* This was it. He was going to inform her of Corrine's murder. Pain shot through every part of her body and she began to bawl like an infant. Troy rushed to her side.

"Baby, what's wrong?"

"I know what you're going to say, but I can't take it right now. I don't want to hear you say she's dead."

He held her tight. "No, baby, calm down. I have no news about Corrine—good or bad."

"Then why were you—" Natalie took a deep breath. She knew how macho Troy was. It would probably crush his ego if he knew she'd seen him. She needed reassurance one last time. "She's *not* dead?"

"Not that I'm aware of. I'm sorry to frighten you. I was checking to see if you were awake."

"Why are you here? Why aren't you out working on Corrine's case like you do with all the others?"

Troy hung his head before looking back at her. "There's no easy way to tell you this. I've been officially taken off of this case."

"What!"

"Don't worry, I'm still going to work it and I promise to do everything to find our daughter."

Natalie was startled. Troy had never referred to Corrine as *their* daughter before.

"I don't know how this will end, but I'm praying God keeps her. Whatever happens, we're going to get through this together, okay? I love you." A tear fell down his cheek and Natalie wiped it at the same time he did hers. He gave her an awkward smile. "Allergies…"

"Thank you," she said, staring into his determined, pain-filled eyes, "for being so wonderful to me despite my dishonesty. I'm really sorry, Troy."

"Let's not talk about this right now."

"We have to talk about it eventually and I don't think there's ever going to be a *right* time. I have a lot of insecurities and I'm scared that I won't be able to handle working with two kids. I don't want to be dependent on any man. I've been in that position before and did a lot of shady things to have a man take care of me."

"I am not *any* man, Natalie. I'm your husband. I wish you would have talked to me instead of leading me on. Given my family's history, I'm scared, too. I don't know what the future of our marriage holds, but I know that I love you more than anything in this world. We have to be honest with and trust each other. More importantly, we have to trust God. I know I've been slipping big time where He's concerned, but I'll get it together, I promise."

Natalie was too choked up to respond. She still wasn't sold on the baby thing, but maybe she would be willing to discuss it more after Corrine was found. The last thing she wanted was for this issue to drive a wedge between them. Troy looked as if he would say something else, but before he could speak, she grabbed his chin, pulling his lips to hers. She tasted the saltiness—her tears or his? In another day or two she'd be on her cycle and in times past, she and Troy made a valiant effort to feed their hormones before the drought. Her emotions were all over the place and it was the immediate need for consolation that overtook her more than the desire for physical pleasure. Like in Genesis when Abraham's servant brought Rebekah to Isaac after Sarah died, the Bible says that he took her into his mother's tent and was comforted. Though Corrine was still believed to be alive, the possibility of death was very imminent. While God held her spiritually, Troy took care of her every physical need. At least for the moment, she was able to escape the cruelties of this world into her own universe of ecstasy.

CHAPTER 37: A LEVEL HEAD

"Corrine, you have to eat something," The Avenger spoke lovingly while trying to force oatmeal in her mouth. Corrine's lips stayed firmly pressed together. "It's not time for you to fast yet. We'll begin that process before you go to meet the Lord. If you don't eat, then we can start right now and this will all be over sooner than later."

She said nothing. She would look like her mother if it wasn't for her swollen eyes from crying all night and her red, flared nostrils. There was innocence in her eyes that the others didn't have. The Avenger almost felt sorry for her, but sin did not deserve sympathy. It must be eradicated or it would spread like cancer. If Corrine slept with one married man, she'd sleep with another! The mere thought incited the Avenger, and without warning, Corrine was slapped. "Eat!" This time Corrine opened her mouth as the Avenger shoved the spoon in. "Good girl. Obedience is an essential element to your walk with Christ."

"Why are you doing this to me?" Oatmeal drooled from the corners of her mouth as she cried.

Like a mother gently cleaning her child's face, the Avenger cleaned Corrine's softly. "Honey, I've already answered that question. You have sinned against God."

"W-w-hat gives you the right to judge me about anything?"

"Scripture. In the last two verses of 1 Corinthians 5, Paul says that we aren't to judge those outside of the church because God will, but we can judge those who are inside the church. In verse 13 of the New International Version, he says to 'expel the wicked man from among you.' I'm simply following orders. What happened to me will not continue to happen to other couples."

"You are misusing the Word."

"And you are living contrary to it."

"Please, let me go. I promise not to say anything. My family was expecting me yesterday and I know they are out looking for me."

"They can search high and low, but there's one thing I am confident of: they won't find you until I'm ready for your body to be discovered. Eat up! This is getting cold and I need to get to church."

Natalie woke up a little after nine Sunday morning to an empty bed. Troy had left a note on his pillow saying that he was in the basement. She smiled. *God, please give him wisdom.* While Troy did his part, she'd do hers. Faith without works was dead. Yesterday she cried, today she would take action. She heard Aneetra fussing at Nate to stop writing on the walls and got up to see what was happening.

"Hi, Mommy!" He ran and hugged her legs.

She picked him up and gave him a kiss while greeting Aneetra. "What are you in here doing?"

"I color on 'da walls and it go away."

"Girl, he *loves* that disappearing ink set that Diane sent him, but I'm trying to get him dressed so we can get out of here. I was going to take him to church and come back later and get his clothes."

Natalie took one of the ink bottles from her and read the label. *Magically disappears within minutes.* "I hope this stuff doesn't stain."

"No, it doesn't. It's really neat though. She got him seven bottles and he's already used two. I just hope he doesn't think he can write on the walls with everything."

"Don't you write on the walls unless you ask permission first. You hear me?"

"Yes, ma'am. Can I write on 'da walls now?"

"No. Aunt Nee Nee told you to stop. You're going to spend the night over her house."

"I wanna go over Sissy's house."

That was a tug on her heart string that she didn't need. She hugged him, not knowing how to respond. She was thankful that Aneetra stepped in.

"We'll go over my house and get ice cream later and watch one of your *Spider-Man* movies."

"Yay! I wanna go to Aunt Nee Nee's and eat ice cream and watch my *Spider-Man* movie."

"Okay, baby, but first you have to listen to her and get dressed for church."

"'Kay." He got his pants, attempting to put them on.

"I spoke with Pastor Giles this morning. He told me to tell you that he's praying for you and if there's anything you need, ask. He said he tried calling you."

"I haven't even checked my phone. Please tell him I said thank you." Natalie was not one to get hung up on preachers, but she absolutely loved Pastor Giles. He was humble and not one of those super-star mentality types always surrounded by armor bearers and distanced from his mid-sized congregation. Despite being extremely busy, he seemed to go the extra mile to show how much he cared about members. If he couldn't do something himself, he made sure someone else on the ministerial staff did. "Where are Lauren and Ashley?"

"Marcus picked them up about an hour ago. He asked if he could take them to breakfast and hang out with them today before they leave for my sister's in the morning. I think he wants to talk to them and explain what's going on in his own way."

"Then you don't have to take Nate. He'll be all right. If your kids are gone, no need of looking after anyone else's."

"It's not a problem. I'll have plenty of alone time when they are in Louisiana. Let me help you."

"I can't get 'dis!" Nate whined. He'd gotten both of his legs stuck in one pant leg.

"I'll get him together, but will you please take this?" She gave Natalie the other bottles of ink she had. "You know Nate didn't open these by himself, right? Feel free to keep them out of eyesight until we're gone. No need to take *everything* to my house."

Natalie laughed and stuffed them in the pocket of her robe while Aneetra attended to Nate. Her motherly instinct wanted to take over. She felt like she was delegating a very important role, but she quickly got over it. Aneetra was an awesome godmother and Natalie told herself she'd step back and let her do her thing. She'd be getting Nate dressed again soon enough. Now that she thought about it, she'd better enjoy the break while she had it. It was too bad it had to come at Corrine's expense.

Natalie was far enough down the basement stairs to witness Troy close something on his computer real quick. "What's up?"

"I was going over crime scene photos. Nothing my pretty wife needs to see and worry her head over." He held out his arms, welcoming her into his lap. "Did you sleep okay?"

"Yeah. I'll feel better once this is all over, I'm sure."

"Ouch! Babe, whatever you have in your pocket is cutting into my stomach."

"Oh, my bad." She removed the squeeze bottles, explaining to Troy how they had made it there in the first place.

"Leave it up to my mama to get stuff like this. She loves getting loud or messy gifts."

"Nate needs to call and thank her."

"Yeah, but finding Corrine is more important right now."

"True." Curiosity took over Natalie and she opened one of the ink containers and began writing on the wall. Troy looked at her like she was crazy, but seemed to use her diverted attention to cover up additional things on his desk. She wanted to know what he was hiding, but figured whatever he was hiding from her was for her own good. "Oh wow! This *is* neat."

He turned around as the words "I love you" lingered on the wall for a few moments then began to fade. Her excitement disappeared just as quickly. Troy caressed her back while ignoring the vibrating cell phone on his desk for about the third or forth time. "Who's Cheryl Hunter?"

"Oh, um, someone who works for the FBI. She put together the profile of the suspect."

"Then why aren't you answering!" Natalie grabbed the phone and forced it to his ear.

"Hel-*lo?*" Troy didn't sound like himself. "No, it's not…uh, we're fine…thanks for your insight and concern…um, I have to go now."

"Everything all right?"

"Yep. She'd heard about Corrine."

He looked stressed, so she switched her focus. "I shouldn't have come down and interrupted you. I wanted to say hi. I should probably get going anyhow. I'm going to pass around fliers of Corrine."

"That's a good idea. I'm supposed to meet Jon somewhere later, but I'm waiting on him to call me back. Will you send Nate down here before they take off?"

"Sure thing." She got up to head back upstairs.

"Hey, Nat…I love you, too," he said and went right back to work.

Jon wouldn't risk sending him official photos of Corrine's apartment, but he did promise to resend the ones of Mindy Lee that he'd neglected to attach yesterday. Troy was cool with that. He had enough pics from Corrine's apartment on his phone to get an accurate assessment. He uploaded them from his Droid onto his computer and printed them, studying the image of the note: WITHOUT THE SHEDDING OF BLOOD, THERE IS NO REMISSION OF SIN. THEY HAD TO DIE SO THAT OTHERS WILL COME TO REPENTANCE. GOD WILL NOT BE MOCKED BY SIN! SOON THE WAGES OF SIN MISSION WILL BE COMPLETE AND SOULS WILL BE SAVED. *Corrine Shepherd* WILL BE THE LAST DEATH. Corrine's name had been handwritten after being whited out. Why didn't the killer retype the note instead of handwriting the name? Troy was getting restless waiting for Jon. He got the key from Natalie, said good-bye to Nate, and drove over to Corrine's, ignoring another incoming phone call from Cheryl.

The door was slightly ajar and Troy could hear someone rustling around inside her apartment. He pulled out his gun and went in. "Hold it right there!"

A dusty-blond Caucasian man, dressed in blue jeans and an Ohio State football T-shirt and matching sun visor, looked frightened enough to pee his pants. He dropped his car keys and held his hands up like he'd been placed under arrest. "I-I'm s-s-sorry. I didn't break in, I promise. I have a key."

"What are you doing here?" Troy, with his gun still pointed, slowly approached him.

"I came to check on Corrine. She is my g-g-irlfriend. I haven't been able to get a hold of her all weekend."

"Place your hands on the wall!" Troy patted him down, pulled out his wallet and confirmed his identity: *Brent Ellis, 5'11", blue eyes, and 175 pounds.* "Says here that you live in Mansfield. An hour is a long way to drive for some booty." For some reason, he'd never pictured Corrine with a white man. He figured she'd take after both her mothers and go for that tall, dark type. Then again, he'd never thought she'd settle for being a mistress, either. "How did you and Corrine become involved?" Troy put his gun away and gave him back his wallet.

"We work together, sir. I'm her supervisor."

"Sounds like sexual harassment to me."

"*No!* It's not like that at all. We keep our personal relationship separate from work . We only see each other in the evenings and on the weekends."

That saddened Troy. Corrine was such a bright and talented girl. She didn't have to compromise her integrity to get ahead. "When is the last time you saw her?"

"Thursday. We came back from a business trip in Chicago. I didn't go to work Friday because…um…I had some personal issues to deal with. Oh, my gosh, did something happen to her? Her brother's birthday party was yesterday and I'm assuming that's his present on the table."

"Did you talk to her at all Friday or yesterday?"

"Not at all yesterday, but Friday, when she was on break. Then later that night, um, she was dialed by mistake."

"What do you mean she was dialed by mistake? Did you talk to her that night or not?"

"Not really, but she answered. I wasn't the one who called her. It was a…um, friend of mine."

Troy could tell Brent wasn't being completely honest and, having been a player in his younger days, he could pretty much piece together what had happened. "What time did the call take place?"

"Around ten or so, I guess."

Brent fit the profile: Caucasian male, anywhere between thirty and forty years old. Troy didn't believe he had anything to do with Corrine's disappearance though. The killer made it clear that Corrine was part of his collection. This guy didn't seem tough enough to pull something like that off. He was bright red and shaking like an epileptic. Plus, if he was in Chicago with Corrine, then he couldn't have killed Mindy Lee. The information was useful in establishing a timeline for Corrine's abduction, which had to take place sometime between ten o'clock Friday night and late yesterday morning when Natalie had first tried to contact her.

"Sir, am I going to have to testify in court if something bad has happened to her? Can I just give a sworn affidavit? If this goes public, it can ruin everything for me."

The more this guy opened his mouth, the more Troy wanted to deck him. He wished he could arrest him, if for nothing else than being stupid. "I'm not worried about your image or keeping your wife and kids from finding out you're a lying cheater! My only concern is finding Corrine."

"Wh-h-hat makes you think I'm married?"

Did this dummy really not know he still had his wedding ring on? "I ask the questions; you answer. Who knows about your affair with Corrine?"

"No one except her mom. I guess she sort of flipped out when Corrine told her about us. I certainly didn't tell anyone."

He pulled out a pen and notepad. "Leave your name and number so I can contact you if you're needed further. I don't know what game you're playing, but if you come near my daughter again, your image will be the least of your worries. The first chance you have to take another position at your job, you better do so. In the meantime, if Corrine gets fired, demoted, or has any problems at work that can be traced back to you, I will make a personal trip to your job to see that a full sexual harassment investigation is launched and then I'll escort you to Mansfield and explain how you have been pretending to work late while screwing around with a young innocent girl."

"Yes, sir, I understand. I swear this is the first time I've done anything like this. I—"

"Just shut up and get out of here." Brent ran like he was on fire. *Jerk!* What did Corrine see in him? Troy would bet money that he was messing around with other women in the office before he picked Corrine as his latest conquest. A wife, alone, was enough for one man to deal with. Why would anyone want a mistress, too!

Troy looked around Corrine's apartment some more, hoping to find some missed clues. He tried calling Jon again.

"Hey, man, I was getting ready to call you. Where you at? You want to ride with me to Freeman's? I want to interview him again."

"Sure, but what makes you think he'll be home on a Sunday afternoon. You sure he's not at his church in Sandusky or in Heaven talking to Jesus."

"He must've taken the day off because I spoke with him after talking to you this morning and he said I could come around one-thirty."

"Okay. I'm at Corrine's poking around."

"You find anything?"

"Nope." He quickly filled Jon in on Brent. "I have his information if you want to question him further."

"Cool. We have someone trying to decipher whose name was whited out on that letter. It may not do us any good, as common as names are, but it's worth a shot. By the way, I sent the pics of Mindy to you. They should be there when you get home."

"Thanks." Troy wanted to tell him that he'd received an email notification on his phone before Jon called, but he didn't feel like trying to explain how he'd set up an email account on his phone. He'd look at it later. "You headed to Freeman's now?"

"Yep. Meet me there in about twenty. Come with a level head, man. Don't make me regret this."

CHAPTER 38: DOWN-TO-EARTH

"God bless you!" Natalie said to the manager of the local print-ing shop. She'd gotten the flier together and took it there to get a hundred of them copied and the store manager didn't charge her one dime, even after she'd told him she wanted them all in color.

"It's the least I can do to help. Good luck in finding her."

"Thank you so much!" She was headed to meet Lisa at a park not too far from where Corrine lived. She'd called this morning for an update on the situation and offered to help. Natalie didn't even try to object. She'd pretty much figured she'd be on her own with Aneetra watching Nate and Troy working.

The picture she chose was one from last month when the two of them had a girl's day out and went to the outlet mall in Jefferson-ville. The photo was taken outside the Coach store with Corrine modeling a new handbag she'd bought. Natalie managed to crop it to a head shot. Corrine's smile was so charming. Staring at it brought back memories of their day together and caused Natalie's eyes to well with tears.

"Are you ladies sisters?" the sales associate had asked.

"Nope. Mother, daughter, and absolute best friends," Corrine replied, winking at Natalie.

For Corrine to regard her so highly was an honor. As close as

Natalie had been with her mother, she didn't confide in her mom like Corrine did with her. There's no way Natalie would have told her mother that she was dating a married man. She appreciated their non-conventional relationship, but she also hoped that it was balanced with proper guidance and wisdom. *Lord, please don't let Thursday be the last day that I will ever hear my daughter's voice.*

"INCOMING CALL FROM TONI. SAY 'HELLO' TO ANSWER OR 'IGNORE' TO SEND THE CALLER TO VOICEMAIL."

Natalie could feel every knot that formed in her stomach. She deliberated so long that she'd missed the call. *Whew!* She knew she'd have to speak with Toni eventually, but at least she'd bought herself a little time. Turned out, it wasn't much time because Toni was calling again within seconds. Lisa wasn't yet there and reluctantly Natalie accepted the call.

"*When were you going to tell me that Corrine is missing!*"

"I'm sorry. I was going to call you. I needed some time to process everything first."

"*You needed time?! From what Sylvia says Corrine may not have much time! The minute you knew something was wrong, you should have called me!*"

"You're right, Toni, I'm sorry. I promise I was going to get around to it."

"*Get around to it?* You selfish, inconsiderate skank! *I* am the one who raised her. How dare you keep information from me when my daughter's life is in danger?!?"

"Toni, I…am…*sorry!* What more do you want me to say? Maybe subconsciously this is the reason why I didn't call because all you ever do is bring up the fact that you raised her. *Who cares?* Your pulling rank does nothing to find her!"

"And what are you doing besides *processing* everything?"

"I'm about to hang fliers until my fingers are numb and Troy is out busting his butt working. You're not the only one who loves her."

"I do know she wouldn't be in this mess if you would have left us alone!" Toni broke out in tears. "Why'd you have to take her? She would be alive and well if it weren't for you meddling in our lives."

Venom flowed through Natalie despite her aunt's tears. She was so sick of Toni blaming her for Corrine's move. It's the same tired argument they'd had the last three years! She felt her conscience telling her to let Toni's words roll off like water on a duck's back, but her emotions took over. "You're nothing but a jealous old wench! Have you ever considered that maybe you drove Corrine away by being so overbearing???"

"Oh, so you're the cool mom and I'm the mean one? Under my watch, Corrine finished high school without getting pregnant and graduated Magna Cum Laude from college! Under yours, she gets kidnapped! You better be glad Mama's not here. If she wasn't already dead, you'd kill her!"

"YOUR CALL HAS ENDED."

Natalie leaned her head against the steering wheel and cried. The mention of her grandmother tore at her heart. They'd only been reunited for a few years when Big Mama died in her sleep from a heart attack when Nate was a baby. She'd know exactly what to do and say right now. So down-to-earth and yet so heavenly minded. Her wisdom and spiritual guidance were missed. *"Chile, quit worryin' and let God do what He gon' do."* Natalie could hear her saying.

How am I not supposed to worry when my child is in the hands of a killer?

"What's worryin' gon' fix? Either you trust God to handle this or

you don't. He wants her found more than we do. She was His before we ever knew her."

"But—"

"You cain't trust Him and worry, too. This is too big for you, but God's got it all under control."

"What if Corrine dies?"

"It broke my heart when you're daddy died, but I never turned my back on God. You need to decide if you're still willing to serve Him even if things don't work out the way you want…"

"I'll be hurt, but yes, I will serve Him."

"Good. Now wipe your face, chile, and get busy. All this cryin' ain't doin' nuthin' to bring my grandbaby home."

Acting as if this had been a real conversation, Natalie followed instructions and looked through the mirror on her sun visor, wiping tear remnants from her face. The knock on the passenger side window startled her. Lisa opened the door.

"Sorry I'm late. I was waiting for RJ to get back. He had to go take care of some crisis at the center. I take it these are the fliers?" she said, picking one up from the seat. "She is so beautiful. She looks so much like you."

"Thanks."

"Are you okay?"

At peace, Natalie smiled, gathering her belongings. "Yep. Let's get this show on the road."

CHAPTER 39: WILD GOOSE CHASE

The Avenger was turning down the street when Evans pulled into Eric's driveway. *Dang!* All hope of speaking to Eric first, perhaps for the last time before the mission ended, was gone. Eric had been such a crucial part of the plan and would have been the fall guy if things hadn't gone wrong with the Lee girl. *No worries.* There wasn't anything new Freeman could reveal now anyhow.

Plan B was inevitable. With all natural and spiritual affairs in order, there was no fear. Like Jesus in the Garden of Gethsemane, the Avenger had prayed for this cup to be removed, but there was no other way. But not before Corrine was held accountable for her sins.

Troy pulled up to the quaint white house with dark purple shutters expecting Jon to be there by now. He waited a few minutes before calling him. "Hey, man, where you at? It's been a pretty long twenty minutes."

"My bad. Um, you go ahead without me. I need to check something out first."

Frustrated, Troy hung up. Besides his mother, what did Knight have to do that was more important than helping him find Corrine? Jon's ears must have been burning, as he must've known what Troy would be thinking, Jon sent him a text. *I am looking into a possible lead. I will explain everything to you later. You go ahead and talk to Freeman without me, but be cool!!!*

Eric seemed unpleasantly surprised to see Troy. "Detective Evans, what can I do for you?" He spoke through the screen door.

"I know you weren't expecting me, but my partner couldn't make it. May I come in?"

Reluctantly, he obliged. "Remember this house is holy. The last time I allowed your people to do a search, my sacred items were disturbed. It took several days to restore the ambiance. This time you will need a warrant or you're not going past the living room."

"I only wish to talk to you."

Eric nodded and led him to the white plush sofa. Eric's house, though immaculate, was a bit eerie. The living room looked more like the inside of a sanctuary than anything. Scriptures were on every wall. A large copy of the Bible sat on a stand on a desk that didn't seem used.

"Can I offer you anything? Perhaps you would like a cup of herbal tea or some water?"

"No, thank you."

"I saw on the news that another lady was found and they think it's the same killer?"

"It's true. That's partially why I am here."

Eric rolled his eyes. "I can understand all the questions, to an extent, because the carnal mind is unable to understand spiritual things. But, the Lord didn't reveal her death to me. I don't see how I can help."

Having expected Jon to do most of the talking, Troy had only a minute or so to ponder his approach and had decided to play into Freeman's ego. It went against his own beliefs about the flaunting of titles, but he had to lay his pride aside. Corrine's life was at stake. "Pastor Freeman, I need you to come clean. Whoever murdered those women now has my daughter and if you don't tell me your connection to the killer, she will be next."

Eric stared at him oddly. "My heart sincerely goes out to you, detective. I discern how troubled your spirit is about this matter and if there was any way I could help you I would. I have been as forthright about things as I can be. I've told the truth, but your people do not want to believe me."

"Believe you? Your story is ridiculous!"

"It's ridiculous to you because you're obviously a man of little faith, but to my prayer partner and me, it is the truth."

"So someone other than you has seen these mysterious messages?"

"No, not exactly. When I told my prayer partner about what was happening to me, not once was my integrity questioned. My word was enough."

"The only reason you're not in jail is because we can't find any evidence to tie you to the murders. Your story is a bunch of crap. God does *not* write messages on walls. Look, man, I don't think you're solely responsible, but I think you know who is. The sooner you talk, the better it will be for you in the end."

"As a police officer, I understand that you like to deal with scientific evidence, but God does not operate within the confines of man. He works supernat—"

"Whatever, Eric, I'm tired of your biblical jargon. In this farce to be so holier than thou, you're jeopardizing my daughter's life and you better pray that she doesn't die because of your lack of cooperation." Troy proceeded to leave, more irritated with Jon for orchestrating this wild goose chase and leaving him hanging than he was with Eric.

"You're wrong, my friend." Eric was surprisingly calm. "The Bible speaks of how God wrote a message on a wall for King Belshazzar that only Daniel was able to interpret. I may be many things, detective, but I am not a liar. When I tell you that God supernaturally revealed to me the location of those women, that is what happened. Your lack of belief doesn't negate the truth."

The passion in which Eric spoke was so sincere that Troy didn't have the energy to argue with him. "Okay, if you say so." Troy walked away, remembering that Eric had been able to pass the polygraph because he actually believed his own story. Could it be that he suffered from a multiple personality disorder and doesn't remember his involvement with the crimes? Though no treatment for mental illness had been discovered thus far, there was no doubt in Troy's mind that there were a few flaws with his cerebral functions that would be worth checking out.

"I'll be praying for your daughter," Eric yelled as Troy got into his truck.

"Jon, where are you? Speaking with Freeman did no good, but someone needs to look into his psychological background ASAP. Call me, man. I need to know what you're up to."

CHAPTER 40: WORKING FOR THE DEVIL

Corrine had been trying to find some way to escape all afternoon. Her left arm had been handcuffed to the railing and there was nothing else in her reach except for the Bible her abductor had left for her to read. Though she'd been given a thin blanket to lie on, the basement floor was chilly. The cracks in the concrete started to form creases in her thighs.

She was scared, cold, and lonely, but ultimately determined not to die at the hand of this psychopath. "God, *please* help me," she cried as thoughts of her family went through her mind. She kissed the locket with Nate's picture, hating that she missed his party yesterday. She'd looked forward to giving him his swimming pool and had purposely bought a gift that Natalie and Troy would have to keep at their house. She had enough of his little gadgets all over her tiny place.

She thought about her parents and wondered if Natalie called her mom. She'd hoped the two of them were able to remain cordial to one another and that her mother wouldn't use this as an opportunity to lash out at Natalie. Had Natalie told her about Brent like she'd done Troy? Though it troubled Corrine a great deal that Troy told his friend about her affair, she was the only one to blame for her current state.

Corrine felt like such a fool. She had bad luck when it came to men. Her very first boyfriend was during her freshman year of college and turned out he was messing around with her roommate behind her back. Corrine was mad, but not devastated because they hadn't done anything except kiss. Her heartbreak came two years later when she gave her virginity away to Juan Robinson, whom she'd met at a party one night. They were together for several months before Corrine had decided to go all the way. It was something she'd wrestled with, knowing she wasn't holding true to her Christian upbringing and it was something that she and Juan even talked about. Ultimately, she gave in to temptation only to later learn that the night they'd met, Juan had bet his friends that he could eventually get her to give it up.

Corrine was crushed. Although Juan apologized and sincerely seemed remorseful, she refused to give him a second opportunity to make a fool of her. After that, Corrine was done with dating. She focused on her grades, graduating Magna Cum Laude, and then moved to Ohio to help with Nate.

She'd known Brent ever since she started working for Victoria's Secret. Though he was her supervisor, the two became great friends. She had no reason to doubt his claims of being trapped in an unhappy marriage because, over the years, his story had stayed consistent. Besides, he was nearly a decade older than her with kids. Surely he'd outgrown the childish games that men her age liked to play. Boy was she wrong!

That night she'd gone for a walk, thinking about all the warning signs she'd ignored or missed. Obviously, her mind was so consumed that she didn't practice the good situational awareness techniques that she'd often heard Troy speak of because she hadn't noticed that dark vehicle next to her until the driver blew the horn. It startled her, but once she saw that it was a friend of

Troy's whom she'd recently accepted a Facebook friend request from, she relaxed, even accepting a ride after realizing how far she'd ventured from her apartment.

Now she was trapped in this basement with virtually no way out. The windows had been boarded, but the dimwit was kind enough to leave the overhead light on so she could read the Bible. Corrine stared at the leather-bound book, wondering if Samson had felt this helpless after he'd revealed the secret of his strength to Delilah and was taken by the Philistines. Tears swam down Corrine's face. Though Samson had managed to kill his captors, he also died in the process. Corrine hoped her adulterous behavior would not lead to her death. She wasn't ready to die. "God, I'm sorry!"

After enduring two days with no shower, little food, and memories of loved ones she may never get to see again, Corrine continued to cry as she reached for the Bible. She recalled the days when her grandmother was alive. Corrine could talk to her about anything. In fact, Big Mama was the only one who knew about what happened with Juan. Corrine refused to tell her mom because she didn't want to hear her preaching to death about virtue and although Natalie knew she was no longer a virgin, she didn't want to share the details because she didn't want to dredge up any negative feelings for her. Big Mama had a way of keeping it real and gentle at the same time.

"There are always consequences when we choose to disobey God's Word," she said, holding Corrine firmly against her healthy chest. *"We don't get to choose what they are and how they will play out. But, know that there is always restoration, too. When we sincerely ask for God's forgiveness, He can be merciful enough to lessen the severity. What's done is done, baby. You cain't change nuthin', but you ain't gotta wallow in self pity over your mistakes. Get back in the Word and get on track."*

Ironically, the New King James Version of God's Word had been left in her reach by someone working for the devil. Corrine instinctively turned to the book of Psalms, which had always been one of Big Mama's favorites. She'd started from the beginning and now found herself already at Psalm 34. *The Lord is near to those who have a broken heart and saves such as have a contrite spirit. Many are the afflictions of the—*" She was about to start the nineteenth verse when she heard an upstairs door open.

Great! Psycho was back from church. Corrine was still scared, but calmer. Reading had done her good. Corrine put the Bible back down, clinging on to the final words she'd read. It was taking longer than usual for her abductor to come down and check on her. She laid her head against the cold wall, hoping that if she pretended to be sleep, she'd be left alone for a little while longer. She tried to relax as she heard the footsteps coming down the stairs.

"*Corrine...*" Her ears recognized a familiar whisper.

When she opened her eyes, Jon was standing before her with his gun in hand.

CHAPTER 41: A STUPID TECHNICALITY

Troy left Eric's and went straight over to Chad Gordon's, whom he hadn't heard from in over a week. It wasn't until the calls stopped that Troy realized how much of a motivation they had been to him.

Troy drove around the apartment complex a couple of times before he had found the Gordon townhome. After several knocks, no one had come to the door. *Darn!* Just as Troy was walking away, someone came to the door, hidden behind weeks of unshaven facial hair. *"Chad?"*

"Hi, detective, what's up?"

"I'm sorry to drop by unannounced. I need to speak with you about the case."

His face lit up. "Sure, come in. Did you find out who killed Lolita?"

"No, I'm sorry, not yet."

"Then what can I do for you?"

Inside the Gordon home, the drawn shades were a perfect match to Chad's ominous demeanor. Troy found himself stepping over pizza boxes and other items all while trying to ignore the smell of rotten trash. "We've come up with a theory of why each victim was targeted. The other women appeared to have been involved in adulterous relationships. I know you and Lolita had a great marriage, but is there any reason someone would *think* she was unfaithful?"

Chad shook his head. "She would never do anything like that to our family. There has to be something else."

"I understand your position and I hate to break it to you like this, but unless we find the killer another woman will soon die. We are certain about the killer's motive. Did Lolita have a close male friend that someone could possibly misconstrue to be something more than what it was?"

"I appreciate how diligent you've been working, but my life sucks enough without you coming in here insinuating that my wife was not who I have known her to be. She was a good woman and if it hadn't been for some monster stealing her away, she, Miguel, and I would be spending time together right now like we always did on Sundays after church. Instead, Lolita is dead and it will feel like my son is, too if my in-laws win this custody suit they've filed. Honestly, if Lolita cheated on me, I don't want to know. Memories of her are all I have left. Sometimes, detective, ignorance is bliss."

"What grounds do your in-laws have for seeking custody of your son?"

"I'm not his biological father. You'd think it wouldn't matter since I have been with Lolita ever since she was pregnant. I never officially adopted him, but he has my last name for goodness sake and they want to strip me of my son because of a stupid technicality." Chad cried shamelessly. Troy had to wait until he calmed down before proceeding further.

"Do you know his biological father's name?"

"Samuel Keller or Kingsley…something like that. I can't remember. She told me they'd met online. It won't do you any good. He was killed shortly after Lolita found out she was pregnant. That was a tough time for her because she saw his murder on the news. I didn't ask many questions. I wanted to be there for her. It didn't matter to me that…well, that the circumstances weren't ideal. I've loved her since high school and wanted to be there for her. I promised to raise her baby as my own and I did."

"What aren't you telling me?"

Chad looked away. "I've told you everything. Anything else isn't relevant to the case. I refuse to say anything that will tarnish my wife's name. She was an amazing woman."

Troy had had enough of tiptoeing around Chad's fragility. "Look, man, personally, I don't care if your wife screwed a dozen guys on the same night she got knocked up. I only want to find her killer, so quit farting around and tell me everything you know about your son's father."

He blew out a long, deep breath. "I know nothing besides the fact that he was married."

CHAPTER 42: PLAIN AND SIMPLE

I t was a few minutes before six when Troy got home. He immediately recognized the almond-colored sedan parked in front of the house and ran in, praying he didn't walk into an explosive situation.

"That must be my husband," he heard Natalie say. She came around the living room corner, followed by Cheryl.

What in the heck is she doing here? Troy thought.

"Hi, babe."

"Um, hey, what's going on?" He stared fiercely at his ex.

"I'm sorry to drop by unannounced. I was telling your wife how concerned I was about your daughter. I thought I'd come by and see if I could provide any additional insight to the case."

"I'll leave the two of you to work. I have some phone calls I need to make. Nice meeting you, Agent Hunter."

"Please, call me Cheryl. It was nice meeting you, too."

When Troy was certain that Natalie was completely out of ear shot, in not so kind words, he asked Cheryl what she was doing at his home. He felt convicted for cursing in light of the new leaf he'd turned over yesterday. Traces of his last conversation with Jon zipped through his mind as she stuttered her reply.

"I wanted to check on you. You didn't sound well earlier and I got concerned because you haven't responded to any of my texts or calls since."

"My daughter is missing. I don't have time to answer your freakin' calls," he spat through gritted teeth.

"Calm down." He backed away as she came closer. "I know solving this case is even more critical to you than before. I want to help any way that I can."

"You've helped enough. I can take it from here."

"Troy, I know you've been taken off the case. I have a lot of friends on the force and I can likely gain access to information that you are no longer privy to."

Troy had never hit a woman in his life and yet he was mad enough to slap the black off Cheryl. "I have friends on the force, too, and I'm sure I can get whatever information I need to work this case. I don't appreciate you coming by my house. How'd you even know where I lived? Did you follow me home Friday night?"

"I'm an FBI agent. It wasn't that hard."

"Your actions are inappropriate and completely unprofessional."

"We don't exactly have a professional relationship."

"We don't have *any* kind of relationship."

"I'm sorry. I—I thought we could be friends." The look on her face was the same as it was the night they'd broken up.

"Why won't you tell me you love me?"

"Because that won't be enough. You'll want more."

"We've been dating for over a year now and you can't even say you love me. Elvin and Nicole haven't been together as long as we have and already he's proposed to her."

"We are not them! I don't want to get married because my best friend is."

"But you will spend seventy-five dollars on a stupid stuffed animal to keep up with him."

"I am not ready."

"Do you love me?"

He looked down at her petite frame, wishing he had never allowed their contact to extend beyond their one-night stand. But, she'd called him the next day and before he knew it, they were dating. She was a nice person whom he'd had a lot of fun and great sex with, but she wasn't someone he wanted to spend the rest of his life with. "I can't give you the answer you want."

"So what are you saying?"

"This is obviously an issue that won't go away. Maybe it's best that we end things."

Cheryl went into a hysterical rage, screaming how much she loved him and wanted to be with him forever. She punched him repeatedly until he'd finally grabbed her arms and held her to his chest. To be so small, she hit hard. He felt horrible, but he refused to lie and play with her heart or any woman's for that matter, by admitting to feelings he did not have. He apologized profusely for hurting her. She kicked him out of her apartment and that was the last he'd ever seen or heard from Cheryl until recently.

"I'm sorry if I have done anything to mislead you into thinking that we could reconnect in any way. It's not wise, given our history."

"I truly just wanted to help. Guess I'll see myself out."

She turned to leave and Troy swore he saw tears in her eyes. After watching her drive away, he immediately locked the door and turned on the exterior alarm before going up to check on Natalie.

"That's fine, Toni," he heard her say. He put his gun in the safe and signaled that he'd be in the basement, anxious to get back on the case.

He still hadn't heard from Jon. Maybe something had happened with his mom? Still, he could have communicated that. To completely disregard Troy's calls and text messages at such a crucial time was plain and simple ignorance. He gave texting one last attempt.

Where r u? Call me asap! Need 2tell u sumthn!!! Spoke 2 Chad Gordon.

He was in the process of printing out one of the official photos that Jon had sent earlier of Mindy Lee's body when Jon finally replied. *Sorry ddnt answr ur calls. WorkN on sumthN. Find out what u can abt Darnell Thompson. DT is r guy. Promise 2fill u n l8r.*

Troy was confused by Jon's message. Something wasn't right. Who in the world was Darnell Thompson? Troy was scanning through witness interviews when Natalie came down to the basement. "Is your friend coming back?"

"No. I got everything I need from her." Now wasn't the time to explain Cheryl to her. "How'd things go today?"

"Great! We walked until our feet were raw. Robert sent some staff members to help us and other people saw what we were doing and joined in."

"That was nice of him and everyone else."

"Yeah. Lisa is so encouraging. I really appreciate her. Anyhow, afterward I stopped over Aneetra's to see Nate. I hadn't too long gotten home when Cheryl came."

"How was li'l man doing?"

"He was good. I thought he might be bored since the girls were still with Marcus, but Aneetra kept him entertained. He did ask for Corrine a couple times. It's going to be so hard if—"

"Shh, baby. Don't say it." He pulled her into his lap.

"Did you find out anything?"

He wanted so desperately to erase those worry lines in her forehead. "Nothing concrete, but I'm trying, babe, and I swear I won't stop." She nodded, staring at the crime scene photo he'd printed. "Who is this?"

"Mindy Lee. The last victim."

"This is—*was* the girl Marcus cheated with?"

"Yeah."

"I've been getting a bunch of phone calls about Corrine. She's all over the news. I was so glued to what the media had been saying about all the other women, but I can't bring myself to watch it now."

He gently grabbed the picture from her and set it next to the ones he'd printed from his phone earlier. "You don't need to be looking at that nor watching the news. These things will only upset you."

"Based on the other victims, how much time do you think Corrine has left?"

Troy could tell from the sound of her voice that she was fighting back tears. He didn't want to add any additional stress. "Honey, I'm trying to find her. Don't get yourself all worked up about things."

"I'm not. I want you to keep it real with me. How much time does she have?"

He sighed heavily. "From all accounts, it seems she was taken late Friday night. Worst case scenario, she has another day. Best case, she has until Thursday."

"What determines how long he keeps them alive?"

"I honestly don't know."

Natalie chewed her bottom lip. "I refuse to panic. I'll prepare for the worst and pray for the best."

As the tears finally rolled down her face, Troy felt his eyes filling as well. This could not happen again. What would she think of him? How could he be there for her if she saw him as emotionally weak? "Um, I should probably get back to this." He willed himself to break her intense gaze, but her eyes held him captive. *Get it together, man!* She was the one who looked away. *Whew!*

"Toni and Kenny are in town."

"They flew in this morning?"

"I'm assuming. I didn't ask. She called when I was at the park going off because I didn't call her. She was blaming me for everything, even called me a skank. I got so mad that I snapped. I called her a jealous old wench."

"You didn't exactly say anything that wasn't true."

"I can only imagine how she feels. She gave up a lot to raise Corrine and had her all to herself before I came into the picture. I should have called her immediately."

"Don't be too hard on yourself. It's not like you intentionally tried to keep her out the loop. She'll have to get over it."

"Toni is not one to forgive easily. I got off the phone with her a few minutes ago and she still has an attitude. She did tell me that Richard pulled some strings and arranged for her and Kenny to hold a press conference. They're offering a twenty-five-thousand-dollar reward for anyone who has information about Corrine."

"Do they have that kind of money?'

"They must."

"We can pitch in if necessary. I'm willing to do anything to find her."

"I do sort of feel responsible. Corrine came to Ohio because of me and look what's happened to her."

"This is not your fault. If my theory is correct, she was targeted because of her involvement with that fool." Troy filled her in on his encounter with Brent.

"Why'd you let him go? What if he's the killer?"

"He's not, babe, trust me. The killer is on some type of moral mission. I've been able to confirm that all the women, except one, were involved with married men. There's no proof about the second victim, Myesha Turner, to support this theory, but I'm ninety-nine point nine percent sure this is why she was chosen."

"But how would the killer know about Corrine?"

"Maybe she told someone."

"I doubt it. I think I'm the only one she confided and I certainly didn't tell anyone but you."

"And the only person I told was J—" A sickening feeling came over Troy. The scratches…the excuses…and now his sudden disappearance—*could it be?*

"*Who?*"

"Jon." He said with a shoe-sized lump in his throat.

"You don't think he…he couldn't do this to us, could he?"

"It's hard for me to conceive, but he was extremely bitter about his wife's affair and his behavior has been very odd lately." Troy thought about something Cheryl had said the day she gave the profile. *He had a troubled childhood or a traumatic event later in life. Either way, something has triggered this string of killings.* "It's been a year since Belinda left him."

Troy hadn't realized he spoke out loud until Natalie said, "What does that mean?"

"Hopefully nothing." Troy's gut was telling him that Jon was a good guy. Still, it was worth checking out.

"Has anyone you've interviewed said anything to make you think Jon is involved?"

"No. I spoke with the husband of the first victim today. He promised to go through his wife's things and get back to me if he finds anything. I stopped by another guy's house earlier, but talking to him was a waste of time. He has this insane story about God writing him messages on the wall. I believe that happened in the Bible, but who in their right mind would buy that crap about mysterious writings disappearing, unless…" At the same time, he and Natalie turned their attention to the bottles of fading ink Troy's mother had gotten Nate for his birthday. "Maybe Eric has been telling the truth after all," he whispered. A quick glance at the two photos of Mindy lying next to each other revealed another troubling fact.

CHAPTER 43: RECENT DEVELOPMENTS

With the two pictures of Mindy Lee side-by-side, Troy noticed a huge discrepancy between the ones printed from his Droid and the ones Jon had sent. In his, Mindy had a closed fist, but in Jon's her hand was open. It wouldn't be a big deal if any of the photos Jon had sent resembled his as CSI sometimes had to move bodies, but they also took pictures every step of the way. There were no official photos of Mindy with her fist closed. Someone had been looking for something.

Troy drowned out all sounds of Natalie as he compared other official crime photos to the ones he'd taken himself. There were no other discrepancies, but there was a startling discovery when he compared the notes of the crime scene reports—*Victim was lying on back with arms spread out wide.*—with the letter left at Corrine's apartment—*Corrine Shepherd* WILL BE THE LAST DEATH. It was very apparent that the person who had written the report and the note was one in the same. Everything was starting to make sense now.

Curious about the DNA results, he called one of the techs on her cell, knowing he'd have a better chance of reaching her that way than by calling the lab. "Do you have the results yet from the Lee case?"

"Yep. We made it a priority as requested. I left a message for Detective Knight earlier today."

She had been given strict orders not to speak with anyone except Jon. But, Troy was able to finagle the information out of her
with relative ease since she had heard that Corrine was missing
and wanted to do what little she could to help. "Thanks, Kel. I
owe you one."

Troy immediately called his Superior, explaining how the DNA
results confirmed his theory.

"These are strong allegations you're making, Evans. Are you
certain about this?"

"Yes, sir."

"As much as I hate to think that one of our people could be
responsible for this nightmare, I'm going to back you up on this
in light of Knight's disappearance. If you're wrong, this could land
you in hot water for quite some time," he said sternly.

Natalie paced back and forth between the living room and the
kitchen, praying and wondering what Troy had discovered. When
he started tuning her out and curtly ordered her to "chill with all
the questions," she knew he was on to something. Natalie watched
from behind as he'd flipped through crime scene photos, mumbling
things under his breath that she couldn't comprehend. She'd never
seen so many pictures of dead people in her life. It freaked her
out. She had to come upstairs to get out of his way and to keep
from imagining Corrine in one of those photos.

After moving from room to room, her pacing driving her to the
point of feeling useless, Natalie thought of a way to be productive
and possibly help out with the case at the same time. She grabbed
her iPad and started looking up the disappearing ink. It sounded
so far-fetched that the killer would sneak into someone's house to

write messages on their wall. The stuff his mom got Nate faded in minutes. She wanted to see if there was anything that lasted longer.

To her surprise, disappearing ink was more common than she'd thought. Many were gag gifts or toys. The most legitimate thing she found was a Russian KGB disappearing ink spy pen. Supposedly it was the type used during the Cold War. There were all kinds of sites advertising ways to chemically create fading ink. Time for the writings to last varied from fifteen minutes to twenty-four hours. It seemed ludicrous, but in a crazy world, anything was possible.

Troy came from the basement at lightning speed and ran upstairs to their room.

"What's going on?" she yelled, following after him.

He unlocked his gun safe faster than she'd ever seen before. "I know who has Corrine."

"Is it Jon?"

"*No!* The DNA did not contain a Y chromosome."

"What does that mean?" He was already back down and nearly out the door.

"The perpetrator is a woman!" His tone was impatient, a mixture of urgency and irritability that she had not paid more attention during her grade-school biology classes. He ordered her to "lock up!" and sped out the garage so quickly that the top of his SUV scraped the garage door as he backed out.

A woman? That seemed even crazier than the disappearing ink! She immediately called Aneetra to give her the latest.

"Girl, I'm watching the news and was about to call you."

Natalie flipped on her TV. "*—live on Columbus' Southside where officers have surrounded the home of a suspect believed to be the Bible Butcher. CPD has not yet released the name of the individual, but sources* *say that it may be someone employed with the department. Officers are concerned that this is a hostage situation as neighbors reported hearing gunshots and the whereabouts of Corrine Shepherd remain unknown. Corrine's adoptive parents were scheduled to give a press conference at eight o'clock this evening. We do not yet know if that will still happen due to the recent developments in the case. Stay tuned as we will bring you the most up-to-date information the moment it comes in."*

Gunshots! Natalie could barely control her breath or slow down her speech. "Oh my gosh, Nee, what if she shot Corrine!"

"She who? Don't think like that."

"Troy said it's a female. She's been killing women sleeping with married men."

"Why in the world did she go after Cor—"

"I'm sorry I shouldn't have said anything. Please don't think bad of my baby. I just…" Natalie had to slow down to catch her breath. "I want her home!" she exploded in tears.

"I do, too, honey. Try and calm down. Nate and I are on our way."

Since it was getting late in the evening, Aneetra planned to sleep over and take Nate to preschool and go to work from there. Before Natalie could hang up with her, Lisa was calling. She'd heard the news as well. Upon hearing tears in Natalie's voice despite her claims of being "fine," she offered to come by. "I have Chandler with me because RJ's at the center. Is that okay?"

Overwhelmed with emotion, she got herself together long enough to call Toni. She hadn't expected Sylvia to answer Toni's cell, but she was relieved to avoid any conflict at the moment. Sylvia stated that Toni and Kenny were out back. Of course, they had already been informed about what was happening. The press conference had been postponed, depending on the outcome.

"By the way, I wasn't trying to start trouble when I called Toni about Corrine. I—"

"It's fine. I'm glad you did call. I don't think I would have been able to handle talking to her right away."

"She feels threatened by your relationship with Corrine, but she's also your aunt and she loves you, Natalie. Don't you dare for a minute think she doesn't."

How Toni felt about Natalie was the least of her concerns right now. "I know we both love Corrine and that's truly all that matters right now."

CHAPTER 44: GOODNESS AND MERCY

"Move it!" she ordered Corrine. Cuffed with the gun in the small of her back, Corrine stepped over Jon's lifeless body.

At first Corrine hadn't known what to think when she saw him with that gun. Her level of fear skyrocketed thinking that he, too, was somehow involved in this craziness. The hushed softness of his voice convinced her that he was there to help. He said, "Hang on, sweetie, I'm going to get you out of here," as he hurriedly unlocked her cuffs and put her mind at ease. Corrine cried and trembled with hope that the nightmare she'd lived for the last two days was finally over.

Bang! Bang! Bang! Bang! A series of gunshots ended her jubilation and Jon fell to the ground. Neither of them had heard her coming.

Corrine screamed until psycho lady yelled *"Shut up!"* and fired her weapon. She felt the heat of the bullet surging past her. The basement stairs were across the room. The door was left open. She'd never make it. Her legs gave out and she fell against the wall so hard, she hurt her shoulder.

Jon's phone vibrated constantly. Crazy lady stomped back and forth, going from extremes of yelling about "the plan" being messed up to softly reassuring herself that everything would be all right. Eventually, his phone went silent.

"I'm sorry that I scared you." Eyes still closed and body trembling uncontrollably, Corrine hadn't known that the lady knelt next to her until she spoke. "Troy may be very close to finding us and I can't let that happen. We need to get out of here." Her voice was eerily gentle.

The next thing Corrine knew, she was in the back of a car with the trunk release conveniently missing. Had she walked or been carried? She didn't know and she didn't care. *Ouch!* She felt a sharp pain in her upper thigh.

"This should keep you calm until we get there."

Corrine felt herself losing consciousness, resolved to the thought that she would not get to see the look on Nate's face when he opened his *Spider-Man* swimming pool, tell her parents and Natalie she loved them, or celebrate her twenty-fourth birthday next month. Those thoughts were too distressing. If this was her final moment, she was determined to go in peace. Confident that all was right between her and God, she silently repeated the twenty-third Psalm. "*...Yea, though I walk through the valley of the shadow of death, I will fear no evil: for thou art with me; thy rod and thy staff they comfort me. Thou preparest a table before me in the presence of mine enemies: thou anointest my head with oil; my cup runneth over. Surely goodness and mercy shall follow me all the days of my life: and I will dwell in the house of the LORD for ever.*"

Knowing that Evans had spoken with Chad Gordon made the Avenger very uneasy. What had Lolita told her husband over the years? Evans was smart. The name Darnell Thompson would only detour him for so long. They needed to get out of there. Hang out elsewhere until the final phase of the mission could be complete. She had the perfect place.

On the way, she stopped by the post office to mail the letter she'd intended to give Eric. Earlier this afternoon she'd planned to stop by his place and say good-bye. He was a good guy and though she had hoped to pin the murders on him, the mess up with Mindy and the young boy accelerated Plan B. Though he was an extremist when it came to the Word, she had grown to really like the guy. She respected his integrity. His warped view of himself made him an easy mark.

The first time she had ever heard of Eric was when he appeared on an investigative news report as a guest. The media had done an exposé on the criminal activity of several Abundant in Life Church members.

"We are live with Eric Freeman who once served on the ministerial staff at this church. Eric, did you have any idea what members of your former congregation were involved in?"

"It's Minister Eric Freeman, soon to be Pastor, because the Lord has given me the unction to start the Tabernacle of Jesus Church in Sandusky, Ohio. And to answer your question, no I did not. Had I had any inclination I would have gone to the authorities after consulting with my Father who I know is displeased with this behavior. The Lord—"

"Okay, sir, let's move on. We have reached out to the former pastor of Abundant in Life for comments, but he has not responded to any of our requests. Have you spoken with him and if so, what has he said about everything?"

"Proverbs 27:17 says that Iron sharpeneth iron; so a man sharpeneth the countenance of his friend. He is not iron in my life and thus as the up and coming Pastor of the Tabernacle of Jesus, I have not spoken to him. I have prayed for him daily because God is—"

The interview continued with the reporter getting visibly irritated with Eric's drawn-out replies and the need to insert his church name into every answer. When asked about the future of Abundant in Life and whether or not he would ever consider rejoining if the doors reopened, Eric stated, "Absolutely not! I am soon to be Pastor Eric Joshua *Free*man. I would be crazy to go back into bondage there when the Lord has given me the Tabernacle of Jesus as my new assignment."

"Okay folks, you heard it here first from Pastor *Free*man, clearly one of the sane former members of Abundant in Life church."

"Yes, sir. Thank you for your acknowledgment," he said, oblivious to the fact that the reporter was mocking him. "If anyone would like to learn more about the Tabernacle of Jesus, please call me at 614-555-2765."

She'd copied down the number, knowing that Eric would somehow be involved in her plan. She called him about a week later using the name Esther Roman because it sounded like a good biblical name. She'd make sure to stroke his ego about what an anointed man of God he appeared to be and how she would like to learn about his church, but it was too far for her to travel each week.

"Do you currently have a church home?" he asked.

"No sir. I have been unable to find a strong spiritual leader thus far. I know this may be an odd request, but would you mind being my spiritual mentor? I believe I could learn a lot from you. I'm willing to pay you for your time."

"That won't be necessary. My God provides all of my needs according to His riches in glory in Christ Jesus and I feel Him giving me unction to start an outreach ministry. I'll tell you what…" He said that he'd been planning to move to Sandusky, but was having a hard time selling his home, so he planned to stay. "Maybe the Lord wants me to stay because of you." Eric began to lay out a plan for them to meet on a regular basis at a neutral location. After several months, they were meeting at his home and eventually, sometimes she joined him, by phone, in his 4:00 a.m. morning devotion sessions. Over time, she had been able to learn his daily schedule and routines. A creature of habit, Eric made it easy for her to determine the right times to sneak into his house and leave messages for him. The writings only lasted a few hours, if that, so she had to be strategic, but in the end, she pulled it off. Eric was so full of himself that he believed God had spoken to him. She had felt a slight twinge of guilt for planning to make him the culprit for the murders, but she figured anyone that gullible needed to be locked up for life.

There was part of her that enjoyed befriending Eric. He was an interesting character, to say the least, but he was sincere. She didn't want to complete this mission without telling him how much she appreciated their time together. She'd written a letter that she was going to mail to him, but at the last minute decided to drop by his home one last time. That's when she saw Evans out front in his truck. Luckily, he didn't see her. She'd parked down the street a while to observe him and a glimpse of her rearview mirror revealed that she was being watched by Jon Knight. She drove away, pretending not to notice he was following her. Instead of going home, she stopped at the store, expecting Jon to follow her inside where she would casually confront him. When he didn't come in, she panicked. Something, which she now contributed to the Spirit of God, told her to go home immediately and that's when she found him in her basement, about to let that little slut go free. She shot him without hesitating and consequently was forced to expedite her plan. A few more hours and this would be all over.

CHAPTER 45: A SPECIAL UPDATE

Troy raced over to the Groveport address, praying Corrine was still alive, not wanting to entertain any other possibility. No matter what, he'd purposed in his heart not to turn away from God. If Corrine was dead, being mad wouldn't bring her back, but trusting Him would hopefully make it easier to help Natalie.

He was certain that something had happened to Jon. The last text supposedly received from him gave way to that thought. *Sorry ddnt answr ur calls. WorkN on sumthN. Find out what u can abt Darnell Thompson. DT is r guy. Promise 2fill u n l8r.* Not only was the name completely out of left field, but the whole message was uncharacteristic of Jon's texting abilities. He'd never used shortcuts like that. She must've gotten a hold of his phone, which meant she also knew that Troy was on to her. Hopefully, she hadn't hurt Corrine.

SWAT had already surrounded the house by the time Troy got there. No movement had been detected and everyone was pretty sure that the house was clear. They went in, Troy and other officers followed. He headed to the basement where Jon was found lying in a pool of blood. No sign of Corrine.

"He's alive!" someone yelled, calling for paramedics.

Troy rushed to his friend's side. His eyes were open and he choked from gurgling blood as he tried to speak. "It's okay. I know you tried. Hang in there, buddy."

Troy held Jon's hand until he was put on the gurney and whisked away. An APB was put out and officers searched her home for clues. Seven expandable folders were found with the victims' names, numbered in the order they had been killed. Inside each one was surveillance photos of the victims and pages of online communications with them and various men. Corrine's folder only contained printouts from her Facebook profile.

She had been planning these murders for quite some time. Pictures of Lolita Gordon went back years. There were even pictures of her and Chad leaving the hospital with their son. A folder with Freeman's name revealed that he, too, was a victim in all of this and not an accomplice as originally thought. Details of his personal schedule were chronicled on a daily basis. Various colored markings on her walls, some words barely visible, indicated that she'd been the one leaving messages in his living room. How she'd gotten the words to last long enough for him to read them and then fade without a trace was a mystery to be solved at another time.

Troy needed to find Corrine and so far there was nothing in this home that led to her whereabouts. Pictures on the mantle showed her and a man Troy assumed to be her late husband. There was one with him standing in front of a cabin holding a big fish. Then Troy remembered something she had said the day Mindy Lee's body was found. *"My family owned property around here."*

"Police have identified thirty-eight-year-old Paula Kyser, seen here, as the prime suspect in several murders throughout Franklin and Hocking counties. Earlier this evening, officers surrounded her Groveport home, but neither she nor Corrine Shepherd, believed to have been abducted by Kyser, was found. Officers did discover Detective Jonathon Knight who suffered from multiple gunshot wounds to the back. He's been taken to OSU Medical Center and listed in critical condition. Paula Kyser is described as a Caucasian female with red hair approximately five-eight, weighing 117 pounds. She drives a light-brown Mazda 626 with license plate KYSER 17. If you see her, call police immediately. She is considered to be armed and dangerous. We will continue to bring you updates as this story develops."

Natalie hated hearing what was going on through the news. She began praying for both Jon and Corrine, wondering why Troy hadn't called her yet! She sat on the edge of her bed, staring at the phone, willing it to ring.

She had come up to get away from the small crowd that had gathered in her living room. Lisa and Aneetra hadn't been there long before several neighbors and other church members started dropping by to offer their support. Appreciative of their concern, she'd started to feel claustrophobic. Dozens of people checking to see if she was "okay" every few minutes was overwhelming. Definitely not a people person, there were only so many times she could answer them without exploding.

"Knock-knock." Aneetra walked in. "You okay?"

"I won't be if everybody keeps asking me that."

"Sorry; I—"

"No, I'm sorry. My nerves are shot."

"Understandable. Toni's here. She's asking for you. What do you want me to tell her?"

"Nothing. Go ahead and send her up." Natalie had been expecting her as Sylvia had texted to see if they could all come by and wait this out together. She took several deep breaths, praying for the

Lord to calm her spirit, unsure of what her encounter with Toni would entail.

"She's right in there," Aneetra could be overheard saying from the hall.

It took Natalie a few seconds to find her voice after Toni knocked. It seemed like it took her nearly as long to enter. A few additional seconds of staring at each other and tears flowed from both their eyes. Hurt feelings were put aside. Corrine was the tie that bound their hearts and arms together in a tight embrace.

"Have you heard from Troy?"

"No. I keep hoping he'll call. I'm going to wait another half hour or so and then I'm calling him."

"I'm as anxious as you, but I don't think you should interrupt him. I'm sure he'll call when he has something concrete to share. All this waiting is torture. I wish Mama were here. She always knew how to keep everyone calm no matter how stressful things were."

"I miss her, too," admitted Natalie. Though she was good and grown, Natalie would love to be in her grandmother's lap right now. A huge chest, but an even larger heart, Big Mama had been the matriarch of their family.

"I haven't gotten over her death yet and now this is happening with Corrine. It's all too much!"

The older Toni got, the more she resembled her mother, minus all the extra packaging. Once on the road to becoming a prominent attorney, she sometimes came across as very crass. Her tough shell was visibly cracked as she stood in Natalie's room. Worry lines decorated her dark-skinned face. Combined with the strands of gray peppered throughout her hair, she looked older than her early to mid-fifties. Natalie was reminded that Toni's love for

Corrine was as strong as hers. "I'm sorry for the way I've handled things. Sometimes I am selfish when it comes to Corrine. I don't mean to be."

"I think we both are." Toni took a seat on the ottoman while Natalie resumed her position on the bed. "You know I don't really think you're a skank, right?"

"And I don't really think you're a jealous old wench."

"Ha! I probably am at times. This likely won't be the last time we bump heads about that girl."

"Of course not. That would be too much like right."

Toni laughed and the two of them spent the next hour or so sharing Corrine and Big Mama stories, even giggling about silly arguments they'd had over the years. "If she ever gets married she may need to have two separate ceremonies because I can see us going at it for sure. No disrespect to Troy, but I think Kenny should be the one to walk her down the aisle. She should also get married in Jackson. It's her hometown."

Natalie chuckled to herself. Apparently Toni had been giving this some serious thought. "I have no objections."

"Now watch Corrine go off and elope just to spite me. I bet she—"

"We interrupt your programming to bring you a special update. Police have now located Paula Kyser."

Instinctively, she and Toni grabbed each other's hands. Aneetra was heard shushing everyone downstairs so she could hear the television.

"We are live in South Bloomingville, Ohio, where officers believe Paula Kyser is secluded inside a cabin in the woods of Hocking County—the *same* woods where bodies of another woman and a young teenage boy were discovered last week. We do know that

Corrine Shepherd is with her, but police have not been able to confirm whether she is dead or alive. Hostage negotiators have—"

"Oh God, I can't take this!" Toni cried, running out of the room.

Natalie sat frozen, able to feel the intensity of her heart beat. *Prepare for the worst, hope for the best.* Within seconds Aneetra came asking if she was okay.

CHAPTER 46: BREAKING THE RULES

Gun in hand, Paula frantically paced around the room. Years of planning had gone into this day and now the stupid cops were messing things up! They had surrounded the place, ordering her to surrender. She prayed for God to give her direction, but the annoying sound of the helicopter circling above made it hard to hear what the Lord was saying. As long as the cops believed that Corrine was alive, she still had a chance to complete this mission.

Paula hated having to improvise so much! It all started with Mindy Lee. She should have never kept her alive so long. Mindy was a lost cause. Rebellion was her way of life. Not only was she having an emotional affair online with someone she thought to be a married man named Kurt, but she was also pregnant! That whore didn't deserve forgiveness. She should have been shot dead on the first day. Because of her, detrimental mistakes had been made.

Paula hadn't realized she was missing one of her stud earrings until she was on her way back to process the scene. She feared that Mindy had somehow grabbed it in her final attempt to escape. When no one was around, she pried Mindy's hand open, hoping to get her stud before anyone else found it, but it wasn't there. Learning that it was later discovered near the young boy she'd killed posed a huge problem because she hadn't gotten that close to his body. No one else seemed to notice, but she knew Troy would figure it out sooner or later since he'd ordered her to let the others take care of Stephen and for her to be in charge of Mindy. She hoped by taking Corrine, Evans would be too distraught to focus entirely on the case. Her actions had only seemed to motivate him even more. His voice dominated the megaphone outside, pleading with her to give up. The cops were not supposed to find the cabin so soon! Paula needed more time. If she was unable to complete this mission then the world would not be saved.

She recalled the first time the Lord spoke to her regarding this unique assignment. It was after she murdered Sam. He'd been an accident. She'd sensed the growing distance between them, but it never crossed her mind that he was having an affair. Decent Christian folks didn't do that and she and Sam had been faithful followers of God since their freshman year of college when they met at Campus Crusade for Christ. Though Paula had taken note of how attractive he was with his hazel eyes, curly brown hair, and athletic build, getting in a relationship with him was the furthest thing from her mind. Guys seemed to be into the voluptuous girls and she was as flat-chested as a ten-year-old boy. She and Sam had developed a genuine friendship that didn't turn romantic until their senior year when, in a moment of weakness, she gave him her virtue.

Paula was so distraught afterward that she became suicidal. She'd never even had a boyfriend and here she was playing the floozy after her first kiss. She stood on the ledge of the balcony, threatening to jump, recalling her mother's words of wisdom after a bottle of scotch: "Paula, dear, beauty has escaped you. You'll never be a pretty bride, but you should aim to be a pure one. Give a man something to love you for." Upon sharing this with Sam, he promised to marry her if she would come off the ledge. The very next day, they married at the justice of the peace. He would later claim he felt pressured and was worried about her mental stability. That was a lie. He was in love with her because she hadn't been with any other man, like her mom said.

She'd labored hard to be the perfect Christian wife for him and yet they seemed to grow apart. He was always going off on some kind of trip. Prior to that fatal night, he'd been held up in the cabin, finishing the report for a research project. Paula's plan was to surprise him, give him a little love, and then go back home. She drove up the steep hill, winding through the trees and was a little taken aback to see the car parked behind Sam's truck. Maybe one of the locals had stopped by to see him. She'd never forget that sensual music she heard upon entering the cabin. Had Sam known she was coming? And then came the rhythmic sound of their squeaking bed with cries of pleasure and "I love yous" being exchanged. Paula tiptoed toward the bedroom, peeked in and got a front row view of her husband doing things to a woman that he'd never done to her.

Heartbroken, Paula drowned herself in tears on the way back home. All night the images tortured her, but by morning she was certain that everything would be all right. She called to alert him that she'd be at the cabin that evening—she couldn't bear to walk up on any more surprises. With brand-new lingerie in the trunk, she embarked on a journey to restore her marriage.

All traces of his rendezvous the night before were gone and he seemed irritated by her presence. "I don't understand why you came out here to bother me. I told you that I'd be working."

She didn't beat around the bush. She told him what she had seen, adding that she forgave him and that she was confident they could get past this. Her pain was magnified when Sam revealed that he was in love with this other woman and wanted a divorce.

"No. Divorce has never been an option."

"I can't live like this any longer. I have been miserable ever since we said 'I do.' Paula, it's over."

She grilled him with questions. How did he meet her? "Online." Did she know he was married? "Yes." What would God say about this? "She and I both know that our relationship is unorthodox, but we believe that God will forgive us. She's pregnant and He's the only giver of life. We were destined to be together."

"B-but, you said you never wanted kids. That's why I've been taking birth control all this time. I can give you a baby if that's what you want."

"I never wanted kids with *you!* I never even wanted to marry you, but you gave me no choice when you said you would kill yourself if I didn't. I figured once you calmed down, we'd have it annulled. I've been in this loveless marriage for too long. I want out!"

She'd never seen him that angry before. Shamelessly, she begged for them to go to counseling, talk to their pastor, or something, but he refused to listen. "I think it's best if you leave now," he said coldly and turned away. Without thinking, she picked up the iron poker and cracked him in the head. She didn't stop until there wasn't an ounce of life left in his body. That's when it hit her. Sam had loved Paula no matter what he'd said. This whole situation would have never happened if that Hispanic tramp had never in-jected herself into their lives. It was then that she received her calling to restore order.

Luckily, there'd been several break-ins in the area. She smashed a few windows, trashed the place, and confiscated his electronics as well as took money from his wallet to make it seem like a burglary gone wrong. For the next several days, she went about her business as usual, even leaving messages on his cell phone to make her claims of a concerned wife more legit. Several days later, she returned to the cabin and "discovered" his body.

She was determined to find this woman who had ruined her life. It wasn't hard. She was able to track down Sam's slut through phone records and other evidence on his computer. Paula had to kill her so that she didn't do this to another couple. She thought Lolita would be the only one, but it dawned on her that if she wanted to free marriages of this temptation of adultery, she had to kill seven women as the number seven held biblical significance. It represented completion.

Initially, Paula wrestled with her assignment. After all, murder was a sin. Then she realized she was exempt from punishment because she was following God's orders. In the Old Testament, He clearly gave instructions to the children of Israel to smite nations that were ungodly. In fact, in 1 Samuel 15, Saul got reprimanded because he didn't completely destroy the Amalekites as God had demanded, but kept the king alive.

If God allowed the destruction of nations that did not know Him, what more would He allow to happen to those who claimed to be His children. That's when Paula decided to find more Lolitas by entering chat rooms and assuming various male identities and engaging in online relationships with Christian, single women. She was appalled at how sympathetic these whores were to a cyber stranger claiming to be stuck in a bad marriage. Very few encouraged her in the Word and broke off the relationships. The majority continued to engage in online relations, despite the circumstances. Though it took two to tango, she blamed the women. Men were powerless against the female persuasion. These women knew they were destroying marriages and didn't care.

Paula would arrange meetings with them and go see if they

showed up. When questioned about her absence, Paula made excuses about not being able to get away from the nagging wife. Some left her alone after that, but others still held on for hope. It was from those women that she chose her targets. This, the seventh year of Sam's death, was the perfect time to carryout her divine mission and now thanks to the immoral Mindy Lee, nosey Jon Knight, and overly determined Troy Evans, things were severely screwed.

Troy couldn't wait any longer. "I'm going in," he said to the hostage negotiator.

"No! She may kill your daughter if she feels threatened by your presence."

"For all we know, Corrine is already dead." With the bulletproof vest secured around his body, he slowly approached the cabin door, ignoring the objecting voices of those behind him. "Paula," he spoke gently through the megaphone. "I'm coming in so we can talk, okay?"

"Go away, Evans, or I swear that I will blow Corrine's brains out!"

"If Corrine is still alive, then why don't you let me speak to her?"

Silence.

He saw Corrine's bare body lying against the wall through the front window. He prayed God would give him the words to comfort Natalie. He couldn't save Corrine, but he could at least bring her killer to justice. Fighting back tears, he sat the megaphone down and slowly tried the door. It was open. By the time he'd crossed the threshold. Paula was on the floor with Corrine's body propped up in front of her as a shield and a gun pressed against her temple. Paula was also naked. *Corrine's not dead!* Troy thought to himself, but restrained his emotions. "What's wrong with her?"

"I am so close to saving the world from adultery," Paula sobbed, "but I can't shoot her without giving her an opportunity to read the scriptures. I have to wait until the sedative wears off. *Wake up!*" Paula screamed, giving Corrine a hard punch to the side of her head.

Troy quickly reached for the gun tucked in his back. "Drop your weapon, Paula!"

She gave a wicked laugh. "Shoot to kill, right, Evans? That's how officers are trained. I bet I can kill her before you kill me."

"But, you won't do that because then you would be breaking the rules of your mission. Corrine needs a chance to repent for her sins like all the others."

"You understand?"

"Of course, I do." There was no way he could get a good shot at her without also injuring Corrine.

"All along I've been doing God's work, but the world has made me out to be a criminal." Paula cried as she detailed her pain that her husband's affair with Lolita had caused. Troy indulged her ranting, if only to find his opening. "I didn't mean to kill him. His mind had been poisoned by that whore. People don't realize the sanctity of marriage. It was God's first institution between man and woman and the world has made a mockery of it. All this lobbying to redefine marriage and celebrities marrying and divorcing a new person new every other year...no one respects the sacredness of vows anymore. I *had* to do something."

"I know..."

"People don't believe that Jesus is coming back. 'Do you not know that wrongdoers will not inherit the kingdom of God? Do not be deceived: neither the sexually immoral nor idolaters nor adulterers nor men who have sex with men nor thieves nor the greedy nor drunkards nor slanderers nor swindlers will inherit the Kingdom of God.' Are you a Christian, Troy?"

He didn't answer right away, knowing that his behavior hadn't always been exemplary.

"*Well?*"

"Yes."

"What scripture did I quote?"

"I-I don't know."

"It was the New International Version of first Corinthians six, verses nine and ten. You're like millions of others who claim to know God, but fail to study His Word. It's pathetic!"

Her gun was still on Corrine and his was still on her. "You're right. I need to step up and I will from here on out." That part he meant in earnest. "Right now I need you to put the gun down. Killing her isn't the answer. They are not going to stay outside much longer. Let me help you."

"There's no help for me," she cried. "I have failed my assignment and am forced to plan B." Staring coldly at him, she began reciting various scriptures. Troy thought he recognized a verse in Psalm 51. "Then I will teach transgressors thy ways; and sinners shall be converted unto thee..." The more she talked, the more she struggled to hold Corrine upright. Troy kept his gun steady, waiting for a clear shot. "Father, forgive them for they know not what they do. Show this world that sin is destructive and that the wages of sin is death. Naked I came into this world and naked will I leave." With those final words, Paula quickly brought the gun up to her own head and fired.

CHAPTER 47: A BIT OF DRAMA

Not knowing where she was, Corrine was initially afraid to open her eyes. The beeping noises and distant voices sounded familiar. Something was irritating her nose. *Tubes.*

"I think she's awake!" She heard her mother shriek and soon felt her presence hovering over her.

Corrine willed her eyes to open. "Hey, guys…" Had the words come out?

"Oh, baby! Thank God you came to!" She was crying. Even her dad's eyes were glossy, contrary to his normally stoic demeanor.

Medical personnel walked in, gently moving her parents out of the way. "Let us check her out real quick and she'll be all yours. Welcome back, young lady," one of them said, shining a light in her face. As they poked and prodded, Corrine had so many questions. The last thing she remembered was watching Jon being shot to death and being stuffed in a trunk. What happened? What day was it? Where was Natalie? Corrine thought maybe she might be in Mississippi. Oh well, it didn't matter. What she knew for sure was that she was safe!

Natalie was home mopping the kitchen floor for the umpteenth time when she got the call from Toni about Corrine. She rushed upstairs to wake Troy whom she'd barely had a chance to speak to since he called after that lady killed herself. He'd spent most of the night at the station doing paper work while Natalie stayed at the hospital with Toni and Kenny. Both came home as Aneetra was leaving to take Nate to school.

"You look like crap," she said to him with a smile.

"Then we must look like twins." They hugged, she cried, and they thanked God together. Natalie offered to make Troy some breakfast while he took a shower. When she came up with his food, she found him fast asleep on the bed where he'd been ever since.

Natalie wanted to camp out at the hospital, but knowing how territorial Toni was, she'd decided to lay low and enjoy the truce between them for the time being. While Toni sat at Corrine's bedside, Natalie couldn't find anything useful to do with herself except clean everything Aneetra had already done. The house was now super immaculate. "Troy, get up! We have to go to the hospital. Corrine's awake!" She shook him frantically until he responded.

"Okay. Go ahead without me. I promise I'm on my way," he said, yawning and throwing the covers back.

He didn't have to say it twice. Natalie was sure she was out the door and down the street before his feet hit the ground.

Troy was anxious to see Corrine, but he also knew everyone would be vying for her attention and he wanted to let things calm down because of what he had in mind. He was so glad she was okay. He'd seen a lot in his eighteen years on the force, but he'd never witnessed someone as passionate about the Word and correct about its principles, yet as wrong in its application as Paula. She'd been right about him needing to know the Bible. He couldn't be the spiritual head of this household if he was ignorant to what the Word said. Starting today, he would read at least one scripture a day and he prayed that God would help him, not only to memorize scriptures, but correctly understand and apply them. He started with the first chapter of Proverbs, since it was known as the book of wisdom.

When he received a text alert, he assumed it would be Natalie telling him to hurry or something to that effect. It was Cheryl, congratulating him on a job well done. *Delete.* Troy got dressed and an hour later he walked into Corrine's hospital room accompanied by Nate.

"Sisssy!" he exclaimed, trying to climb on the bed.

She seemed happy to see them both and with a raspy voice, thanked him for saving her life.

"I'd do anything for you, kiddo."

She smiled as Natalie lifted Nate onto the bed. "Why you not come to my birday party?"

Troy was not sure how Corrine responded. Surprised to see Natalie there alone, he'd asked where Toni and Kenny had gone.

"To the cafeteria. I'm sure they won't be gone long. Kenny had to practically pry her away. I think he was trying to give me time alone with Corrine."

"I'll be right back, okay?"

The girls understood. Both giving him a message to carry.

Troy found his buddy's room in no time. He wasn't prepared for the many tubes and monitors sprouting from his body. Jon was staring out the window. "What's on your mind, man?"

"Hey, brotha! I heard about you on the news. How's Corrine?"

"She's okay. She thanks you for everything and Natalie sends her love."

"Ain't no thing. I'm glad you found her."

"I wouldn't have been able to do it without you. Why didn't you tell me you'd suspected Paula? As elusive as you were being, I almost thought it was you."

"Why is it always the white man?"

Troy laughed. "Hey, man, I was going by the profile. Paula was a complete surprise."

"Yeah. I didn't really put two and two together until I saw her watching you at Freeman's. Then I knew something was up. It was stupid for me go in without notifying anyone. That's why I'm in this condition. They say I may never walk again."

"I'm sorry. I don't know what to say." How could one guy's life be filled with so many unfortunate circumstances?

"Sometimes words aren't necessary. People need you to listen. Don't go getting all anti-Christ because of what's going on with me. I'll be all right either way it goes. You make sure you take care of your family."

"Deal. You need me to check on your mom while you're in here?"

"I appreciate the offer, but my sister is on her way up from Florida. She should be here any time."

Troy's phone buzzed violently. "I better take this."

"No problem. Thanks for coming by. I love you, man."

Troy smiled. "Yeah, yeah, you're all right, too. I'll be back a little later...hello?"

"Why haven't y'all had Nate call me? I'm sick of chasing after y'all black a—"

"Sorry, Mama, we ran into a bit of drama."

"It's gon' be some drama all right if I don't get to talk to my grandson." She cursed Troy out all the way from Jon's room back to Corrine's.

EPILOGUE

Three Months Later...

Troy was thankful that the remainder of the summer was uneventful. In July, he and Natalie celebrated their fourth wedding anniversary in the comfort of their home playing games and eating pizza with Nate. Corrine was in Jackson at the time. She'd gone there shortly after her hospital release and stayed for well over a month where she'd celebrated her twenty-fourth birthday. When she returned to work, she learned that Brent had been placed on administrative leave, pending a sexual harassment allegation by one of the office assistants.

Aneetra's girls spent the rest of their summer with her sister in Louisiana. She and Marcus were still separated and Troy hadn't yet heard whether they were planning to divorce or reconcile. Natalie and Aneetra continued to attend the Wise Wives meetings each month. He desperately tried to be available so that he could watch Nate. Sometimes the two of them would tag along so they could hang out with Robert and Chandler.

The more time passed, the more everyone seemed to put Paula's madness behind them. However, Eric Freeman was in denial. Though he had confirmed that Paula looked very much like his prayer partner, Esther Roman, who had sent him a letter saying she was leaving the country on a missionary trip, he'd refused to believe that they were one in the same or that the messages on his wall came from anyone other than the hand of God.

Unfortunately, Jon had not yet regained his ability to walk. Doctors were hopeful that continued hard work and aggressive therapy may yield minor results, but they didn't think he would ever make a full recovery. In the meantime, his sister was still in town, looking after him and their mom. Sadly, his ex-wife hadn't even cared enough to send a "get well" card. No matter what, Jon never stopped smiling, praising God, or singing love songs to pretty women.

As fall began, Natalie was nearing the end of her first trimester. She'd apparently missed a few pills during the ordeal with Corrine. Troy was elated and tried to remain sensitive to the fact that she had mixed feelings. They still hadn't come to an agreement about her working, but he would make an extra effort to be more available without her having to ask. He was even planning to take time off after she gave birth—something he hadn't done with Nate.

In the meantime, Troy tried to make the most of every moment with his family. While Natalie, Corrine, and Aneetra had orchestrated some girl weekend getaway, it would be him and li'l man for the next several days. They'd spent nearly the whole afternoon at Magic Mountain. Exhausted, Troy had finally been able to lure him away with the promise of a new *Spider-Man* movie. They'd seen the new one over the summer, but it had not yet been released on DVD. Troy usually didn't resort to bribery, but his parenting style was a little less stringent when Natalie wasn't around.

"Can I have bofe movies, Daddy?"

"No, pick one."

"Well, if it isn't the two handsome Evans boys." Troy's entire body tensed at the sound of Cheryl's voice. "Hey, little fellah, you must be Nate." She bent down to make eye contact with him.

"How you know my name?"

"Your daddy told me."

"C'mon, Nate, pick the movie and let's go."

"How's your wife and stepdaughter?"

"Fine. Forget it. I changed my mind. You can have them both."

As he hurried away, Cheryl yelled out, "Good to see you, Troy! I miss talking with you."

It hadn't dawned on him until they were in the parking lot that Toys R Us was an odd place to run into her. "You know better than to talk to strangers, don't you? Even if someone knows your name, but you don't know them, you are not allowed to speak to them if your mom or I aren't around, okay?"

Nate wasn't paying attention. He was too busy making up a song about his two movies. Later that night, Troy repeated himself.

"Yes, sir."

"Okay, bud, let's say prayers."

"God, I thank You for my *Spider-Man* movies. Please bless my mommy, my sissy, my aunt Nee Nee, and my baby brudders." Troy chuckled. Natalie was expecting twins, but they did not know the sex of either baby. However, Nate was determined that they would be boys. "Your turn, Daddy."

Troy smiled. Nightly prayers were no longer a rudimentary routine he participated in to appease Natalie. He took joy in both individual and group prayer time and his faith was continuously growing stronger. He had so much to thank God for. Tonight, as his custom many nights, he started with his family.

DISCUSSION QUESTIONS

1. Eric is insistent that he is addressed by his title. Why do you think so many church people with titles find them so important? What are the advantages/disadvantages of titles in the church?

2. What are your first thoughts regarding how Eric came across the information about Lolita Gordon?

3. Eric adamantly insists that he is not a psychic. How can a person discern the difference between a psychic and a prophet? What does the Bible say? Do prophets still exist?

4. Do you or your spouse have a demanding job? What are some of the effects on your marriage? How can one balance the demands of work and family?

5. Has there ever been a time when your faith was shaken? Please explain.

6. Natalie is keeping a very big secret from Troy. Obviously, this is something he should know, but are spouses ever to keep secrets from one another or should they tell each other everything?

7. Natalie's feelings toward Lynn aren't unique when it comes to female relationships. Do you think men have these thoughts/feelings too, or do women read too much into things?

8. Based on the FBI profile in chapter 7, do you have any idea of who the killer may be?

9. Troy doesn't seem to mind Jon's behavior toward Natalie, but what do you think? Is it harmless or disrespectful? If it is okay, under what circumstances would it not be?

10. What would you say, if anything, to a loved one who is involved in an adulterous relationship?

11. Robert mentions doing something that he'd never imagined he would do and contributes his actions to his strained relationship with God. Have you ever found yourself in a situation that caused you to stray far from your true beliefs?

12. Robert says that ministry isn't only in the pulpit. Why do you think so many people aim for that type of ministry, believing that it's the most important?

13. Natalie mentions her past in Chapter 14, fearing that she may eventually reap what she has sown. Are her concerns valid or was Troy's response correct?

14. Natalie mentions having been candid with Corrine about her past. How much should we tell our children? Can we ever share too much?

15. How would you handle things if you were Aneetra? If you wanted to mend your marriage, what are the first three things you would do?

16. In Chapter 16, Natalie says, "the more you know, the more you have to forgive." Do you agree with her advice?

17. What were you initial thoughts about how Marcus was involved in Troy's case?

18. What did you think of Jon's explanation of his injuries in Chapter 20?

19. What's your opinion of Karen in Chapter 22? Was Natalie being paranoid?

20. Some people believe that marriage is forever, no matter what, while others say there's a limit to what a spouse should take and it's okay to get out when things get to that point. What are your thoughts?

21. Natalie and Troy have an argument in Chapter 26 when he discovers her secret. Who do you tend to side with?

22. What do you think about Troy's phone call getting so personal in Chapter 27?

23. Should Troy have gone to Starbucks?

24. Why do you think the word "submission" is a tough one for many modern-day women to follow?

25. What kinds of activities do you engage in to take your mind off worries?

26. Do you have a favorite book of the Bible? If so, what is it and why?

27. Do you sympathize with Cheryl at all in Chapter 42?

28. Should Troy have told Natalie about Cheryl, despite it not being an opportune time?

29. Troy pieces clues together in Chapter 43? Do you know who the killer is now as well? Did you know before him? If so, what tipped you off?

30. How do you think the killer began to embrace the misunderstanding of the Word regarding the mission?

31. Read 1 Samuel 15. How would you explain God's instructions to Saul to a non-believer?

32. Not taking into account the murders, do you sympathize with the killer's story at all?

33. What, if anything, can be learned from this killer's supposed mission?

34. Do you have any predictions about what will happen with Cheryl?

ABOUT THE AUTHOR

Yolonda Tonette Sanders was born and raised in Sandusky, Ohio, and moved to Columbus, Ohio, after high school to attend Capital University. While there, she double-majored in Political Science and Criminology and then went on to get a master's degree in Sociology from The Ohio State University. For three and a half years, Yolonda worked with the state of Ohio as a researcher, but in 2004, she took a leap of faith and resigned from her job to focus full-time on writing. It was a leap that she has never regretted.

In 2005, her first novel, *Soul Matters* (Hachette Book Group), was published. In 2008, *Secrets of a Sinner* (Harlequin/Kimani Press) was released. That same year, Yolonda started Yo Productions, LLC, a Christian-based literary services and theatrical entertainment company. Yo Productions was used to launch Yolonda's first stage production based on her debut novel, *Soul Matters*, which premiered at the Capital Theatre in downtown Columbus, Ohio.

After several years, Yolonda landed a four book deal with Strebor Books, an imprint of Simon & Schuster. Her third novel, *In Times of Trouble*, was released in 2013. The remaining three works she has contracted with this publisher are part of "The Protective Detective" series, which stars a male protagonist. *Wages of Sin* is the first installment. Yolonda's nickname for the entire collection is "mystery with a message" because it blends her fondness for the mystery/suspense genre with her love for Christ.

Yolonda continues to flourish in everything she does. As a writer, she is developing new projects and is even working on a young adult series. As a speaker, Yolonda has been invited to address audiences across the country regarding various topics and enjoys the opportunity to connect with people from all walks of life. As a business owner, she seeks to help other writers develop and perfect their works. Yo Productions has been used as a catalyst to help both self- and traditionally published authors. In addition, Yolonda is planning to tour with her first stage production as well as expand the services offered by Yo Productions nationwide. Currently, Yolonda resides in Columbus, Ohio, and is the loving wife of David, proud mother of Tre and Tia, and joyful caregiver of her mother, Wilene.

Visit the author at www.yoproductions.net, www.yolonda.net, www.yoproductions.net and Twitter @ytsanders

IF YOU ENJOYED "WAGES OF SIN," PLEASE BE SURE TO
CHECK OUT

In Times of Trouble

BY YOLONDA TONETTE SANDERS
AVAILABLE FROM STREBOR BOOKS

CHAPTER 1
A Minor Issue

It took Lisa a few minutes to fully regain consciousness when she woke up and found herself in the living room. She hadn't meant to fall asleep. Tucked away in an eastern suburb of Columbus, the Hampton household had been relatively quiet last night. With her mother and daughter out, Lisa took advantage of the solitary Saturday evening and just relaxed. Considering the many late nights she'd worked the previous week, she needed the break. Lisa spent the evening in her blue satin pajamas curled up on her cream plush sofa where she had apparently fallen asleep.

The sound of snow humming on her flat television screen was irritating and she quickly used the remote to turn it off. Noticing the time was 12:49 a.m., Lisa leapt up and ran through the kitchen to see if her car was in the garage. Nope, just her mother's car, which meant that Chanelle, her seventeen-year-old daughter, had missed her midnight curfew!

"Don't jump to conclusions," Lisa said to herself as she reached for the phone, flipping through the caller ID. She hoped Chanelle had tried to call when she was asleep, but was disheartened to find no evidence supporting her theory. She quickly dialed Chanelle's cell phone, hearing the hip-hop music selection that preceded her daughter's voice mail. She didn't bother leaving a message.

Dashing up the stairs, Lisa knocked on her mother's bedroom door as a courtesy, but didn't wait for a response. "Mama?" She peeked inside.

Hattie lay like Sleeping Beauty underneath a tan comforter that blended in perfectly with her light skin tone. She looked so peaceful that Lisa really didn't want to disturb her. She stood for a split second, admiring her mother's beauty. Though she was in her mid-sixties, Lisa's mother looked great—still-mostly-black hair, a shapely size ten figure and no wrinkles. Lisa hoped she'd inherited her mother's genes and would also age gracefully. So far so good, but if Chanelle kept working her nerves, she'd surely look old and gray within a few years.

"Mama!" Lisa spoke with more force.

"Huh?"

"Sorry to wake you…I want to know if you've heard from Chanelle."

"No, why? She's not home yet?"

"No, but don't worry. I'll find her."

Her mother quickly sat up. "Did you call Jareeka? Maybe Chanelle accidentally dozed off over there."

The girl's name was actually Gericka, like *Erika*, but Lisa didn't bother correcting her mother, who was notorious for renaming people. "Calling there is my next step. I wanted to check with you first."

Lisa ran back down to the kitchen where Chanelle's best friend's telephone number was posted on the small magnetic bulletin board attached to the refrigerator. By now it was a few minutes shy of one.

The phone rang several times before Marlon Young, Gericka's father, answered.

"Hi! I'm sorry to call your house so late. This is Lisa."

"Yes, what can I do for you?"

"Is Chanelle there?"

"No, why do you ask?"

Lisa's throat tightened. "She's not here yet. Do you know what time she brought Gericka home from the movies?"

"I don't know what Chanelle told you, but she didn't go to the movies with Gericka," Marlon firmly stated. "Gericka and Karen went to Louisville on Friday to spend the weekend with my mother-in-law."

"I'm sorry…I thought. Never mind. I'm sorry I woke you."

"It's okay. I'm sure you're concerned about your daughter. I pray she gets home safely," he said, before hanging up.

With no other options, Lisa reluctantly dialed RJ's number, which she had unfortunately memorized by now. She *hated* calling her ex-husband, but figured the situation warranted such an action. It was a waste of time because he hadn't seen or heard from Chanelle either. As if his presence would calm Lisa's nerves, RJ had offered to come over and wait with her until Chanelle arrived.

"No, thanks!" Lisa quickly declined. He always seemed to be looking for an excuse to be near her, but the only man occupying her time was Minister Freeman, whom she had been out to dinner with on several occasions.

"Please let me know the minute you hear from her," RJ requested.

"I will," she assured.

He had some nerve, acting like a concerned father when he was the reason why she and Chanelle had left Baltimore and come to Ohio in the first place. Had she known several summers ago when she moved here that he would follow, she would have accepted another job elsewhere.

Feeling her blood pressure rise with each passing second, she went back into the living room and sat on the couch. She began fiddling with the charm on the necklace she never took off, which had become a habit whenever she became nervous or angry. The time was exactly 1:07 a.m. and that meant her daughter was now sixty-seven minutes past curfew. Lisa was fuming!

Though the "God, please don't let anything bad happen to her" prayer cycled through Lisa's head a few times, she honestly didn't feel a need to panic. For some reason, Lisa knew Chanelle was okay—wherever she was. Chanelle was okay now, but Lisa couldn't promise that she'd be later when she finally brought her behind home and parental justice kicked in.

She did not understand why Chanelle would intentionally lie and violate her curfew. She was fresh off of punishment for talking back earlier that week. Lisa had asked Chanelle to get off the computer so she could type some information for work, but Chanelle had defiantly replied, "No!"—as if Lisa had really given her an option. Already stressed because of her work challenges, Lisa controlled the urge to snatch Chanelle out of the chair by her ponytail and threatened that if she didn't move of her own accord, she would be moved. Chanelle got up without further objection but her attitude had struck Lisa's nerve, so Chanelle had been placed on punishment.

Hearing the sound of her mother's footsteps descending the hardwood stairs, Lisa leaned back on the sofa so as not to appear overly anxious.

"Chanelle still hasn't made it home?" Her mother's wire-framed glasses rested at the tip of her nose while a large green robe concealed her body.

"Nope…"

"Did you call Jareeka's?"

"Yes, her father said that she and her mother are away for the weekend." She felt herself tensing with every word.

"What about RJ? Have you called him?"

"He hasn't seen her either."

"Well, don't come down too hard on her. Maybe she didn't know Jareeka was out of town and when she found out, she decided to hang with one of her other friends instead. Now she should've at least called and told you, but she was probably so happy to get out the house that she forgot. Poor thing; it seems like she's always on punishment. Sometimes I think you're too hard on that girl. I don't want to meddle—"

"Then please don't," the thirty-eight-year-old interjected in the most respectful tone that she could conjure up with a clenched jaw.

"All right. I'll keep my opinion to myself, but I was merely going to say that you may want to consider extending Chanelle's curfew. She's practically an adult and it's time you start treating her like one. Maybe then you'd be less likely to run into this problem."

An electrifying jolt shot through Lisa's body. The way she disciplined Chanelle had become a constant point of contention between her and her mother. Thank goodness Hattie would soon be moving into her own apartment! Lisa could not wait!

"That makes absolutely no sense!" she fired back. "What she is, is irresponsible. Why should I reward her for not being able to honor her curfew? And anyhow, she wouldn't have been on punishment recently had she not been so smart at the mouth."

"I wonder where she got it from…" her mother replied cynically, quickly disappearing into the kitchen and returning moments later. "Good night."

"The same to you," Lisa replied, continuing to stew as the clock read 1:21 a.m. The only other noise she heard was the emptying of the automatic ice machine until ten minutes or so later when a car pulled into the driveway. Lisa's heart began racing when she saw flashing blue and red lights from the window. It wasn't her car as she had thought, but a police cruiser. A gut-wrenching fear fell over her. Had something horrible happened to Chanelle? She felt guilty about being so angry and the missed curfew was now a minor issue compared to the concern that her baby might be lying in the hospital somewhere. Lisa was horrified by the unlimited possibilities of things that could've happened to her daughter. The pit of her stomach knotted as she sprang from the couch and raced to the front door.